Secrets
of the
Vineyard

MARY CAROL

NEWMAN SPRINGS PUBLISHING
320 Broad Street
Red Bank, NJ 07701

First originally published by Newman Springs Publishing 2019

ISBN 978-1-64531-077-8 (Paperback)
ISBN 978-1-64531-430-1 (Hardcover)
ISBN 978-1-64531-078-5 (Digital)

Printed in the United States of America

Contents

CHAPTER 1

Saturday Surprise

THE SUN HAD BARELY BROKEN over the east range of the Napa Valley as the truck pulled into the vineyard on the Silverado Trail, commonly known as the Trail to valley natives, where Robb's dad was foreman. School was only out for the summer a week or so, and Robb already missed the gang at school. Robb's dad warned him as he unloaded his bike off the back of the truck. "Be careful on the Trail and watch for trucks. See you by five," his dad yelled.

"Yeah! I will." He jumped on and sped off quickly up the dirt road to the Silverado Trail, raising his arm waving goodbye, his heart racing with anticipation and excitement over his first little bit of independence.

The air was fresh with the dew of the morning as the sun had not reached the Trail yet. He rode fast with great excitement. He picked up speed, riding past the vineyards and moss-covered rock walls, feeling the cold damp air on his face, admiring the beauty of the countryside.

When he reached the big white gate with the sign "R. G. Rogers Ranch" held by two huge stone pillars, he jumped off his bike, opened it, and pushed through. He had to lay his bike down in order to go back and shut the huge white wooden gate. He hopped back on his bike, passing the famous Moore dog kennel where Annie and Robin Moore lived.

He yelled, "SHUT UP!" at the dogs in the kennel, who were barking at him. Pushing on, he continued up the dusty dirt road through the oak trees. Getting to a sharp turn in the road at a bridge where he crossed over a large creek and up a steep hill, he got off his bike and walked, pushing his bike hard. He enjoyed the smell of the wet dewy grass and the fresh air as the sun started to come through the trees. There were little wildflowers in the grass, of Indian Paintbrush, popping up in the midst of the rocks.

He reached a gate to Jenny's dad's property and stopped for a moment, wondering why there would be a gate here. Then pushing on to the top of the hill where the road flattened out, he stood to look over the valley. The vineyards and ranches were laid out in blocks, with barns, dams, farmhouses, pump houses, and water towers. The hills were already yellow, and the oak trees were a contrast in dark green. He could see all the way across the valley to the towns of Oakville, Rutherford, and Yountville. Never seeing the valley in this way before, he looked off to the north where his dad was on the ranch. He hoped he would see him out in the vineyard.

He pushed on up the next grade to a level place where the vineyard started and the road was flat again. There he mounted his bike and started to ride slowly. A covey of quail and their babies startled him as they skittered quickly across the road into the Manzanita and brush, out of sight. He admired the huge redwood trees at the top of the hill to the east above the vineyard, and there spied a large stone winery building standing high looking over the valley.

Reaching a fork in the road where he knew from Mari's description to go to the right, there it was in the distance, the huge oak trees and in the midst of them, the ranch house. His heart leaped as he pedaled his bike a little faster down the grade and around the bend below a water dam, then up to the house.

Reaching the end of the veranda steps, he dropped his bike carelessly. He crept quietly along the house on the veranda, passing two large windows. Then he saw an open window, stuck his head in, and looking around, saw Mari sleeping.

He stood silently for a moment and then whispered, "Blondie, wake up. Wake up! I rode all the way here to see you." He crawled carefully into the room and knelt next to her bed. "Wake up, Blondie. I road my bike all the way here to see you."

She rose with a start, surprised to see his face so close to hers. "What are you doing? You can't be in here!"

Robb quietly put his fingers up to her. "Shhh, someone will hear you. Where's your dad? RG will kill me if he catches me."

She sat up, covering herself with her blankets. "He must be milking the cow. Didn't the dogs see you? I didn't hear them bark. They must be up at the pasture with Dad and our cow Baby. Get out of here before someone comes and sees you. I'll meet you outside."

He crawled out the window and stood next to it, feeling the crisp morning air as his heart beat a mile a minute.

Mari quickly got out of bed, rushing to get her best jeans and nicest shirt on. She quickly brushed her long wavy blonde hair that flowed softly down one side into a page-boy hairstyle and then ran to the bathroom across the hall, washed her face, and rinsed her mouth. All the while, she wondered why Robb would come up to the ranch to see her. She was confounded to think Robb would be interested in her but found it flattering. She rushed out the door, down the stairs into the breezeway, and around the corner where Robb was standing.

"How did you get here? What are you doing here?" she whispered.

Robb stood awkwardly looking at her. "I thought I would spend the day with you while my dad was doing some stuff at the ranch down the Trail where he works. What do you think?"

Mari grabbed his hand and said, "Come with me to the kitchen, and we can have breakfast."

They went around through the breezeway, on down the veranda to the kitchen door. Seeing the door was already open, they pushed through the screen door and entered the large kitchen looking around.

"Hi, Mrs. Rogers!" Robb said with surprise.

"Well, hello to you, Robb. You are up early today. What's the occasion?" Mrs. Rogers replied in surprise.

Robb explained, "I thought I would spend the day here at your ranch while my dad was working at the ranch on the Trail."

Mari's mom, being quietly surprised, hid her thoughts. She was already getting breakfast for RG before he came down from milking

Baby. The kitchen window was open, and the fresh morning air came through the room, bringing a bit of a chill.

Mari stood in the middle of the room and watched her mom working around and asked, "Is there anything I should do to help with breakfast? I thought Robb would need to have some too."

Her mom was quick to reply, "Sure, you two can set the table. The boys will be down soon."

Mari and Robb went into the dining room and got the dishes out of the cupboard. Robb stood and was amazed at the place. Mari didn't notice as she opened the drawer to get the silver out and handed it to him.

"Put it round." She waved her hand to direct him.

He stood there and wondered what she meant.

"Set it around to each place, silly," she explained with encouragement. He still didn't get it. He couldn't figure out why there would be a tablecloth and settings at the table for breakfast. She took the silver from him and showed him how to place each setting at each chair.

He grabbed the silver. "I can finish it now."

She followed with dishes at each place. Then going to the cupboard, she got the glasses out and handed them to him to place around. Again, he didn't get it. She smiled and nudged him, showing him again how to do it. As he walked around, she followed with napkins and placed them to the left of each setting. They stood at the end of the table admiring it. Then as she tilted her head and turned to go back to the kitchen, he followed.

By then her brothers, Daniel and Mark had bound into the kitchen asking if RG had come down from the pasture. Mama had already started the bacon, preparing bread for french toast. She quietly ordered out directions to each one to get out the syrup, jam, butter, salt, pepper, and anything else they might want on the table.

The boys scuffled at each other, jabbing and whispering.

"What is Robb doing here? He's a big jock at school and gets around with all the girls. We'll have to make him help with the chores. We have wood to cut," Daniel remarked with a sneer.

Mark chided, "He can haul it into the wood box for us. I have to clean the barn. That will give him a great experience."

Mari over heard them and whispered, "He came to spend the day with me, not you!"

RG walked in the kitchen door just then and stopped just inside the door, surprised to see so much activity that early in the morning.

"What the hell! As I was milking Baby, she stepped in the milk bucket and spilled half of it. I was going to make cheese today. What's going on with Mari?" he announced in his boisterous, enthusiastic voice.

The boys snickered and slipped out of the kitchen into the dining room.

Mama replied, "Robb has come up for the day. Shhh! Get cleaned up. I'm almost ready to serve. Mari, get in here and help get the food on the table."

Robb stood around not knowing what to do. Mark looked around the door and grabbed him to get into the dining room. "Come in with us. Have a seat here. Grab a napkin and relax."

Robb sat down and looked around at the room. It was grand by his expectations. Things at home were a lot simpler. The boys started in telling him all about the chores they wanted him to help with. He listened quietly, knowing all along that wasn't going to happen. He had big plans to be with Mari all day.

RG came into the room and sat down with great gusto. He was not real tall but big and muscular, ruggedly handsome.

"Good morning, boys! Getting the wood done today?" RG said strongly.

"Yes, sir," both boys said together.

"Good. Be sure you ask your mother what she needs you to do today. There is plenty to get done this summer. You can join me out in the vineyard and learn how to thin the vines. Mother will have lunch ready by noon. Be sure you are back and cleaned up in time." His enthusiasm was still bursting forth.

Mari and Mama came in with the tea cart stacked with all the serving dishes full of french toast, bacon, eggs, fruit, and all the fixings. RG and the boys stood as they came in the room. Robb followed their direction, and then they all sat down. Mark rose and went to help his mother set the food on the table. Robb was impressed at his manners. The food was a feast to his eyes. The aroma of the bacon, eggs, homemade syrup, and all were amazing to him.

Everything was passed around as each served themselves. Robb watched to see what everyone else was doing. He saw the boys dive into their meal with great enthusiasm. RG praised mama as he served himself up with a huge plate of all that was there.

RG leaned back in his chair. "The bacon is from old man Jones. He butchered some pigs last month."

Daniel chimed in, "I heard they call this cut Canadian bacon. This has a lot more meat on it, doesn't it? In 4-H, we learned about Canadian bacon. I like it a lot better."

Mark mumbled with his mouth full, "Sure is good."

"Thanks a lot, Mrs. Rogers!" Robb added.

Mari sat quietly as she poured a glass of milk, still wondering why Robb would make the trip all the way up to the ranch just to see her.

After a hearty conversation around the table, RG finished. "Thanks be to God for the day, good food, and the company. I'll be off now. You boys get going as soon as you finish. I don't want to hear any fighting. Mari, help Mother in the kitchen before you do your chores. See you all at noon."

He dropped his napkin on the chair, kissed mama, ran his hand through his hair, stuck a little round cap he had made by cutting out the top of a hat on his head, and went out through the kitchen door.

Mari could see him walk up the path to the barn through the large bay window. She loved her dad and was so very proud of him. He worked hard every day maintaining the ranch and his business in Napa as a contractor and architect. There were many days when she spent time with him as he instructed her in all the ways to run the ranch. He taught her to drive the truck when she was nine years old and learned how to drive the tractor at ten. Her dad also taught her how to tend to the vineyard and all that needed to be done. She loved the ranch.

The boys asked mama if they could be excused from the table. They cleared their own dishes to the kitchen. Mari asked if she and

Robb could be excused. After clearing their places, they helped mama in the kitchen with the cleaning up. Mari and Robb worked together. Mari washed, and Robb dried the dishes. They put everything back in the cupboard from where they had taken it all out.

"Come on, Robb," Mari said with excitement. "You and I can go up to the barn now and feed the chickens, ducks, and help Daniel with the rabbits. Daniel raises rabbits for the local butcher in St. Helena. The chickens are my 4-H project."

As they ran up the path RG had taken to the barn, mama shouted out, "Feed the dogs before you run off!"

When they got there, RG was getting the tractor out to make his rounds around the vineyard. The two of them laughed and giggled as they worked together feeding the chickens, ducks, and helping Daniel with the rabbits.

Daniel explained all about the rabbits and how not to stick their fingers into the cage of the buck since he was very mean and would bite your finger off. "We have to keep a record for 4-H. See this book? I keep track of all the rabbits, when to breed them, kill them, and sell them."

"We're out of here, Daniel. We'll see you later," shouted Mari as she and Robb hurried out the front door of the barn.

Her black Sheltie mix dog, Dagwood, suddenly appeared wagging his tail. He followed them as Mari guided Robb around the huge wooden corral fence and up the road to the pasture. There were ducks nesting all along the corral fence as they rushed up the road past the vineyard to the right and a hayfield to the left lined with fruit trees.

Robb gazed up the hill beyond the pasture and suddenly saw the expanse of the ranch. The pasture was just turning dry with barely any green left to it. The sun was up now and warm as they reached the gate to the pasture. Mari pushed the latch open, and they went through.

"Where's the cow? Will it hurt us?" Robb said quietly, so as not to surprise it.

"Don't be silly!" Mari retorted. "Baby won't hurt anybody. She's as tame as the dogs."

They went over to the barn where RG milked Baby and peeked in. Mari grabbed Robb's arm and said, "Come on, let's get up the hill, and I'll show you something."

They walked faster now, Robb taking it all in, loving Mari and the way she loved the ranch. Dagwood was in tow behind them as they rushed up the hill through the pasture. While they walked, Mari showed Robb where she and the boys target-practiced with their guns.

Reaching the end of the fence at the top of the pasture, they turned, tracking along the vineyard. Climbing over some rocks and through some oak trees, they came to a huge concrete watering trough. It must have been ten feet by four with eight-inch-thick concrete walls. The thing was full of water, clear, and clean, reflecting the clouds in the sky.

"We could swim in this thing. It's so huge!" Robb said with amazement.

The windmill was still in the quiet air. Standing next to the watering trough, they dipped their hands in the water. Robb splashed Mari a little, stepping back so as not to get anything in return.

Squealing back, she said, "You devil, don't get me wet now. It's still too cold this morning."

She turned quickly and ran up the path to some rocks and said, "Come on, sit here and see this."

Robb quickly shuffled up to her on the huge rock she was sitting on. They sat close as he put his arm around her. "Are you cold?" he whispered.

"Not much," she replied, shrugging it off. "Just look at the view from up here." She pointed to the valley. Just then, five calves came up the path to the watering trough. Mari pointed. "Look, watch them!" The calves seemed to follow a leader and knew where they were to stand as they got to their respective places at the trough. They drank quietly. Then as the leader led them away north to the pasture above the vineyard, Robb watched with interest.

Mari jumped up and tugged at his arm. "Come on, I'll show you a cave up here."

Following the calves at a distance, they walked along the cow path. Stopping along the way, they saw RG down in the vineyard thinning out of the vines. He systematically walked from one vine to the next, pulling out the young sprouts called suckers.

"Our vines are Mountain Zinfandel grapes," Mari explained. "We're one of only three ranches in the valley that grow them. Dad sells our grapes to Charles Krug winery. You should come up later this fall at harvest and help. We pay a lot more per box than anyone else in the valley." Mari seemed to say this with a bit of pride.

"I've never picked grapes. Is it hard?" Robb said as he gently pushed her.

"Well, yes," Mari said surprised. "The boxes are fifty pounds when they're full. I can do it, so could you. Come on!" She ran up the hill toward the brush through the slippery grass, still wet with morning dew. Robb followed, slipping on the grass. Falling on his knees, he grabbed at the rocks to keep up. Mari disappeared into the brush.

He got to the brush line and yelled, "Blondie! Where are you?"

"I'm here!" Her voice was coming out of the brush. He looked all over and still didn't see her. Suddenly she appeared out of the brush, startling him.

"Come on, silly, look here." They pushed through the Manzanita, the California lilac, and sagebrush.

Suddenly Robb stopped. "What the heck! What's that?"

"It's a cave where they used to keep the wine and stuff during Prohibition," Mari explained. The opening was small, so they crouched to get in. There were still some barrels lined up along the wall.

"Is there still wine in these barrels?" Robb looked closer.

"Probably. But Dad said not to bother with them as the stuff is most likely spoiled. It's history." Mari stayed close to him, staying in the light of the opening.

Robb stopped to look around the cave. "Are there any bears around here? They say bears live in caves."

Mari replied, "We do see tracks during harvest. When they come down, they toss the boxes of grapes that haven't been run into the winery from the final pick of the day. We try not to leave any sitting around overnight because they lose sugar content. We get bobcats too. The dogs will run all night, chasing them all over the whole ranch."

"I think this is creepy. I want to get out of here," Robb said suddenly. He turned toward the light at the entrance of the cave, crouching to get out. He brushed himself off, turning to see Mari crouching out of the small opening. He reached over to help her.

"Thanks. I can manage." She waved him away and brushed herself off. "What do you think? Dad doesn't want us going in there too much because he's afraid it might cave in on us."

Robb had been looking out at the beautiful view and turned. "You think? Thanks for showing me that, but I think I'll do as your dad says and stay out."

Dagwood was waiting in the shade of the oak trees and came up to sniff Robb wagging his tail. Robb pet him behind the ears gently and pulled him close to his leg as they sat down on some rocks. Robb and Mari talked about school and some of their friends. Robb sat as close to her as he could; Dagwood rested his head on his leg. Robb kept moving his knee to touch Mari all the while they sat together. He picked some grass and put it in his mouth.

Suddenly Mari got up, bounding quickly down the hill toward the vineyard. "Come on, silly. Let's see what my dad is doing," she said impishly.

They ran down the hill to the rock wall and the tall deer fence, Mari in front all the way. She climbed over the wall and through a gate in the wire deer fence, jumping down to the vineyard below. Robb, stumbling behind, shouted out, "Wait! Blondie!" She paused and waited.

RG was just getting to the end of a row as they approached. "Where have you two been? I hope you stayed out of that cave," RG said gruffly.

"We didn't go in very far, Dad. We stayed in the light. I wanted to show Robb," Mari exclaimed with excitement. "I'm giving Robb a tour of the ranch. We're out of here now."

The two ran down an aisle of the vineyard toward the barn and passed the second well in the middle of the vineyard. Robb paused and asked, "Does this one work too?"

Mari stopped and said, "It goes dry in the summer. We haven't had any water in it for a week now." She pushed on. They reached the back of the smaller barns surrounding the big barn.

"This is an old pigpen. We never raise pigs because Dad thinks they are too dangerous around us kids. He gets pork from old man Jones." She stood on the edge of the fence peering in.

Robb stopped and peered over the fence next to her. "This is swell. What a great pigpen. It's too bad you don't use it."

"Come on!" she urged. They continued around the small barn where the boys were chopping wood in a small corral.

"Get over here and help us haul wood over to the house, you guys!" Mark shouted. "We can get this done twice as fast with all of us working."

Robb was anxious to help. "Sure. What do you want me to do?"

Daniel was clever and said, "We like to see who can win by carrying the most wood over to the wood box. Here, hold your hands out like this. I'll load you up. How much can you hold?"

Robb held out both his arms so Daniel could load him up. Daniel stacked the wood in his arms clear up to his chin.

"I can hold more than this," Daniel said braggingly. "How about you? How high can you go?"

Well, Robb was not about to have Daniel win. "Oh, go a little higher," Robb boasted. Daniel put three more pieces on. Robb wobbled a bit and said, "Okay, where do I take this now?"

Mari grabbed a few pieces of wood and pulled his arm, "Follow me."

Robb could hardly see over the wood in his arms. He struggled along the path to the house while Mari guided him along and told him to stop when they reached the house. The door to the wood box was on the side of the house. Mari opened it and started taking the wood off Robb one piece at a time, stacking it inside the house.

"Whoa! Do you think I packed more than Daniel?" Robb said excitedly.

"Don't be fooled by him. He just does that to get you to take more wood so he doesn't have to do it. He tricked me long ago with that. Come on, we aren't going to help them anymore." They walked around the house between the stone milk house and under a big oak tree.

Robb stopped. "What's this?"

"Oh, those are the steps down to the old wine cellar. The house is built over two wine cellars. We keep jars of canned food down there. Want to see?" Mari went on.

They hopped down the rock stairs through the wooden door and into the dark room. Mari pulled a chain and turned on the light. Robb stood on the wet dirt floor in amazement as he looked at jars of peaches, pears, apricots, applesauce, green beans, pickled beets, jams and jellies. He had never seen such beautiful glass jars of all sorts.

"We will be canning all sorts of stuff this summer. Those empty jars will be loaded with all kinds of stuff. It's a lot of work. Everyone in the family helps when we do it." Mari was excited to talk about it. On the other wall were bottles lying on their side.

"What's that?" Robb stepped closer to look.

"Oh, that's root beer that Daniel and my dad made. It's really good. You want some?" Mari answered, smiling.

"Sure!" Robb stepped even closer to the shelves to admire it all.

Mari reached up and took two bottles in each hand. "You take some too. We'll have it for lunch." Robb grabbed two in each hand, turning quickly as Mari pulled on the light chain as they hopped up the stone stairs. They headed to the veranda and bolted up the stairs to the kitchen.

"Look what we brought up from the cellar, Mama," Mari said with great enthusiasm. Mama turned from the counter where she was already making pie crust for the peach pies she would bake for dinner.

Mari's mom quietly motioned an order, waving her floury hand. "You kids wipe your dirty feet! Set those down and get out of here! Go and wash up before you come back into the house."

Mari and Robb quickly set the bottles down and went out on the veranda. There was a wash station outside on the veranda down from the kitchen door where they washed up. Robb washed his arms and face, filled with dust and dirt from the cave and vineyard. He checked his shoes for mud and kicked at them. Mari reached up to the rack and handed him a towel to dry.

Robb grabbed at the towel playfully while Mari held it high over her head.

"Thanks," he said as he grabbed it.

She leaned over and washed her face; her blonde wavy hair shone in the morning light. Robb stood and admired her. He handed a towel to her when she finished.

Dagwood, close by, wagging his tail, sniffed at Robb. "What a great pal you have. I wish I had a dog."

Mari explained, "My dad's dog Pat had puppies when I was five, and he let me keep one. I always liked Dagwood Bumstead in the funny papers, so I called him Dagwood. Dad would read the funnies every Sunday morning to us kids. He used to read to us kids all the time. Come up with me. I'll show you the library."

She turned and led him down the veranda and up the stairs to the other part of the house. The house actually was two houses with a breezeway that separated them. There were five steps up to that part of the house. The bedrooms and library were in that part of the house. Robb had already been by the bedrooms that morning, but only figured out where Mari's room was.

Mari nodded toward the door on the right. "If you need to use the bathroom, there you are. My room is across the hall where you were this morning."

He slipped into the bathroom quickly and shut the door. Mari went on down the hall to the library. She plopped down and waited in the big green armchair. Robb found his way and stood at the door, looking in with great pleasure and surprise. Three walls from floor to ceiling all filled with books! The stone fireplace on the north wall near the corner stood cold with signs of having a fire the night before. A large window on the north wall next to the fireplace gave a view of Mount Saint Helena. The window on the west viewed the vineyard and some walnut trees.

He stepped quickly over to Mari and squeezed into the big green chair and snuggled close to her. They looked around at all the books.

Robb nodded to the right at the piano. "Do you play?"

"Some," she said shyly. "Daniel always makes fun of me because I sing when I play. I practice my choir music that Mr. Lee gives me for school and for church on Sunday."

"You go to church?" he said, surprised.

"Sure. I walk down the hill and wait at the gate on the Trail for anyone who is going into town to get a ride," she said nonchalantly.

"You what?" He looked at her, shocked. "What do your parents think?"

She tossed her hair and looked firmly with a haughty air. "They usually don't even know I'm gone because I get up early and get out on my own before they even get up. If I get there soon enough, the Baptist bus comes out and picks up a bunch of us kids. They bring us all home in the afternoon."

Robb wondered, "How is it you sing at the Methodist church if the Baptist bus brings you in?"

"Oh, they don't mind if I go there because they don't have a choir," she replied with a bit of a toss of her head.

Robb got up, sat at the piano, and started to play from the sheet music on the piano.

"Well, look who can play now!" Mari spoke a bit sarcastically. She got up and stood behind him as she started to sing the song from memory as he played. Robb joined in, "Blessed assurance, Jesus is mine. O what a foretaste of glory divine. Heir of salvation, purchase of God, born of His Spirit, washed in His blood. Perfect submission, all is at rest, I in my Savior am happy and blessed. Watching and waiting, looking above, filled with His goodness, lost in His love."

They sang out loudly, "This is my story, this is my song, praising my Savior all the day long. This is my story, this is my song, praising my Savior all the day long!"

They laughed as he turned around, grabbing her around the waist, and hugged her. Mari was surprised and pulled away.

"What kind of books do you have anyway?" He stood up and started to look at the shelves.

"My mom and dad read a lot. All the books are in order according to category. We always get a book for our birthday or Christmas from my dad's sisters in Illinois. Here…see all this section? These are mostly children's books we got as gifts."

She pulled one off the shelf. "I love this one about fairies. Each fairy is a flower, and then there is a poem about it. Don't you just love the artwork?"

He took the book from her and paged through it. "That's nice." As he put it back on the shelf, he found several books he liked. He had never known anyone with such a huge private library and was amazed as he looked around at the beautiful room. They spent quite a bit of time in the library since Mari saw how much he enjoyed looking at all the books.

"Come on, let's get out of here," Mari urged.

Leaving the library, Robb looked down the hall to the right, observing the rest of the house. As Robb came down the stairs into the breezeway, he noticed more stairs on the left. "Where do they go?"

Mari came back and looked over the railing. "Oh, that's the other wine cellar. Come on, I'll show you."

As they went down the veranda past the kitchen and down the steps, they turned back in front of the house over to the stairs leading to the cellar under the part of the house where the bedrooms and library were. Stepping carefully down the stone steps, she rolled the huge wooden door open. Robb stepped into the dark as Mari turned on the light. The dirt floor was damp like the other cellar. But this one had four huge ten-foot wine tanks standing off to the left corner.

"This is great!" shouted Robb. "Are they full of wine?"

"No, we don't make our own wine. They're left from the old days and the previous owners from years ago." As they walked around looking at them, the little frogs that lived there jumped around.

Mari flinched and moaned. "Let's get out of here. I don't like these frogs."

"Boy, your place is really great with all this stuff," Robb said with amazement. They both left, turning out the light as they bounded up the stairs.

Mari took this opportunity to walk down to the dam together, Dagwood following right behind. They stood at the top of the dam and looked back toward the house. Robb turned back to the north and noticed he could see Mount Saint Helena from there also. "What a view!" he expounded.

Mari stood close to him. "I love each time of the year. Sometimes there is snow on it." The sun was higher now, Mari noticing her shadow. "I see it's almost noon."

Looking around, Robb asked, "How can you tell that?"

Mari stood still and instructed him. "Okay, look down at your shadow. If you think about a clock, your shadow will point like the hands of the clock. See? Our shadow is at eleven-thirty."

Robb stood away from her to see his shadow. "Whoa! How neat is that?" he exclaimed.

"I can always tell when to get home on time," Mari explained. They walked back up to the house and on to the veranda. Robb opened the kitchen door, letting Mari in first.

"Is there anything we can do for you, Mrs. Rogers?" he asked politely.

"Sure, wash your hands and set the table for lunch," she responded quietly.

Mari and Robb washed up and went in the dining room to set the table. This time, he knew what he was doing. They walked around the table following each other as they put things out. Mari held her head down a bit and looked his way and smiled. "Thanks, I've been having a great time."

"Me too," he replied.

Everyone rallied round the table and sat down for lunch. RG sat down, flipping his napkin onto his lap. "What have you boys been up to?"

"Oh, nothin'!" Daniel mumbled with his head down. "Mark beat me at getting all the wood in again," Daniel said smartly.

"That'll never happen again, jerk face!" Mark argued, kicking at him under the table.

"Yeah, I won too. I'm on to him now," Robb said, smiling.

"Well, now, Mari, what are you and Robb up to this afternoon?" RG looked right at Robb.

"Sir, I will have to get down the hill before my dad leaves from the ranch. I've really had a great time already, thanks. And thank you, Mrs. Rogers."

RG grabbed a large piece of bread. "Next time stay out of that cave!"

Mama looked over to Mari. "Don't forget you still have to feed the dogs today."

"Oh, I'll get them done right after lunch, Mama." She looked over at Robb.

They were all excused from the table once they were finished eating. The boys shuffled at each other and pushed their chairs in as they cleared their own dishes away. Mari and Robb cleared theirs too.

"Can we help you, Mrs. Rogers?" asked Robb.

"No, go on you two and get out to the barn and do Mari's chores."

They rushed out the door and ran up to the barn. Daniel was already waiting for them, yelling, "Robb and Mari sittin' in a tree, K-I-S-S-I-N...G!" He ran off, laughing.

"Oh, never mind him," Mari said, embarrassed. They went into the barn where they had been that morning. There were two galvanized garbage cans sitting back in the tack room behind where all the rabbits were. The shelf above held four stainless steel dishes. Mari reached up and took them down, placing them on the concrete floor. She lifted the lid on one of the cans and measured out two scoops of dog food for each dog. By then they had all come running with great anticipation, wagging their tails. Robb was startled to see so many dogs since he hadn't noticed the other dogs before.

"Where did these guys come from?" he said in surprise, dodging around the pack. Dagwood was right among them. They all chowed down as if they had never been fed in their lives.

Mari explained, "They usually are running around the vineyard following my dad wherever he goes. They spend a lot of time running around the ranch checking things out for us like guard dogs."

Mari showed Robb how she checked the water for the chickens and the ducks. They filled the water pans carefully.

"We have to be careful not to waste any water because we always run out in the summer. Dad has to bring water up in that big tank on the back of the truck. We fill water bottles up for the house for all the cooking. I can wash my hair with one gallon of water," Mari said casually, but with a bit of pride.

"You mean you only use one gallon of water for your long hair?" Robb was amazed.

"It's easy. You only need a little to lather up, then the most to rinse with. Nothin' to it." She threw the bucket over by the barn door.

"Come on, look over here. I love this old barn. It's very old. You can see the huge timbers they used to build it. It's sectioned off in three parts. The center section is used for hay. It has a great wooden floor. This part is where they used to keep the cattle for milking. You see my dad turned it into a place for Daniel's rabbits. On the other side, you can see through the huge timbered walls to where all the tractors and equipment are kept. That section will hold the old pickup, dads' truck, the tractor, and all the disks, harrows, and other stuff. Someday I want to have a party in the middle," she said with excitement.

Robb followed her along with amazement.

"What a beautiful place!" he said quietly. They walked through the open walls and out the big doors.

"I better get down the hill before my dad leaves for home. I wouldn't want to ride my bike all the way into town," Robb said anxiously.

"No, I should say not. I think it's at least twelve miles," Mari replied.

They went down on the path to the house where Robb had dropped his bike at the end of the veranda. He picked it up, and they walked together side by side as he pushed his bike until they got down a little way near the dam where they had been earlier.

"Oh, I think I should tell my mom I'll walk you down the hill." She turned quickly and ran back to the veranda in front of the kitchen door and yelled, "Mama, I'm going to walk down the hill with Robb. I'll see you later." She ran quickly to catch up with Robb.

They were around the dam now and up to the fork in the road. Robb stopped and looked back. "I've had a great time. Be sure and tell your mom thanks for me. I didn't think to go in before we left."

Mari stood with Robb and looked at the view of the dam and the house. They turned and pushed on just as a covey of quail scurried across the road into the brush.

"WHOA! What was that?" Robb shouted.

"Quail, silly. Haven't you ever seen quail?" Mari squealed.

"Not until this morning when I came up!" he exclaimed.

"Yeah! We see 'um all the time. Dad won't let us shoot 'um because they're the state bird," she said proudly. "We do shoot the deer though. They come in and eat all the tender shoots on the grape vines. Dad has a permit to protect the vineyard. I think all the ranchers do," she said, a bit breathless as they walked.

As they walked, Mari explained how they repair the road in order to keep the rain from washing it out.

"Dad and the boys come down the hill every year with the tractor and smooth out the gullies the rain makes. They make these culverts to divert the water from one side of the road and down at an angle so the water flows into the ditch on the other side. My brother Mark crushed his foot last year with the big piece of concrete they were using as a drag to smooth the road." She was very casual about it all.

They stopped now to look out over the valley where Robb had first stopped that morning to see it. "What a view!" he exclaimed as he took in a big breath.

"You should see it later this fall when the vineyards turn color. It looks like a patchwork quilt." She smiled as she paused and looked at her shadow. "It must be two-thirty by now. What time do you need to be at your dad's?"

"Oh, I have time." They pushed on slowly as Robb didn't want to go. When they reached the bridge at the bottom of the hill, Robb stopped, Dagwood at his side.

"Come and sit with me on the bridge, Mari." He laid his bike down, and they sat together, hanging their feet over the side. The water looked cool as it ran under the bridge beneath them.

Robb scooted closer and put his arm around Mari. "You're the best! We could be together forever! When we get out of school, we have to get married. What do you think?"

Mari pulled away a bit and looked at him. "What are you saying?"

"I love you, Mari. You are the best," he said quietly.

"Oh, silly, we're too young to think about that. I've known you since grade school, and you only come around for my sandwiches at lunchtime," she explained.

"Well, it would be swell if you were my steady girlfriend. Wouldn't it?" he pleaded.

"Sure. It's a deal. I'll be your steady. No one else," Mari said enthusiastically, hugging him.

Robb grabbed her and gave her a big kiss right on the lips. She was astonished and kissed him right back. They hugged for a bit and sat in silence.

Mari said with a start, "Look at the shadow! I think you better get going before it's too late." They jumped up, and Robb hopped on his bike and sped off. He turned his head, his brown hair shining in the sun, looked back, and waved. "See you later, Blondie! You're *my* girl now!"

Mari walked back up the mile road slowly, Dagwood at her heals. She talked out loud to Dagwood, wondering why Robb would be in love with her since he was so popular with all the other girls and so big in sports. They had known each other all through grade school, and now they would be sophomores in high school in the fall. *I don't know what came over me. I've never been so impulsive.*

Robb came up several times during the summer to see her. In July, he and the gang from school came up for Mark's seventeenth birthday party. She and Robb spent time reading in the library, playing the piano, and singing. He helped her do her chores, and they went hiking around the ranch. He learned to leave his bike near the bridge and walk up the road.

Mari always found great relief from the huge production of canning fruits and vegetables, making jam and jelly, and just keeping up with all the work around the ranch, when Robb or any of her girlfriends came to visit.

All the while during her family's summer preparation for winter, she pondered why Robb would be interested in her, just a country girl, not sophisticated like all the town girls.

She kept Robb's declaration of love for her a secret from all her girlfriends since she didn't quite believe her dream of having a steady boyfriend like Robb. Was this too good to be true?

CHAPTER 2

Back to School

MARI WALKED DOWN THE HILL with her two brothers to meet the school bus at 7:15 a.m. as they usually did. Summer was over, and the excitement of the new school year as a sophomore in high school was almost too much for Mari. They waited patiently shivering in the cold with Robin and Annie.

"I hate waiting for this old bus!" Mari said impatiently.

"Oh, you are such a sissy," retorted Daniel.

"Augh, leave her alone," snipped Mark.

Just then, they could hear the bus up the hill and around the bend on the road by Jenney's. The bus came to a screeching halt in front of the big white gate where they were waiting. Daniel piled in first. Mark waited for Mari, Robin, and Annie to jump in, and they all stumbled down the center of the bus to get a seat as the bus jerked and started up the road. The half-hour ride was not especially new or exciting except for one thing: Mari was really looking forward to seeing Robb today.

Mari sat with Jenny, and they talked about their summer. Mari didn't say a word about Robb coming up to the ranch on Saturdays and the other days.

"How's your summer, Elzbeth?" Mari leaned over the aisle to her. "Are you going to the game on Friday?"

Elzbeth shyly looked over with her head down a bit. Her hair was hanging down around her face and apparently had not been combed. She wore a tattered old sweater covering a wrinkled cotton dress. She clutched a handmade cotton bag with her things in it.

"I won't have a ride. I don't think my dad would let me go anyway." She moved her bag closer to her chest.

"We could come over and get you if you can make it," Mari offered with enthusiasm.

"Don't bother. I won't get to come anyways." Elzbeth turned her head to look out the window.

Mari looked sadly at her and turned to Jenny. "Are you going?"

"I wouldn't miss seeing Robb and the guys for a minute." Jenny squirmed in her seat with excitement.

They piled off the bus with all the rest of the kids when the bus pulled up in front of the gray stone building. Jenny and Mari took the path to the girls' washroom at the end of the building to go to the bathroom, comb their hair, and put on lipstick.

"I have to get something out of my locker, Jenny. I'll see you in class," Mari said anxiously. She pushed the door and went out into the hall to her locker. The combination was easy, but she always paused to think about it.

"Hi, Mari, getting your books for class?" Robb whispered behind her.

"Oh, you devil! You know I was just waiting here to see if you would be around," she whispered.

"I'll walk you to your class. I'm just down the hall," Robb said as he took her books in his arms. He was only carrying one book of his own.

"I'm going out to the gym for PE. That will be out of your way. I'll see you later." She took her books back and turned quickly to go.

Mari looked forward to PE every day. This time of the year when they were out of water up at the ranch, it made it easy for her to take a shower first thing in the day.

They played soccer this time of the year. Mari was captain of their team. She and the girls on her team were fierce: Blayne Alexander was center forward, a very beautiful tall black girl with a perfect body; Joan Barnes, left guard, medium build, honey-colored hair, fast thinking, and a fierce player; Rue Alberts; Pauline Banks—the "gang" that all hung together in everything.

She stood in the shower after playing and thought to herself, *What I wouldn't give for this and hot water at home.*

Suddenly looking over at Elzbeth, she asked, "What on earth, Elzbeth? What happened to you? How did you get those big black bruises on your back?" Mari said as she started to dry herself off.

Elzbeth covered herself up quickly with her towel, pulling her clothes over quickly to get dressed. "Oh, leave it, Mari. I'm all right," Elzbeth said defensively.

They dressed and left quickly to get to their next class.

Mari met Robb in the hall. Robb took her books as he had done before, and they walked quietly up the stairs to the second floor where Mari paused, took her books from him, and went in the door, taking her seat. She looked up to see Robb still standing there, watching her. Then he quickly turned and went out of sight.

The whole time in class, Mari had a difficult time concentrating on the lesson. She worried about Elzbeth. The bell rang, and Joan and Jenny approached her.

"Have lunch with us, Mari. We're going out on the front lawn after we get something at the student store," Jenny said as she held her books close to her.

"I didn't bring anything today. We were so late getting going this morning," Joan said with an air of carelessness.

"I have a class with Mr. Patrick out in the new buildings for science. Where are you, Mari?" Joan asked as they walked down the hall to the back stairway.

"I'm going to Mr. Brown for history. Then I will see you at Mrs. Bird's for English." Mari waved to both the girls as they separated.

"Hi, Robb," both Joan and Jenny sang out together as they rushed to their classes. They giggled and looked at each other.

Robb was with three other guys on the football team. "What a dish, look at those…" Charlie motioned with his hands blowing at his fingertips. Charlie was tall and lanky. He always wore blue jeans with a big belt buckle and cowboy boots. He was really an awkward, shy boy.

"Yeah, that isn't all there is to a girl," Robb said with an air of confidence.

They were walking out past the new buildings where they passed Mari. "Hi, Mari," Robb said in passing. "Now that is what I'm talking about."

"You say?" Charlie replied as he looked back to see her go in the classroom door.

"I bet she wouldn't give you a second look." Steven sneered.

"Those girls she runs with are hot. I wouldn't mind getting in with them." Bill skipped ahead, turning around and facing the others walking backward. Bill was an Ivy League sort of guy, khaki jeans with a neat shirt always pressed—the studious one, always a leader.

They got to the Quonset hut where their agriculture class was, and Mr. Henning shouted out, "It's about time you guys showed up. We were starting without you."

The bell rang at the end of class, and the boys cleaned up at the wash tray. They made their way to the student store where they could buy soup, sandwiches, soda, milkshakes, and snacks. None of them had any lunch from home. They wouldn't think of being cool with a homemade lunch.

"I think I'll get out to the front lawn and see what's going on," Robb said as he waited for the other guys while they were getting their orders. He couldn't wait any longer. He headed for the door, jumped off the three steps, and off to the path past the main gray stone building. He stood and waited near a redwood tree and looked over the lawn to see who was there. His friends came up behind him.

"Where do you want to go, Robb?" Steven asked, nudging him in the back as he walked along with the gang. Steven was the Presbyterian pastor's kid: confident, sure of himself, and not particularly athletic.

"I see a good place over there where we can get a good look at Harper and those other girls," Bill said as he darted ahead a little, leading the pack.

"What did you bring for lunch, Robb?" Steven asked, checking him out.

Just then, they walked past Mari, Harper, Jenny, and Joan.

"What do you have there, Mari? Looks good to me." Robb leaned over and took her sandwich and bit a huge bite out of it.

"You can have it now!" Mari knew he hadn't brought any lunch with him. He wouldn't want the other guys to think he wasn't cool.

The thought of eating her mother's sandwiches with thick slices of homemade bread, spread with only butter and thick slices of roast beef or ham was more than she could stomach.

The boys walked a little way over so they could be close enough to talk to the girls and yet not be too conspicuous as to their intentions.

"Are you girls going to the game on Friday night?" Steven asked shyly. "You know there is a dance at the Presbyterian church afterward. Everybody will be there. My dad wants the kids to have someplace to go after the game so they won't get into trouble," Steven said with a bit of pride.

"As if kids aren't going to find trouble anyway." Robb sneered.

"I wouldn't be able to get into trouble even if I wanted to," Jenny said with an air. "My parents will probably be there, out in the parking lot, smoking with all the rest of the parents."

"All *you* country kids have to put up with your parents being at anything you go to since they have to bring you into town," Joan said smartly.

The warning bell rang, and they all got up.

"We have home economics next. If you guys hang out after, you might get something we made," Jenny said with hope they would come.

The boys did come and hang out for a handout. The girls were delighted to share and show off what they could cook.

Jenny, Mari, and Joan took off their aprons and rushed to their lockers. Mari ran up the west stairs to the library for study hall. Not giving her friends Jenny and Joan a thought, she looked for Robb in hopes she could sit close by in the library. As she got to the top of the stairs, she looked across to the east stairs and saw Robb. Her heart raced. She darted into the library and took a seat where she knew Robb would see her. As she set her books down, Robb and Jenny came in the door together. Mari didn't think a thing about it and waved Jenny over to her table.

"What took you so long? I saved a seat for you." Mari pushed a chair out for her to sit.

"I saw the guys, so I walked up with them," Jenny said coyly.

"Good job. Who do you think you want?" Mari said quietly.

"Robb, of course! He's captain of the football team now and will be captain of the basketball team and the baseball team. What a catch!" Jenny said with such assurance in her voice.

Mrs. Windom came in the library just then, and they had to be quiet and act like they were studying. The rest of the boys came sauntering in as if they were the most important people in the world.

"What excuse do you boys have this time for being late? Sit down and get to work." Mrs. Windom waved her hand to have them take a seat.

At the end of the hour, the bell rang to dismiss everyone to go home. Mari grabbed her books and rushed out the door to her locker.

"Hey, wait up," Robb called to her.

She was down the stairs in a flash, didn't pause a second at the combination to her locker, and got everything she needed. She turned quickly. "Oh, what do you want?"

Robb was right there blocking her way. "What's the matter with you?" Robb asked, touching her arm.

"I just didn't care for the way everyone was acting today," she replied as she turned her face away.

"I thought after summer, things would be different today. I have to catch the bus. I'll see you tomorrow."

Mari pulled away, dodged around him, and out the south entrance of the gray stone building, then out to the front where the buses were waiting.

"See you tomorrow, Blondie!" Robb shouted after her.

Jenny came down the center aisle of the bus and sat next to Mari. "I didn't know Robb called you that."

"Only just since the sixth grade," Mari replied, looking out the window so as not to let her see how she really felt.

The forty-five-minute ride out to the ranch was long that day. Mari paid attention to Elzbeth to see how she was.

"Hi, Elzbeth, did you have a good first day after summer?" Mari leaned over to look at her.

"It was okay, I guess," Elzbeth said quietly.

"Did you see any of your friends or see anyone you knew?" Mari pushed on to get her to talk.

"A few, but they were busy." Elzbeth turned her face to look out the window.

"What are you bothering with her for?" Jenny whispered.

"Never mind," Mari said impatiently.

The bus rumbled down the Oakville Road, letting Elzbeth and some other kids off. Mari waved to Elzbeth as she turned and looked back. Jenny was next at the Silverado Trail. Mari, her brothers, Annie, and Robin were the last to be let off the bus that day. They waved goodbye to the driver, Mrs. Jones.

"See you in the morning!" she said as she closed the door to the bus.

Mari went to the mailbox and gathered the mail.

"Don't you dare cross the creek to make the shortcut," Daniel shouted.

Mark was already well on his way up the road. Mari stood and watched to see Daniel disappear into the oak trees. Her books were as heavy as her heart as she walked slowly up the one-mile-and-a-tenth road, the long way around to the bridge where she and Robb had sat on that first Saturday. There was nothing but routine about that night.

The next day, she rose and grabbed her barn jeans and slipped them on quickly. "Oh my God! What the heck!" She pulled her jeans off quickly only to find a potato bug in the leg of the jeans. "I'll get you, Daniel, so help me, I'll get you!" she yelled.

Running out and up to the barn, she caught Daniel and yelled, "How dare you come into my room! Who do you think you are anyway? I know it was you who put that bug in my jeans." She charged at him, stopping short.

"You think you are so hot with those friends of yours. All your Jesus friends and your stupid songs," Daniel yelled. He grabbed her by the hair and threw her to the ground, kicking at her.

"Leave me alone, you fart face! I'm going to tell Dad on you!" She was in tears by now. Mari left the barn after she took care of the chickens and ducks.

"What happened to you, dear?" Her mother came over and looked at her face. "You're a mess. Get into the bathroom and get ready for school."

Mari was crying at this point. "You never do anything to him when he beats up on me. Why not!" she wailed.

Her mother just went on with what she was doing. RG came in and asked, "What the hell is going on with those two again?"

"Oh, just the usual. Don't pay any attention to that. I have breakfast ready," her mother said without much care.

Mari rushed through breakfast and ran up to her room to change her clothes. She rushed through the bathroom as quickly as possible. She wanted to look her best today to be sure she got Robb's attention. She felt a little threatened by Jenny and her thoughts about Robb.

Rushing down the steps into the kitchen to grab her lunch bag, she hollered out, "Bye, Mama. I'm going." Mari hopped down the steps and across the front of the house and down the road. She had no idea where the boys were or if they had already gone down to the bus. She walked briskly with determination, barely noticing where she was in the mile she had to walk. It troubled her that she had not finished her homework the night before. She hoped she would have some time on the bus or between classes to jot some of it down. Joan always was the one she could count on to help her with her math. It seemed there was never any time for schoolwork, only chores around the house and ranch. Daniel and Mark seemed so smart and never had any homework. The town kids always seemed to have so much of an advantage since they didn't have chores like she did.

The bus roared to a stop as usual. Daniel on first, Annie, Robin, Mari, and then Mark. Mari looked around for Elzbeth.

Jenny spoke up right away, "Here, sit here."

"Sure, thanks," Mari said, still wondering where Elzbeth was.

Mari took out some of her homework and started to work it out.

"What are you doing?" Jenny leaned over to see. "Can I help?"

"I think I've got this part easily. I just never have time with all the work I have to get done on the ranch. By the time I get home by four-thirty, feed all the animals, help with dinner, do the dishes, clean up other stuff my mom hasn't done yet, practice my piano—whatever!" She almost started to cry.

"I won't bother you now. Just get it done before we get there," Jenny said quietly as she turned and looked out the window.

The bus rolled in, and they all piled out. Mari hopped off the bus and walked around the front of the bus. To her surprise, Robb was standing by the redwood tree waiting for her.

"Hi, you're here early this morning," Mari said cheerfully.

"I just wanted to see you first thing and hope I can make it a better day today. I really meant what I said on that Saturday. We had a great summer. Didn't we? I just was afraid to tell all the guys." Robb was apologetic in his tone.

"The first day back after summer is always tough. I didn't tell anyone either." Mari motioned to walk down the path to the south entrance to the gray stone building.

"Did you get your homework done, Mari?" Jenny came up behind them.

"Yeah, I still have some math to get done before class." Mari looked at Robb, a little embarrassed. He seemed so capable, and it looked as if everything came easily to him.

They walked over to the lockers where they all sorted out what they needed for the next few classes.

"I'll see you later, Robb," Jenny said with confidence.

"Sure, see you in class." Robb nodded in passing. "Come on, Mari, I'll walk you to the gym. I won't be late this time." They walked quickly to get to class before the bell. Robb nudged Mari on the arm.

"Have a great day."

Lunch came quickly, and the girls met up and went out to the lawn again and sat down. All the girls had full skirts on with crinoline slips to make them full. They all sat so their skirts were fluffed and full.

"Mind if we join you today, ladies?" Steven came in and knelt down nearest to Joan.

33

"Sure. Where are your pals?" Joan replied.

"They stopped at the student store for some lunch." Steven laughed out loud. "They never bring anything to eat."

"I know. Robb always steals my sandwich. He has been doing it for years," Mari said with a smile. "He likes my mother's roast beef sandwiches with thick slices of bread."

Just then, Robb and Bill came up and sat down with the group. Robb reached over and grabbed Mari's sandwich as if he were entitled to it.

"I saw a list of all the clubs we can sign up for on the board in the student store. What are you guys going for?" Robb said seriously. "I'm going for FFA this year."

"Don't you have to be a country kid to do that?" Steven replied with interest.

"I don't think so," Bill interjected musingly. "I bet he could get a rabbit in his backyard to keep the lawn cut." Everyone laughed.

"No, seriously, I think having a ranch would be just the thing for me. My dad works out on the Trail as foreman on a ranch. I want to learn more about the vineyard and winemaking. I wouldn't mind having some cattle too." Robb was very serious. They all were so surprised to hear him talk this way since he had always been the big sports guy.

"I want to take auto shop and learn how to customize trucks and cars," Bill chimed in with enthusiasm. "I have my eye on an old truck up at Angwin a guy has for sale. I could fix it up and have my own wheels."

"I don't know what I want to do. My dad wants me to be a preacher like he is," Steven said hesitantly.

"What would you want to get into, Mari?" Robb turned to her with interest.

"I think I'll join the Red Cross club. Mrs. Blanchet is the counselor for that, and I like her. They meet during lunch once a month, and I would be able to get to that," Mari said seriously.

"I think I'll run for cheerleader this year," Joan added. "Will you guys support me?"

Mari and Jenny jumped in. "Really? How fun! We'll support you," Jenny said with great excitement.

"That is one thing I dream of doing, but since I live out, I would never be able to get to the practices," Mari said a little sadly.

"You would be great, Mari. There should be some way you could get to do it. Run and see if you could get it. You and Joan would really be great," Robb said seriously.

"What about me?" Jenny said with indignation. "The three of us would be a great team."

Just then, the warning bell rang to go to class. They all got up and brushed themselves off.

Robb and Mari walked together. The guys broke away as the girls went to their classes.

"What's with you and Mari, Robb?" asked Steven. "I was going to ask her to meet me at the dance Friday night."

"I wasn't going to say anything yet, but I'm taking her myself." Robb rushed ahead to get to class quickly.

Raising his voice, Steven shouted after him, "We'll see about that!"

Friday night came, and everyone was at the game. The whole town. The first game of the year was always exciting. They played Cloverdale every year, and the game was always close. Some years they would win, but the last two years Saint Helena had won. There was rivalry between them now.

Joan made the cheerleading squad with Hydie, Babs, Pauline, Rue, and Tammy. They were great! They had made their own pom-poms and changed the uniforms from the years past. That had created a big stir with all the parents. They were shorter! The skirts came just to their knees, not below.

The band marched out on the field playing with Zack leading the Star-Spangled Banner. Everyone screamed and applauded.

The two teams ran out on the field, and everyone cheered loudly with enormous pride.

The game was wild with excitement the whole evening. Cloverdale won! A very close game with a score of 14 to 13.

"Come on, Mari, everyone is going over to the Presbyterian Parish Hall to the dance. Are you coming?" Jenny asked, grabbing her arm.

"I have to meet my parents, and they will take me over," Mari said, looking for them. "I'm waiting for Joan."

Joan was with all her cheerleader friends now, laughing and picking up their gear.

"Joan, great job! Who you going with over to the dance?" Mari shouted over the fence to the field.

"I'm going with the team on the bus," Joan shouted. "See you there." She bounced off with the other girls and through the bleachers out of sight.

"I guess we'll never see her anymore now that she's so hot," Jenny said scathingly.

"She's just excited with her new job. We'll see her as usual," Mari said reassuringly.

Mari searched out her parents to get a ride over to the church. All the parents were excited to see one another. Football was a great time of the year where the community all came together. Some of the parents were in charge of the refreshment stand. Daniel's freshman class took it on this year as a fund-raiser to earn money to put on the school's senior graduation dance when they become juniors. This formal dance was called the Senior Ball.

Once they got everything put away and packed up at the refreshment stand, they all piled in RG's truck and drove over to the church. Everyone was already there. The music was blaring from inside the hall. People were standing outside with their sodas and sandwiches the church had provided.

Mari jumped off the back of the truck and quickly went to find everybody.

"Hi, Zack, great band! Have you seen Robb?" They both rushed in, looking around.

"I saw him with Joan and Jenny inside a while ago." Zack waved his hand in that direction.

Mari cruised around the hall looking for them. Robb was leaning against the wall with his left hand and arm on the wall. Jenny was leaning against the wall just under his arm, looking up into Robb's eyes. They were talking quietly to each other. Mari walked over quietly.

"Great game, Robb! You were right on as usual. I had to wait for my brother to clean up the refreshment stand before I could get here," Mari said as if nothing about this bothered her.

"Jen and I were just talking. Want to dance?" Robb said with a bit of surprise.

"Sure, see you, *Jen!*" Mari turned to the dance floor with a toss of her hair.

She and Robb danced close. "Are you mad about something?" Robb whispered in her ear.

"It just looked funny, you leaning against the wall looking into her eyes like that," she said, pouting.

"I was just tired. It didn't mean anything," Robb defended himself.

"I was really proud of everybody tonight, weren't you? The band, Joan and the cheerleaders. I think your team really gave it a huge effort. You'll win next time." Mari changed the conversation to a lighter subject. They danced several dances together.

"Hey, Robb, give her up. I would like a dance with Mari," Steven said, touching his shoulder.

"I don't know, if you want to, Mari?" Robb said reluctantly.

"Sure, just this once," Mari said to be polite.

Robb swung her out and around to let her free to dance with Steven.

"I'll be back to get her, preacher man." Robb pointed his finger at him.

"I sure would like to see you, Mari. We could go to the movies on Saturday," Steven said as they danced.

"I don't think I could since I have to take my eggs to the farmers' market, and Daniel has to take his rabbits to the butcher on Saturdays."

Mari was excited to think Steven thought enough of her to ask. She couldn't bring herself to tell him she and Robb had made an agreement to be steadies since Robb hadn't said anything to anyone yet.

"Thanks for the dance, Steven." Mari met Robb on the side of the dance floor.

"Why haven't you told your friends that we're going steady, Robb?" Mari said, rather annoyed.

"I just haven't gotten around to it yet." Robb swung her around to start the next dance.

"Does that mean you have changed your mind?" Mari pulled back to look him in the face.

"Ugh, come on, let's have a good time." Robb swung her around again as they danced. "I need something to drink. Let's go outside and see what we can find."

"What do you mean, go outside? There's plenty in here." Mari pulled at his arm as he started to walk toward the door.

"Shhh, I know some guys who got some beer. Keep quiet." Robb put his arm around her waist as he pulled her along.

"I don't want to, thanks anyway." Mari pulled away and went back into the building.

"What happened to Robb, Mari?" Steven rushed up to see her. He took the opportunity to cut in as he watched the whole thing. He knew what was going on out behind the hall.

"Oh, he and all the jocks are getting some beer. I'm not interested. Besides, my parents are here out in the parking lot with all their friends visiting," Mari said, annoyed.

"Here, have some punch and a cookie." Steven handed her a cup and a napkin with a cookie in it.

"Thanks. I need to sit down for a while." Mari went over to a table where there were some chairs.

Jenny came over and sat down. "I still haven't seen Joan. She's too good for us now."

"I don't think so. I saw her dancing. We will see her Monday as usual," Mari reassured her.

"All the jocks hang out together now, so I am on the edge too," Steven interjected.

"Come with me, Jenny. I'll introduce you to Chris. He's a friend of mine here at church."

They all got up and walked across the room where Chris and some other guys were standing around.

"Chris, I want you to meet a friend of mine, Jenny Hayward. She's a pretty good dancer." Steven gently put his hand on her side and nudged her closer.

"Hi, Jenny, want to dance?" Chris took the chance, and off they went.

"Now, Mari, you and me." Steven took her hand and swung her around and pulled her in close.

"I really want to see you, Mari. Give it some thought. We would be good together." Steven gave her a little squeeze.

Mari didn't say anything in return. They just danced quietly.

"I see my dad at the door looking for me. I think he wants to get home." Mari took a breath and looked at Steven. "I've had a really nice time tonight, thanks." She squeezed his hand and pulled away and headed for the door.

RG said gruffly, "Had a good time tonight? Daniel and Mark are already in the truck. Your mother is talking with the 4-H leaders and will be right along."

They got to the truck, and Mari piled in the back of the truck and sat on the bench with Daniel and Mark. She strained to look for Robb but couldn't see him. The ride home was cold and long. She washed up and was off to bed.

CHAPTER 3

Robb

SLEEPING IN A BIT ON a Saturday, Mari got up, dressed, and washed up across the hall. Down the steps along the veranda to the kitchen, she popped in to see if she had missed breakfast. There were some biscuits on a dish covered with a towel. She took one, spread some butter and jam on it, and pushed out the door to get up to the barn to get her chores done. She quickly fed the dogs.

Dagwood at her heals, she walked out under the big oak tree in front of the barn to see where everyone was. She figured she would have to help with the laundry today since she got out of it last weekend.

Back down to the house, she found her mother up in the bedroom wing stripping the sheets on the beds for the laundry.

"Well, there you are, sleepyhead. You going to help today?" Mama said gently.

"Sure, I don't mind this at all. What opera is playing today?" Mari enjoyed listening to the radio on Saturday with her mom while they hung the laundry out on the line. *Don Giovanni* by Wolfgang Amadeus Mozart was playing that Saturday. A light opera, said to be Mozart's greatest light opera. Dad had set up a place on the veranda where mama set the radio out and plugged it in so they could hear it out in the yard.

"I think I'll go down the hill later to see Annie and Robin. I haven't spent much time with them lately," Mari said as they ran the water in the wringer washer. She sorted the white things from the colored and the jeans in a big pile. They always washed the sheets first, ran them through the wringer into the rinse water in the wash tray. Then they washed the white things while the sheets were in the rinse water. She ran them through the wringer and into the basket. She and her mother went out together and hung them on the huge clothesline her dad built them out near the edge of the creek just next to the vineyard on the east side of the house. Everything always smelled so fresh and good in the sunshine.

Suddenly Mari heard her mother shouting out, "Get off me! Get the hell off me, you little critter!"

Mari lifted the sheets and peeked around to see Hermon the duck pinching at her mother's ankles. Her mother was kicking at the duck and waving her hands to shoo the duck away. Mari quickly rushed over and chased Hermon away.

"We may have to eat him yet, huh, Mama?" Mari laughed.

Mama suggested, "That old duck would be too tough to eat." They went back to the wash, mama quietly singing along with the opera. She was a soprano and had sung on the radio when she was in college. They washed and hung several loads.

"Do you think you will be all right on your own now, Mama? I don't want to get down the hill too late to see Annie and Robin." Mari was anxious to get going.

"Sure, I have things under control as long as Hermon is away," mama said as she took some of the dry things off the line and into the basket.

Mari ducked under the clothes and quickly ran up the veranda to her room where she changed her clothes into something nicer and . clean. She darted into the kitchen and grabbed a quick drink of milk and another biscuit. She ran down the steps past her mother, brushing her with a kiss on the cheek. "I'll be back to help with supper."

Her mother stood on the veranda and watched her run down the dusty road past the dam and out of sight.

Mari made good time down the road and past the bridge where she and Robb had sat and talked. Her heart beat a little faster thinking about it. When she got to Annie and Robin's, they were outside raking up the yard.

"Hi, you guys! Thought I would come down and see you since I hadn't had a chance for a while," Mari said, catching her breath.

Annie stopped raking. "This is great! I didn't want to do this anymore anyway! Robin, let's get something to drink and sit out here."

Robin put the rake against the little building where the tools were stored. "I know there is some lemonade in the fridge. Come in and help me."

They all went inside through the back door to the house.

"Hi, Mrs. Moore, how are you today?"

Mrs. Moore was so happy to see Mari. "We're wonderful, Mari. The girls and I have missed you. Bring us up to date and fill us in on the latest," Mrs. Moore said cheerfully.

They all went outside and sat down on the chairs under the small oak trees. Everything was dry and dusty. Robin had brought a large tray out with the glasses and lemonade. Mrs. Moore had some cookies she and the girls had made that morning.

"Where is your dad today, Annie?" Mari asked.

"Oh, he's at another dog show in Nevada. The last one he went to, he came home with three huge trophies, four blue ribbons, and a plaque for Best in Show. He is one of the top breeders on the west coast of whippets and greyhounds," Annie explained with pride.

Mari was really excited to hear about it all. She had seen Mr. Moore training the dogs down the Silverado Trail in one of the fields near a vineyard once.

"The greyhounds always look so sleek and fast when they run," Mari commented with excitement.

"Did you and Robin get to the game and the dance the other night, Annie?" Mari was fishing to see if they had any gossip that might interest her.

"We didn't get to go since my dad was out of town, and we really didn't have any way to get there," Robin said with a tone and a bit of bitterness. "I was wishing we could have seen your brother play. He is so dreamy."

Mari laughed. "Oh sure!"

Robin leaned over to Mari. "Do you think he has ever noticed me or said anything about me?"

"I guess I haven't. I will have to make it a point to see what I can do for you," Mari said very sincerely. Annie snickered a little, and Mrs. Moore got up and took the tray inside.

"Thanks, Mrs. Moore!" shouted Mari as Mrs. Moore walked away.

"It's hot out here. Let's go inside and sit out front where we can watch the people drive by." Annie jumped up to lead the way. They all went inside and sat in the front room by the huge window overlooking the Silverado Trail below. They talked and chatted at length about school, their classes, their teachers, and other kids.

Just as Mari was about to say she needed to get home, Annie jumped up and said, "Look who's coming down the road on his bike!" The girls jumped up and went to the window.

"I wonder where he's been?" Robin said curiously.

"He's coming from Jenny's house!" Mari said with displeasure.

"What would he be doing there?" Annie almost shouted with alarm. "I thought you two were pretty thick since I saw him here during the summer several times riding his bike up from his dad's place!"

Mari stood and watched as Robb rode by on his bike with his head down pedaling fast, not seeing them standing at the window. She walked back to the big chair nearest the window and slumped down.

"Oh, Mari! What do you think…what are you going to do?" Annie said as she came close and put her arm around her.

"Oh well…he was acting like a total turd at the dance the other night anyway…what do I care?" Mari stood up. "I need to get up the road before it gets too late. I told my mother I would be back in time to help with dinner."

As she walked through the kitchen, Mrs. Moore spoke softly, "I am sorry, Mari. Don't let it bother you. Just move on and make your way with someone else and be happy."

"Thanks for the lemonade and cookies, Mrs. Moore. I'll see you later. My mom says to say hello." Out she went up the dusty road, her heart heavy. She passed the bridge and thought about Robb and all his words.

"What a lowlife!" she spoke out loud as she picked up her steps getting up the hill.

Mari stood at the top of the hill where the road was flat and looked out over the valley with all its beauty. She could name every owner of every ranch she could see. They were all known to her parents and one another. With a sense of home and pleasure in it all, she walked on. When she reached the fork in the road, she paused again and looked up the hill to the left where the neighbors would drive, and to the right, to the road leading to her home. There was Dagwood waiting in the shade by the big rock next to the little oak tree. "Hi, Dagwood! Come on, let's run." She and Dagwood lit off as if in a race.

When she got to the house, she met Mark. "Robin said to say hello. She's really pretty, don't you think?"

"Oh, I haven't noticed." Mark brushed past her as if he hadn't paid any attention.

Daniel overheard and said with a sneer, "Oh, he noticed, all right. She's a looker, all right."

"Oh, shut up, asshole!" Mark shouted from the other room.

Mari went on to see her mom and help out in the kitchen.

"How were the girls? Did you say hello to Mrs. Moore for me?" her mother inquired.

"Everyone is great! Just great!" Mari said, a bit out of sorts.

"What's wrong with you? Didn't you have a nice time?" Her mother stopped to listen.

"Oh yeah! Only we saw Robb coming from Jenny's house on his bike while we were in their front room overlooking the Silverado Trail watching all the cars go by."

"What was he doing there?" her mom said with surprise.

"Who knows? What do I care anyway? He was such a butthead at the dance doing stuff and leaving me off by myself. I had more fun with Steven anyway. Steven is a real friend and a gentleman. Maybe I won't be bothered with Robb anymore," Mari said as she finished peeling the potatoes.

Daniel and Mark rushed in and said they had seen their dad up at the barn, and they figured he would be down pretty soon.

"What did Robin say about me anyway, Mari?" Mark said quietly.

Mari answered all the while setting the table, "Oh, just hello. Why? Why don't you just say hello to her yourself? I bet she would like that." Mari continued setting some dishes on the table. "I know she doesn't get to go to all the stuff at school because her parents only have the one truck, and her dad is often away showing his dogs at a show. Why don't you arrange for her to get a ride to some of your games?"

"I might just do that." Mark sat down at the table.

"Are you that hungry?" Mari said, looking back as she left the room.

That evening, everyone was quietly reading. Mari got up and said good-night to everyone.

"You just might get a seat on the bus next to Robin on Monday," Mari quipped as she left the room.

Mark pretended to not hear her. Daniel perched his lips and made *kiss, kiss, kiss* sound.

"Asshole!" Mark replied as he got up and went upstairs to his room. As he passed by Mari's room, he leaned in the door.

"Thanks, Mari. Night."

Mari woke early Sunday morning and took a bath. She put on one of her nicest dresses and her clean shoes. Finding her coat, she ran down to the kitchen. No one was around; it was cold. She grabbed a quick glass of milk and a biscuit. With her Bible in hand, she took off down the road at a fast clip. She didn't mind the cold, crisp weather as it was quiet and peaceful. She hoped she had not missed the Baptist bus. She looked out to see the Oakville Road and didn't see anyone. She picked up her pace and rushed a little faster. By the time she got to the gate, she was out of breath. She opened the big white gate, slipping through. Just as she shut it, she heard the bus coming around the bend. Getting out to the edge of the drive, she waved, and the bus stopped.

"Good morning, Mari! You going our way? Staying with us or over to the Methodist church to sing?" Pastor Bob said with a smile.

"I don't think we're singing over there today. I'm looking forward to being with you today," Mari said, out of breath, as she took her seat.

Jenny was already on the bus sitting in the back.

"Oh, hi, Jenny. I didn't see you there. Have you seen Elzbeth?" Mari moved to the back to be closer to Jenny.

"I haven't seen her in days. Have you?" Jenny said without a care.

There were a lot more people on the bus today. Mari sat quietly and took notice of everyone. She had not realized so many people took the Baptist bus into town for church. She wondered why they just didn't drive themselves. They stopped and picked up Margot and the two boys at the Martin Ranch. They were high school kids who rode on the school bus every day too.

Margot sat near Mari and asked, "Where is Elzbeth today?"

Mari replied, "She missed a lot of school last week. I thought someone would know where she was."

One of the adults turned and made a comment that when they passed by their place, it seemed very quiet.

Mari leaned up and said, "Don't you think someone should go over there and check things out and see what is going on? I think there is something wrong with Elzbeth. She seems hurt or something."

The boys started to sing and clap their hands, interrupting them. Everyone joined in, smiling and clapping.

The bus pulled up to the little white church where everyone piled out and went into the church. The Martin boys waved as they left to get over to the Catholic church.

The service was wonderful. Mari was so happy. Pastor Bob preached about the feeding of the five thousand. The little boy had a basket of bread and fish and shared it with everyone. When Mari started to go out to the bus after church, she stopped to speak to Pastor Bob.

"Have you seen Elzbeth? I am worried about her. That place where she lives is really awful, and she seems sad all the time. Do you ever get out that way?" Mari was very concerned. Pastor Bob said he would drive out there and check on things that week.

Once Mari got back from church that afternoon, she came in to speak to her mother.

"It seemed to me Robb and I had something in common this summer, Mama. Now he flirts with other girls and has never kept his word that we would be steadies. What should I do?" Mari sat on the window ledge in the kitchen while her mother was working.

"He seemed to be such a nice boy. I thought you were telling me about this boy Steven. You're too young to tie yourself up with one person, so don't worry about it. Just have a good time with all your friends. Be happy with every one of your friends you see every day," her mother said as she cut large chunks of bread dough to put in each greased pan.

"Well, Robb is the big football star and always struts around as if he knows everything. For years he has always been my friend and takes my sandwiches at lunch. *Oh*, I shouldn't tell you that! I never have liked those huge slices of bread with thick pieces of meat in them." Mari laughed out loud. "I think he's really smart and does well in his classes. All the guys like him," she added, still trying to convince herself Robb was what she wanted.

She went on, "The thing is, I told you, when I was at Annie and Robins' house yesterday, we saw Robb riding his bike down the Trail coming from Jenny's house. That just seems strange to me. Jenny didn't tell me she was having friends over. I would think she would have asked me over too." Mari was kicking her feet up and down while she sat on the windowsill.

"Well, now, that puts a different perspective on the issue," her mother replied. "I want you to just have a lot of friends and not stick with one person. I'm sure you will have much more fun that way. Now get off that perch and make yourself useful around here," her mother said in an encouraging manner.

Mark walked in at the end and heard part of what was said. "Mama is right. Don't get sucked in by that guy Robb. He isn't all he makes out to be. Do what I do. Make everyone your friend. Dad does. That is how you do business in this valley. Know everyone and be everyone's friend." He reached over and stuck his finger in some jam and licked it off.

Dinner was a round table of conversation as usual. Arrangements were made to get into town to sell rabbits, eggs, and do some shopping in St. Helena the next weekend.

"Blayne Alexander's mother just opened a shop called 'The Elegant Closet'. I sure would like to see what she is selling," Mari said with excitement. "Maybe I could see some of my town friends then?" She had great anticipation in her voice.

"My friends on the football team talk about the Weston's Men's Clothiers. I could sure use a new sweater this year, Dad," Mark interjected.

"Me too, Dad," Daniel said. "I'll have some money of my own after I sell some rabbits."

"Oh, all right! Your mother will want to make the trip too." RG looked over at Helen and winked. He placed his napkin on the table and stood up. "Very fine vittles, Mama. Very fine. Everyone to your duties."

Mari went to bed with great hopes and satisfaction. She decided to take mama's advice. Sleep came easily that night.

CHAPTER 4

Elzbeth

Monday morning, Mari looked around the bus to see if Elzbeth was anywhere in sight. She wasn't there.

"Did you go down to Elzbeth's place yesterday after church, Jen?" Mari leaned in and asked quietly.

"No, why should I? She isn't anything to me," Jen said in a disdainful way.

"What a way to talk, Jen! I can't believe you mean that," Mari said, surprised. "You go to church with her and go to school with her. She lives just down the road from you, and you don't care about her?" Mari moved away and couldn't talk to Jen anymore.

The school bus pulled in front of the gray stone building as usual. Steven was waiting by the big redwood tree.

Mari looked to see if Robb was there to meet her. He was nowhere in sight.

"Hi, Steven! Did you have a nice weekend?" Mari said cheerfully.

"I thought I might have seen you in church on Sunday." Steven walked up close to her.

"I went to the Baptist church because I rode their bus," Mari said as they walked into the gray stone building. "I know your dad is the pastor at the Presbyterian church, and you have to go there. I have to go wherever I can get a ride. My folks don't go to church," Mari stated matter-of-factly.

They got to her locker, and she fumbled to get the lock opened. She looked up at Steven and noticed he was intent on her.

"What?" she said quietly.

"Oh. You look so nice today. I'll see you at lunchtime out on the lawn, okay?" Steven turned and went off to his own locker. She shut the door and turned.

"Hello, Robb. Where have you been?" Mari was startled to see him.

"I was late getting here. I'll talk to you later." He turned and went on.

Mari rushed over to the gym and quickly dressed in her gym suit. When class was over, she rushed through her shower and got dressed.

"Great game, Blayne. We whooped them again, didn't we?" They rushed up the stairs together.

Mari and Blayne went on to their typing class and sat down. After class, Mari spoke to Mrs. Blanchet.

"Have you seen Elzbeth? I am worried about her. I haven't seen her in several days, and the place she lives is really quiet."

Mrs. Blanchet looked at Mari. "You are really worried about her, aren't you?"

Mari went on, "Well, that place she lives in out by our ranch is really strange. The men out there are weird too. She is always sad and never clean and taken care of very well."

Mrs. Blanchet motioned with her hand to walk out with her. "I'll look into it for you and get back to you, okay?"

Mari went on to her next class and looked back. "Thanks!"

Lunch came too soon. Robb came around to get his sandwich from Mari and sat with the guys close enough to seem not too interested in the girls but close enough to talk to them once in a while. Steven took the opportunity when they were picking up to get back to class to walk close enough to Mari.

"I saw you talking to Mrs. Blanchet after class. Is anything the matter?" he asked.

Mari looked a bit surprised. "As a matter of fact, I was asking if she knew anything about Elzbeth. I am worried about her. Doesn't anybody care about her?"

Steven was surprised. "I really don't know her or who she is."

"Well, she lives out by our ranch in a terrible place, and she never has any clean clothes on or seems very happy. She didn't go to church yesterday either. She always makes it on the Baptist bus on Sunday. She wasn't in school several days either."

They got to the lockers, and Steven said, "I'll catch up with you later. Maybe my dad can look into it for you."

Mari nodded and went on to her class.

The day went on slowly. Mari sat on the bus by a window on the side where she would be able to see Elzbeth's place. They got near. Mari strained to look and see anything at all. There were people there now. It looked like a lot of cars were there she had never seen before. Jenny was talking to Robin and Annie while Mari was watching out the window. The bus came to a quick stop, and Jenny jumped off the bus, waving as it drove away.

Robin scooted over near Mari. "Did you say anything to your brother?"

"Oh yeah, I told him to say hello for himself. He said he just might. Why don't you sit closer to him sometime to make it easier to say hello?" Mari said in a whisper.

Robin scooted down the aisle quickly before the bus could get to the big white gate. She sat one seat away from Mark. As they got up to get out of the bus, she stood up and made sure he had to see her.

"Hi, Robin," Mark said with a smile. He walked behind her. They got to the gate together, and Mark opened it, letting her pass through first.

"See you in the morning," Mark shouted. Robin seemed to skip a little as she went up to her house. Mari smiled to herself.

Mari sauntered home that day pondering about Elzbeth. She paused and looked out over the valley when she got to the flat place in the road at the top of the hill. She strained to see if she could see where Elzbeth lived. It was out of sight. Once she was home, she saw her dad out in the barn.

"Do you know about Elzbeth and her people, Dad?" she asked.

"Oh, that bunch. They are a bunch of Oakies who migrated here last summer. They seem to always be in some kind of trouble. Why?" He stopped and looked at her.

"Well, Elzbeth is a strange girl and always seems sad and never has clean clothes. When we dressed for gym, I saw a lot of bruises on her back. She's always really sad. She has missed a lot of school and didn't go to church on Sunday." Mari stood next to the tractor watching her dad work.

He stood up and looked at her strongly. "You stay away from that place, you hear?"

Mari was startled. "I never have gone there. It's too creepy. I don't get it. Why doesn't anyone care about her?" Mari spoke out.

RG stopped working and looked hard at her. "Why do you care so much about this girl anyway?"

"Shouldn't someone care and take care of her if she needs help?" she replied, raising her voice a bit.

"Now don't get excited! I can drive by there tomorrow and see what the hell is going on. Now get on with you and get your chores done. Help your mom in the house." He went back to what he was doing, puzzled over her concern.

Mari turned and rushed off down to the house with hope in her heart that RG would do that for her.

The next day, RG left early after Mari had gone down to the bus. He drove over to the ranch on the Oakville Road where he knew Elzbeth lived. When he drove in, there were four rough-looking men sitting around under the big oak tree. They were dirty and unshaven. One man stood up, walked over to RG's truck, and asked very rudely, "What the hell do you want?"

RG replied, "Just wondered if I could see your girl Elzbeth?"

"How do you know about her?" one of the men sitting around shouted. "She's a good one, if that is what you need."

RG shouted back, "Can I see her first?"

One of the other men got up and went into the old broken-down house. He could hear him shouting, "Get the hell out here. I have someone for you!"

All the men stood up. "She's a good one. Pay up-front! Where do you want her?" one man shouted.

RG was stunned at the casual way they went about it. He didn't expect this at all. Elzbeth came out of the house. RG said gruffly, "Come over here, girl! Let me look at you!"

Elzbeth was barefooted and quickly moved over to RG and the truck.

"What do you think I want, girl?"

Elzbeth looked down at the dirt. "I can take good care of you, mister, whatever you want. Don't make my dad mad."

RG shouted over to the men, "How much you want for her for the whole day?"

"The whole day? About $50!" the one man shouted.

RG pulled out a handful of bills, sorted out $50, and handed the money to the man closest to him.

"Get in the truck, girl. Hurry up!" He slammed the door and got in quickly. RG rushed, backing the truck out and spinning around to get on the road. His heart in his chest, he sped away quickly.

Elzbeth sat quiet as a stone, looking down the whole time. RG got to the big gate and jumped out quickly to open it. Getting back in, he drove through without even shutting it. RG barreled up the hill as fast as he could. He sped up to the front of the kitchen door and jumped out of the truck.

"Mama! Mama! Mama!" he shouted. "Get the hell out here!"

She ran swinging the door open to meet RG on the steps of the veranda. "What is going on?" she yelled.

"I have trouble! I have trouble! What are we going to do?" RG yelled.

"Going to do? What do you mean?" She looked and saw Elzbeth in the truck. "What have you done?" She gasped.

"Done? Nothing! I just saved this little girl. I have to call the sheriff! Get her in the house and clean her up. Get some of Mari's clothes and clean her up. She needs a bath and something to eat."

Elzbeth sat in the truck and started to cry.

"Mister, what are you going to do with me? Don't get me in trouble with my dad and those men."

RG ran back down to the truck. "Come on, girl. We're going to clean you up and get you something to eat. You are not here to do what you usually do."

RG took her hand and helped her down out of the truck. He took her in, and Helen put her arm around her and led her to the bathroom. Elzbeth stood there shivering in fear. The whole time, Helen comforted her. She ran a nice hot bath and told Elzbeth to sit and relax while she went to get her some clothes. When she returned with some of Mari's clothes, she saw Elzbeth still needed to wash her hair. She got the shampoo and told her she would help her.

Helen sang softly as she helped. Noticing the bruises, she said nothing. "Now you dry off and get these things on and come out when you're ready, okay? I'll be right outside waiting."

Elzbeth came out and stood still. "What do you want me to do for you now, lady?"

"I am Mrs. Rogers. You are Elzbeth, aren't you?" Helen said quietly.

"Yes, ma'am," she replied in almost a whisper. "Are you Mari's mother?"

"As a matter of fact, I am," Helen replied.

Elzbeth started to cry very hard. "Don't tell on me. Please!"

Helen took her up in her arms and wept with her. "Everything will be all right from now on, sweetheart. Don't you worry. Come with me now. We'll fix you something to eat. When is the last time you had anything to eat?"

They walked to the kitchen where Elzbeth sat on a stool while Helen made some eggs and toast. She could hear RG yelling on the phone.

"I need to talk to someone right now. Give me the sheriff. This is R. G. Rogers, goddamn it! Get him now. He is a personal friend of mine, and I have a serious problem. I need him right now!" RG was in a panic.

"Hello? Walter? This is RG. I have a serious problem on my hands, and I need you to come up to the ranch right now! I mean *right now*! As soon as you can get here! I'll tell you everything when you get here. You can't tell anyone what you're doing. I can't tell you on the phone! Get up here fast!"

He hung up the phone and came in the kitchen. "Well, don't you look swell! Everything is going to be just fine, Elzbeth. You believe me! Everything is going to be just fine from now on!" He took a white handkerchief out of his pocket and wiped his face and nose.

Helen hummed along, trying not to show emotion. She was intent, serious, and very soft and kind as she took care of Elzbeth. After Elzbeth ate, she took her out to the living room and turned on the radio to her morning breakfast club show. She got the Sears catalog out for Elsbeth to read. "You sit here and be comfortable, okay?"

"Thanks, Mrs. Rogers. What is going to happen to me now?" Elzbeth said with tears about to come.

"I don't know, dear. But you will be safe now," Helen said as she patted her on the shoulder.

About an hour later, a car drove up.

"Who is that? What do they want? Are they looking for me?" Elzbeth shouted.

Helen ran in the room and sat close to her. "You are all right. It's just a friend of RG." She could hear the men talking.

RG was serious, and the other man could be heard saying, "It will be all right, RG. You did the right thing. There won't be any charges against you."

The men came in the house where Elzbeth was and sat down across the room from her. "Where is your mother, Elzbeth?" asked the man.

"I don't know. I haven't seen her for a couple of years. The man I call dad is not my father. I just stay with him and the other men and do what they tell me," she explained quietly with great fear.

The room went silent. RG put his hands over his face for a moment, choking back tears. "What the hell! You know what this is? Come in the other room with me."

They left the room where they could talk privately. "I need a drink." RG got a bottle of Jack Daniels out and poured a glass for himself and the sheriff.

"I think we have to call the County Welfare people in on this. Can you keep her until we can sort this out?" the sheriff said quietly.

"No problem. But this has to be kept quiet. I don't want Mari and my boys to be talked about in this case, no matter what. You keep this quiet, you hear? I mean it! Don't let any of our being in this out to the press. Keep this quiet!" He was stern.

The sheriff assured him that it would all be done discreetly.

"We will make up a story that her parents went somewhere for a job, and we had to keep her until they got back. We'll ride with that until later up the road." RG shook his hand, and the sheriff left, returning to town.

"You will stay with us for a few days or so, Elzbeth. Don't tell anyone what this is all about. Everyone will know you are just visiting at Mari's invitation until your parents get back from a job they went to do, okay?" RG spoke quietly now to Elzbeth.

"Whatever you say, mister. I can keep all kinds of secrets. I know how. I won't get into any trouble? Nobody will hurt me now?" She got up and grabbed him around the waist and held on tight. He patted her on the shoulder and the head as he took a deep breath.

"Now go on with you. The others will be getting home from school this afternoon. You and mama get in there and do something wonderful to take up your time. I'll see you later." R.G. left the room and went out to move the truck from in front of the house.

About 4:00 p.m., he drove down the hill and waited at the gate for the bus. Mark and Daniel were off the bus first. They were so surprised to see their dad waiting. The boys jumped in the back of the truck with their books and sat down on the bench. Mari walked up and started to get in the back.

"Get in up here with me, Brat!" RG said gruffly.

She jumped in. "What are you doing here?" Mari asked.

"I have something to tell you first. I went to see Elzbeth this morning. She is at the house with your mother. No one is to know about this. She is waiting for her parents to come back from a job they got. Your mother gave her some of your clothes to wear. She's all cleaned up and settled in. I'll talk to the boys before we go in the house. She's your guest just like any other of your girlfriends who come up and stay. So when anyone asks you, just let them know she is here as your friend. You hear?" RG was intent as they rumbled up the road.

"Sure, Daddy. Thanks awfully! Whatever we need to do to help her. No one cares about her." Mari started to cry. The boys were listening through the window. They sat back and never said a word the whole time up the road.

Robin and Annie walked up to their house and wondered what RG was doing picking the kids up today.

Annie said, "That's funny to see their dad here at this time of day. I hope everything is all right up at the ranch."

"He is just a great dad, that's all," Robin replied as they got to the back door.

The truck pulled up in front of the big barn. Daniel jumped down from the truck and went over to his dad. "I saw five sheriff cars and a big van at Elzbeth's place when the bus went by. What were they doing, Dad?"

RG put his hand on his shoulder and said, "We will tell you later. Right now keep quiet and be nice to the girl. She is a guest of Mari's now. You boys do the right thing now! Don't make any slip-ups. I mean it!"

They all went into the house trying to take it all in and act as if nothing was unusual about Elzbeth being there.

"Mark, did you see Robin and say hello today?" Mari said to break the ice.

"Yeah, I saw her when we got off the bus." Mark got a book and sat down in the big chair near the window.

Daniel asked Elzbeth, "Did you see the dogs yet? Mari named her dumb dog Dagwood. He's the one to play with."

Elzbeth nodded and sat quietly in the big chair across the room.

Mari came bouncing in and announced she was going up to change her clothes and get up to the barn to take care of her chores. "Elzbeth, come with me. You and I will get things done twice as fast."

They both rushed upstairs with great purpose. Mari took Elzbeth into her room and changed into her barn jeans and shirt. "I am so happy you are here. We can have so much fun. You and I can work together. That way, I can get all my chores done faster, and I'll have a chance to get some homework done for a change." She rushed around while she was talking. "I bet you will have a chance to catch up on your schoolwork too. What about that?" She stopped for a moment and looked at Elzbeth.

"Things are going to be so much better for you now. Really! Come on now. I'll show you the ropes and how much fun this is going to be." Mari was excited.

Elzbeth followed along right behind Mari. They rushed up to the barn where Mari went through the routine of feeding the animals and showing her where everything was kept.

"You know all about me now, don't you?" Elzbeth said quietly while they were working.

"What does it matter? You're here, aren't you? You'll have some people to talk to in a few days to get things straightened out. Then you can make a new life and put this all behind you." Mari smiled and gave her a bucket and walked out to where the ducks were. "Don't be afraid. Just reach down and take the eggs out of the nest and walk to the next one. They will lay some more tomorrow." Mari took some from the first nest.

"See? Easy!"

They finished and started down to the house.

"Besides, Elzbeth, I'm not sure I want to know *all* about you and what is going on. I just want to be your friend like anyone else."

They stopped at the veranda sink, putting the bucket down, and washed their hands.

"Check your feet here and be sure you don't bring in any of the barn with you."

Elzbeth looked down at her feet and took a big rag and wiped them hard. "That okay?" she said.

Mari looked. "Sure."

Dinner was ready, and they all sat down. RG made a comment to thank God for everything that day.

There was little small talk that night. Mama spoke up, "I have a bed ready for you, Elzbeth, in Mari's room. I thought you girls would like to be together for now. Is that all right with you both?"

The girls looked at each other and smiled.

They were both so very tired that night. The boys had nothing to say to torment Mari. After dinner, everyone read for a while and went up to their rooms. They slept well that night.

CHAPTER 5

The New Girl "Beth"

ELZBETH HAD SETTLED IN UP at the ranch for over a week now. There was talk at the dinner table of the Christmas ball coming up at school, Robb and the football games he would be playing in, 4-H projects, and the kids at school.

"When is Elzbeth going to go back to school, Dad?" Daniel asked abruptly with a mouth full.

"I think we have things pretty well in hand now," RG said as he reached for a dish of green beans.

"I saw some strange guys driving down the hill on the way up from the bus the other day, Dad," Mark spoke up. "Who were they? Did they have business up here with us?"

"You kids don't need to know much now, and when it's time, you'll be told only what you need to know," RG spoke assuredly. "Just keep your mouths shut like you are for now."

"Yes, sir, we are," Daniel and Mark said together.

Mari and Elzbeth looked at each other and never said a word. When all was finished after dinner and the dishes were done, Mari and Elzbeth went up to their room.

"You think I can get back to school without anyone knowing what has happened to me?" Elzbeth said quietly to Mari.

"My folks are getting it all taken care of, and you'll be okay."

The next morning, Mari got down to the bus early. She thought she would go over to see Annie and Robin since it was early and it was cold standing around.

"Good morning, Mari. Come on in and get warm while the girls are getting ready," Mrs. Moore said as she waved Mari in to the warm kitchen.

"How are you today, Mrs. Moore? Are you feeling all right?" Mari looked at her closely.

"Oh, I am a little seasick this morning."

"Seasick? How is that?" Mari looked closer into her face. "A baby?" Mari said in surprise. "When?"

"Not till March or thereabouts. What a great Easter present for everyone. What do you think?" Mrs. Moore went on and reached for a cup and made some hot chocolate for Mari.

"Thanks, Mrs. Moore," Mari said, taking the cup.

"Oh, hi, Mari. Didn't know you were here this morning," Annie said as she came into the kitchen.

"I was early and it was cold, so I came over to wait for the bus. We can all go together. Your mom just told me you were getting a sister or a brother for Easter. What you think about that?" Mari said as she sipped her cup.

"Oh, we were sure surprised. That's for sure. It will be great fun," Annie said as she gulped her chocolate down.

"Hurry up, Robin, or we'll miss the bus," shouted Annie.

"Come on, she'll catch up with us." Both girls headed for the door.

"Thanks, Mrs. Moore," Mari shouted as they ran out the back door.

"You really think it will be great having a baby around the house?" Mari said as they walked. "I think your mom and dad are too old to have any more kids."

Annie stopped short. "Sometimes it just happens! That's what my mom said. She cries a lot now."

The bus came around the bend and down the grade to the big white gate. They all piled onto the bus. No more was said about it. Annie and Mari sat together. Jenny was a few seats away.

"Mari, did you get your homework done? Can I help?" Jen said kindly.

"Thanks, I did pretty good last night," Mari said with confidence.

They passed the ranch where the new family just moved in.

"I hear they came from some foreign country. Did you see their two boys? They are really tall and good-looking," Jenny said to Mari.

"They came from Italy. They know a lot about the vineyard and hope to reopen the winery on their place," Mari said with a knowing air about her.

"Really? How do you know that?" Jenny said as she strained to look out the window as if to try and see them.

"My dad met their father right after they got here. He knows everybody here in the valley. Why? Didn't your dad meet them yet?" Mari went on.

"Oh, he's probably too busy for that sort of thing," Jenny said in a huff.

They got to Margot's place, and she jumped on. She sat near Mari. "Have you seen or heard anything about Elzbeth?" Margot asked.

Mari tried to stay sure of herself. "I'm sure she is okay. I haven't seen anyone at the place for a while. Maybe they moved away."

Mark chimed in, "I bet they moved away."

Daniel chimed in, "Yeah, I bet they moved away."

Everyone chatted for the rest of the long ride in. When they rolled up to the gray stone building and everyone piled off the bus, Mari looked for Robb. He was nowhere in sight.

"Hi, Mari!" a voice came from the side of the redwood tree as she walked around the side of the building.

"Oh, hi, Steven. How are you?" Mari said, surprised to see him. "You're here early today. What's going on with you?"

Steven walked close to her. "Well, I told you I wanted to see you. I really meant it. I wondered if you would consider coming to our church and singing in our choir? There are a lot of other kids from school that go to our church and sing."

They got to the lockers, and Mari opened the lock easily. "I don't know how I could get there. I catch the Baptist bus, and when I don't sing at the Methodist church, I go there since they pick me up."

Steven looked around. "No one would mind if you walked down to us. Why not ask the Baptist preacher if he would mind?"

"Oh, I don't know. That's too much to think about. That's really nice of you." She shut the locker door and turned to go to class. Steven was close, and she had to brush close by him.

"I really mean it, Mari. I really would like to see you," Steven implored her.

Mari went on to the gym and thought about Steven. He was very tall and handsome in a quiet, intelligent way.

Lunch came around as usual, and the girls all went out to their spot on the front lawn. The guys all came around the girls. Robb took Mari's sandwich and acted the same old way.

"Thanks, Blondie! Roast beef today?" Robb said smartly.

Steven sat a little closer so as to get into the conversation more. Everyone talked about the game Friday night and the dance at the church. The day wore on with warmer weather. The last bell rang, and Mari grabbed her stuff and headed for the buses out in front of the gray stone building.

"Oh, hi, Steven. See you tomorrow," Mari said as if in passing.

"I am sure you will," he replied confidently.

Jenny noticed all this as she got on the bus. She made sure she strategically placed herself near Mari.

"I saw Steven talking to you. What did he want?" Jenny inquired.

"Oh, nothing. He wants me to sing in their church choir. That's all. He says lots of the other kids are there, and it's a really big choir," Mari brushed it all off.

"The Christmas ball is coming up in December. Who are you going with, Mari?" Jenny said with an air.

"I'm not even sure I want to go," Mari replied.

Jenny turned in her seat and put her feet up, taking up the entire seat. "What happened with you and Robb? I thought I saw you together. He always takes your lunch."

"Oh, shut up! You know I saw him coming down from your place on that Saturday. Don't play games with me about Robb," Mari said sharply.

"Don't get into it with her, Mari," Annie sharply joined in. "She knows perfectly well."

By then, they were coming around the bend on the Oakville Road where Elzbeth had lived. Mari turned her face to look away from Jenny to see anything that might be going on at the place. It was stone quiet. Not a thing was going on. It looked as if no one lived there at all now. The bus came to the Silverado Trail and let Jenny off at her place.

Mari watched while she walked up her driveway to their house. Her dad was moving hay out of the barn and loading it on the big truck he used to deliver hay. When the bus rolled to a stop at the big white gate, the five of them rumbled out of the bus. Mari went to the mailbox, got the mail as usual, while the boys ran up the road in a hurry. Annie waited at the pillar, holding the big white gate open.

"I wanted to talk to you about my mom having the baby."

They started to walk up to Annie's house together.

"I don't think Robin is very happy about the whole thing. She says we'll have to take care of the baby a lot, and she doesn't want it. She'll be a senior next year and wants to go to school in Davis after she graduates. I'll end up with it all when she goes away. My dad is always gone, and that leaves us home to do it all."

They got to the back-kitchen door.

"Don't say anything to my mom. She cries a lot now," Annie whispered.

They came in, finding Robin already getting glasses out.

"Would you like some lemonade before you go up the hill, Mari?"

"Sure, that will be great. It's been warm this week. I think I'll wait and see if I can catch a ride up the hill with my dad when he comes home from Napa. We should go out and keep an eye out for him so I don't miss him."

They all went out under the small oak trees and sat down in the chairs.

"Have you and Mark talked any lately?" Mari asked Robin.

"Oh yes. I see him often now, and we walk to class together. He and I have had a great time together. I hope he will ask me to the Christmas ball. You think he will?" Robin asked, a little excited.

"I wouldn't know," Mari said.

Annie moved to the edge of her chair. "He would be really dreamy at the dance." She was giggling.

"Oh, don't be silly," Robin replied.

"Oh, there's my dad. I better run and get to the gate before I miss him." Mari ran and waved her hand. "Thanks for the lemonade. See you tomorrow."

She got to the gate just in time for her dad to see her and stop. She piled in with all her books and the mail.

"What the hell, why are you still down here? Why didn't you get up the hill and get to your chores?" RG said gruffly.

"Annie's mother is going to have a baby, Robin and Annie aren't happy about it. Mrs. Moore cries a lot about it," Mari chatted on, out of breath.

"Well, now, isn't that something? When is that going to happen?" RG seemed to change his tone.

"Easter or so. What a present! Their dad is never home much, and they'll have to help take care of the baby." Mari went on and on as they surged up the dirt road to the ranch.

"Before we get home, I want to tell you what is going to happen with Elzbeth. We're going to keep her for a few months till things get sorted out where she belongs." RG was very serious. "I think we can send her back to school next week, but since she is all cleaned up now, she looks better, and maybe no one will notice who she really is now. Your mother thinks we can call her Beth and tell everyone she is a friend we have taken in till her parents get back from a big trip to Europe. What do you think?" He looked over as he pulled to a stop at the flat part of the road looking over the valley.

"We have to keep her secret, you know? Protect her. Can everyone do that?" her dad said seriously.

Filled with emotion, Mari started to cry. "Sure, Daddy. I can. Will the boys? Daniel is really mean, and I hope he never tells. Mark will never tell anyone. I know that."

RG started the truck up and went on up the road. Dagwood was at the fork in the road waiting. He ran along the side of the truck until they got to the house. His tongue hanging out and his tail wagging, he was always so glad to see Mari.

Elzbeth stood on the veranda, waiting anxiously. "Hi, Mari, I missed you all day. Your mom and I made all sorts of stuff in the kitchen. I never saw so much good stuff in my life!" Mari got out of the truck and went up the veranda.

"Let me get my stuff down, and I will be right there." Mari unloaded her things from the truck.

She went up to her room and changed her clothes. She held back tears, trying to compose herself before she went down to the kitchen.

"What have you guys made? I bet it's wonderful. Mama always makes the best stuff for 4-H bake sales." Mari stuck her finger in some icing. "I'm going up to the barn to get things done up there. Are you coming?" she urged Elzbeth.

"No, I think I'll stick around here and help your mom some more," Elzbeth replied.

Mari ran up the path to the barn. "Daniel, did Dad tell you about Elzbeth? You better keep your mouth shut or else!" Mari yelled at him.

"Go to hell, stupid. You and your Jesus stuff. Getting out of work on Sundays when you sneak off. Dad will lay into any of us if we say a word about that girl!" He threw a rock at her. Daniel went on down the row of rabbit cages watering each one. "You get the pellets and put some in the dish in each cage. BE CAREFUL OF THAT BUCK!" he warned her.

She hurried from cage to cage. "I have to feed my chickens and the ducks too." She dropped the bucket at the end of the row and went on to the chickens and ducks.

"Did anyone feed the dogs yet?"

"Yeah, I did," Daniel yelled.

Mark was coming down from the pasture where he had been taking care of the calves. He had been checking on the workers out picking grapes. Harvest was in full swing now. Mark had been put in charge of the vineyard this year for his FFA project.

"Did Dad talk to you about Elzbeth yet?" Mari asked.

"Yeah, I think the whole thing is really a mystery. What the hell is going on any way?" Mark was annoyed with it all since he had more responsibility on the ranch.

"Did Robin tell you about her mother?" Mari asked Mark.

"Yeah, what a sad situation that is. Now Robin may not be able to go to UC Davis after she graduates," Mark replied.

They walked down to the house together. They got to the sink on the veranda to wash up, and Elzbeth came out.

"We have some really great stuff we made today. I can't wait for you to see it." She was squirming with delight.

Everyone did their bit to get dinner on the table. Elzbeth sat with great pride and expectation.

"This is really great, Elzbeth," Mark said as he passed a bowl of rolls to her. "I bet you have worked hard all day."

"Oh, it was nothin'. I had so much fun I never had before. What happened at school today? Did anyone miss me?" She was excited.

"What happened to your hair?" Daniel spoke out without thinking.

Mama spoke up, "We decided to give her a new look. Do you like it? A little strawberry blonde and a ponytail like the other girls have. A little twist in the hair as I brought it back like I saw in San Francisco. She looks like a different person. Don't you think?" Mama said with pride.

RG spoke up with a little force. "About school. We think it's time you got back into it. We have made arrangements for you to stay here for several months. No one is to know the deal around here, and you all have to keep it a secret. We will call you Beth now, and no one will remember who you were since you are all cleaned up now, and you look better. You'll be a new person. Everyone will know your parents are in Europe, and they won't be back until next summer. Everyone understand? Mari and Mark will look after you if you need anything at school. If you have any trouble with anybody, just go to the office and call home here. We will take care of anything that comes up. I don't think anything will. You understand? Now, that is it. We aren't going to talk about it anymore. We're a family now. Beth, you will have chores to do just like any of the other kids. Mama will see to what you will be doing. Pass the potatoes."

Mama reached over and touched his arm. "Thank you, dear. Thank you. We're all very happy now."

Monday, September 24 came, and Mari got off the bus in the morning in front of the gray stone building. Steven was there waiting again.

"Have you thought any more about singing in the choir?" he asked as they walked in by the lockers.

"Not really, I have been busy."

Just then Robb walked up. "Hi, Mari. What's up with you?"

"What do you care?" She turned quickly and rushed off to the gym.

"What's with her, Steven? All I said was hi." Robb acted surprised.

"Don't be stupid, Robb. She knows you went to Jenney's on that Saturday. Who do you think you're kidding? She is too good for you anyway."

As they walked to their class, Robb bragged, "Well, she will be going to the Christmas ball with me. You wait and see."

Steven stopped and looked at him. "I wouldn't bet on that!"

They went in and sat down. Robb stared at Steven as he slammed his books on his desk. Steven just went on as if he didn't notice.

Over that weekend, Mari and now Beth talked about how school would be now.

"You have missed a lot, and I don't know what my mom and dad have done about the people at school. I'm sure they set things up for you." Mari was very sure of herself.

"I'll do all right. This is still easier than before," Beth said quietly. They went up to the library and sat at the piano. They sang songs together.

"You ever sing in the choir, Beth?" Mari had never seen her.

"No. I would like to, if I could." They laughed and sang for a long time.

"Ugh! Ough!" howled Daniel as he came down the hall into the library. "Ugh—what a racket. The dogs are howling."

"Get out of here! We're having a great time without you!" Beth said indignantly.

"We were having a good time until you came up here," Mari said. "I'm going to tell Mama on you. Get out of here!"

Daniel turned the pages of the music, and they fell on the floor. He ran off down the hall.

"Don't pay any attention to him. He's really mean to me all the time," Mari said as she picked up the pages.

"Oh, I wish I had a brother," Beth said.

"Well, you have one now! So live it up!" Mari said, smiling.

October 1 came all too soon. They all ran down the hill early that morning. The boys were ahead as Mari and Beth trailed behind at a good pace. They all were excited to see everyone and introduce "Beth" to them all. They held their secret close to their heart with some fear that someone would find out.

Annie and Robin greeted them at the big white gate.

"Hi, Mark," Robin said quietly.

"Mornin'." Mark opened the gate as everyone passed by. He hung back a bit to walk near Robin. "How's your mom getting along? Feelin' any better?"

"No, she still cries a lot. Who's the girl?" Robin asked.

"Oh, some friends of my parents are in Europe, so she's staying with us until they get back next summer. Her name is Beth," Mark said in a passing way.

Annie walked close by Mari and Beth. "My name is Annie. What's your name?"

Mari said, "*Oh*, this is Beth. Her parents are in Europe, and our parents are taking care of her until they get back next summer."

Daniel turned around and looked at them and said, "She and my sister are really stupid and get on my nerves." The bus rolled down around the bend and pulled up to a stop.

They all pilled in and took their seats. Jenny was the first to move from her seat to get close in order to find out who the new girl was.

"My name is Jenny. Are you visiting?" she said, being really nosy.

"No, I'm staying with the Rogers until my parents get back from Europe next summer," Beth replied with confidence.

"Well, you can count on me to get you in with the right people." Jenny was squirming with delight.

Mari was eating up inside with laughter to think Jenny was making such a fuss over Elzbeth and didn't even recognize her now. What a joke!

They got to the new Italians' place, and Jenny strained to see the handsome boys as they boarded the bus. "I will have to introduce you to the new boys from Europe. They are new here too," Jenny said all-knowingly.

Mari smiled even more to hear Jenny go on and on to Beth. Margot boarded the bus and sat near one of the new boys.

"Good morning, Margot," one of the boys said to her.

Jenny just about jumped out of her skin. How could Margot know them? The three of them talked all the way into school.

Jenny made it a point to get right up and see to it she was close to one of the new boys. "Hi, I'm Jenny. How do you know Margot?"

The older boy said, "We know her from church bus. Where do you go?" Just then, everyone was pushing to get off the bus. The boys and Margot walked off together.

Jenny just paused and watched in amazement. "I'll have to find out what church they go to," Jenny said out loud.

Mari smiled, almost out loud. "Come on, Beth. Let's get you up to the office and see about your classes. I'm sure they have them all sorted out for you already."

Steven walked up. "Hi, Mari. Where are you off to in such a hurry?"

"I have to take Beth to the office to get her set up for her classes. She's a new girl. She's staying at our place until next summer when her folks get back from Europe. I'll see you later."

She and Beth quickly went up to the office.

"Hi, I'm here with the new girl, Beth. My folks made arrangements last week for her to start this week," Mari said to the lady behind the counter.

"That's right. You can go on to class now, Mari. We'll take care of her and get her to class." The lady was very insistent for Mari to go on to her own class.

"I'll see you later. Make some new friends, okay?" Mari backed away, holding her books in one arm and waving her hand down by her side.

Mari went on to her class, all the while worrying about Beth and how her day would go. She saw Annie in the girls' room between classes.

"You okay? Don't think about your mom. Just stay on to your classes and do a good job for yourself. That's what I do." Mari was pushing her with her hand. "Go on with you. Smile. We all are," Mari said with a smile.

Lunch came around. Robb came by and got his sandwich from Mari as he always did. "Thanks, Blondie! Chicken today?"

Steven sat even closer so he could talk to the girls and Mari. Robb and the guys were laughing and carrying on as they always did.

The week passed, and no one ever knew who Beth was. Robin and Annie never mentioned they were going to have a baby at their house by March or so. Mark and Daniel went on with school as usual. The weather got colder as the weeks passed.

"Mari, I have been around now, and you know I want to be friends," Steven started one day at lunch. "The Christmas ball is coming up in a few weeks now. I want you to go with me. Will you go with me?"

Mari stood in her tracks. "I'm not sure my folks are going to let me go. They always have to come into town when we have a dance or anything. I will have to ask first. I'll have to let you know later. Thanks for asking." She smiled and walked away.

Steven stood there and watched her as she turned around and looked at him.

"I know you will," Steven said, smiling.

CHAPTER 6

The Confession

THE BUS ROLLED ON AND on while Mari watched out the window at all the beautiful green hills on the west side of the valley. Such a contrast to the east where the ranch was. The rocks and the oak trees were beautiful in their own right. Her mind wandered around all the things that had transpired over the last several weeks. *How do these awful things happen to good people, God?* she wondered.

Margot and the new immigrant boys were having such a nice time talking. Perhaps because her family had migrated from Germany several years earlier, and they still spoke their own language at home, they had a connection. Mari wondered what it would have been like to leave her home and moved away to some foreign land. What was going on in Elzbeth's head with her life? How blessed she knew she was even if she had her thoughts of how hard things were for her.

"Mari?" Jenny spoke up with a question. "S'pose you and Robb are going to the Christmas ball?"

"Oh, I don't think so," she replied without much care. "I have to ask my parents if I can go anyway. 'Sides, I'd need a dress to go." She continued to look out the window as the bus rolled along.

Jenny jumped off the bus at her place. "See you, Mari," she said as she walked up her drive and waved.

She and the others piled off the bus at the big white gate. Mari went and got the mail. Beth was waiting at the gate with Annie. Robin and Mark were walking together and talking. Mari watched to see if she could tell what they were talking about. Maybe Mark was going to take her to the ball. That gave her hope. Maybe if he went, she would be able to go with Steven.

"You seem deep in thought today, Mari," Annie said. "What is on your mind?"

Beth walked along to listen. "I saw you talking with Steven today. Did he ask you to the ball?" Beth inquired.

"Oh, what a dreamy guy!" Annie twirled around as if to dance. "I can just see him tall and smart holding you in his arms…"

"Oh, be quiet, Annie. It's not like that. We're just friends anyway. Besides, I have to ask my parents," Mari said impatiently.

Beth and Mari walked briskly up the road. They got to the bridge and admired the creek as it ran clean and slowly now as the weather was getting colder.

"Soon it will pretty much run higher when it rains. It always has a little water all summer. But not much," Mari said as she pushed on. They got to the flat part of the road at the top of the hill where they stopped to look over the valley to rest.

"What a view!" Beth said. "You are so lucky to live here."

Mari walked on. "Yeah, I know."

Dagwood was at the fork in the road, waiting as usual.

"Hi, Daggie boy! Such a good boy. You always are here for me, aren't you?" Mari leaned down to hug him and pet him. The house was in sight now.

"When we get to the house, let's work out our chores and get them done really fast so I can get some homework done tonight. It seems as if I can never get it done with everything I have to do. What ya say, Beth?" Mari spoke with assurance.

"Sure, I know how to feed the chickens and the ducks already. You feed the dogs and help Daniel with the rabbits." Beth was excited to have an important job to do.

"Rush and change your clothes!" Mari said as they bounded up the veranda. They rushed through the chores and ran down to the house.

"What can we do to help in the kitchen, Mrs. Rogers?" Beth said, out of breath.

"My, my, you girls are here early. Someone has to peel the potatoes, and someone has to get the green beans cleaned and in the pot." Mama waved her hand to show them. They jumped right in and tended to everything she asked them to do.

"I hear your dad driving up. Get the table set," Mama ordered.

Everyone got to the table for dinner. RG said something about how thankful they were for the great day and the great food mama prepared as he slapped his napkin on his lap.

"Daddy, do you think I could go to the Christmas ball this year? I am old enough now," Mari said as she passed the dish of beans his way.

"Well, I don't know. I think I will have to talk it over with your mother first." He looked over to mama.

Mark spoke up quickly, "I would like to go too. I'm a junior this year. I get to go since our class is putting it on."

Daniel snidely said, "Kissy, kiss, kiss! Who would go with either of you anyway?"

"Oh, I think plenty of people would like to go with Mark," Beth spoke up bravely.

"That's nice of you, Beth," mama said. "Your dad and I will discuss it later and let you both know."

The rest of the night went as planned by Mari. They cleared the table, did the dishes, put everything away and got right into their homework.

"Showing off, Mari? Doing homework?" Daniel prodded.

"Oh, shut up, butthole," Mari spoke up harshly.

"I need to catch up since I missed so much," Beth said quietly.

"Well, that's different." Daniel softened up a little. They both shut their books when they finished and smiled at each other.

"Now that I am back in school, I see no one seems to know who I am. I didn't think I was that much different now," Beth announced quietly.

RG overheard her and interjected, "You are healthier now, and that makes a big difference. Mama has dressed you up and changed your hair. You look like a great kid now. Keep it up."

Mark chimed in, "I saw you with some new friends the other day. They seem like nice girls. Who are they? Who are their parents?"

"I don't know. What difference does it make who their parents are?" She seemed surprised at his question.

"We always know who everyone's parents are. Don't we, Dad?" Mark replied.

"That's right, Buck. I don't want any of you runnin' with the wrong crowd and given me a bad name," RG said strongly.

"Maybe it's time you joined 4-H with the rest of the kids. That way, you'll meet all the right people, Beth," Mama said quietly. "You already have a great start with your cooking lessons with me."

Mari jumped in, "I can tell you everyone's name and what farm they own. Just look out over the valley when you stand at the flats on the top of the hill. I can name them all. Any time I go to any ranch, they all know my name and who my folks are." She had an air of pride about her.

Daniel spoke up, "I run with the town crowd. We're the brains of the school and run things."

Beth replied, "The girls I talk to live in town too. They don't seem any smarter than I am. One girl said her dad owned one of the wineries. I don't know which one, but I'll find out for you."

RG quickly replied, "Whatever you do, never tell those girls anything about what has happened to you, or you'll be ruined."

"Never, Mr. Rogers, never!" She put her head down as a tear fell down her cheek.

"Now look what you've done!" mama said admonishingly. "You are doing just fine, Beth. You keep up the good work, and you will be the best of them all, you wait and see. Now everyone get up to your rooms and get to bed."

They all jumped up and rushed up stairs to their rooms.

"Mari? Do you know those girls I know?" Beth asked.

"I haven't seen you with them. I'll have to make it a point to check up and watch. Where do you go when you have lunch? My gang all go out on the front lawn and sit. Maybe I'll have to take a walk around to where you lower classmen sit and see what you are up to. I'll make it look like we just happened to come around, okay?"

"Would you do that? I don't want RG to get into any trouble because of me, after all he has done for me already." They both were in bed looking over at each other.

"That will be fun spying on you. My friends and I will get a kick out of seeing what you little kids are doing anyway." Mari rolled over and smiled to herself.

Mari was looking forward to lunch today. She had a mission.

"I'm not going to stay out on the lawn today. Anyone want to walk with me around campus and see what's going on with the little kids?"

Steven jumped up to take the opportunity. "Sure!"

Jenny said she would rather stay. It looked like she had her eyes on Robb. Mari walked away with Steven toward the other side of the gray stone building near the auditorium.

"Do you know where the little kids hang out, Steven? I'm checking up on my friend Beth to see how she is getting along."

"My little brother is in her class. Actually, they all hang out near the music building behind the gym." They stepped it up a little faster.

"Do you know any of those kids' parents? Who are they?" Mari said anxiously.

"Well, the Richland kid and his cousins are part of it. The girls come from the big winery just out of town. My dad knows their old lady aunts who live in the big mansion just inside the rock wall pillars," Steven said casually. "My brother runs with them all. Maybe she's with them."

They came around the music building and saw them all. Some of the guys were on the field playing catch, and the girls were sitting on some benches watching.

"Let's walk over and sit a little way away and watch," Mari said quietly. "I see your brother now. Is he the one with the red shirt on?"

"Yeah, that's him. He thinks he is a real jock," Steven said with pride.

"Well, we need some good players in his class," Mari replied.

"Did you ask your parents if you could come with me to the ball?" Steven asked as they found a seat near enough to see what was going on without being too obvious.

"I asked. So did my brother Mark. Maybe if he gets to go, he will let me ride with him into town," Mari said as she watched for Beth.

"Oh, if you come with me, I'll come out and get you. I can drive now," Steven said excitedly. "I just got my license the other week."

"Whoa!" Mari was excited. "I'm hoping Mark will take Robin. We'll see."

"Has anyone else asked you to go?" Steven inquired as he leaned in close to her shoulder.

"I don't have a dress. I don't know if Mama will let me have a new dress," Mari said, a little sad.

"I think if I came up to the ranch to see you and meet your dad, he would let you go. Ya think?" Steven said with great confidence.

"It means a lot to my dad to know everyone. I'm sure he knows your dad already," Mari said as she turned and looked at him.

The first warning bell rang to go back to class.

"I think I've seen enough, don't you? Let's get out of here before your brother and his fancy friends see us. Beth wouldn't want anyone of her new friends to see me," Mari said as she hopped off the bench.

"You afraid that you're not good enough for them? You are R. G. Rogers's daughter! Everyone knows Mark and Daniel. They all know your dad and who he is," Steven said, surprised at her.

"What do you mean?" Mari said as they walked between the gym and music building. "My dad does know everyone. He works hard just like anyone else in the valley."

"Well, no one else has the power he has. Everyone knows that! He gets things done and done right. My dad talks about him all the time. He and the ranchers see to it that fair labor and prices are made for the farmworkers. They had a big meeting about it, and everyone had to do what he said," Steven said with assurance.

They reached their lockers.

"Hi, Jen. Have a good lunch?" Mari said when she got in close to her, knowing all along all she wanted to find out was how she did with Robb.

"Nothing happened!" Jenny slammed the locker door. "Why? What do you care anyway?"

Mari replied, "You don't have to be snotty to me like that."

They walked up the stairs to class.

Robb came up behind. "Haven't seen you around today, Mari. What's up?"

"Oh, just changing my routine and checking out my new little sister, seeing if she's doing all right." She tossed her hair nonchalantly.

Robb leaned in. "Oh, she's doing all right, that's for sure. She's got in with the right gang already."

Mari turned and looked him straight in the face. "You be nice to her now, you hear! Her parents are gone, and she's with us now till they get back from Europe."

"Don't worry about me. What are you getting all ouchy about?" They got to their class and went in and sat down.

Mari looked over at him and smiled. He winked and clicked his mouth in a smart way and pointed at her.

That week went by fast. The juniors were planning the decorations for the fall festival in the gym. The home economics class was planning a fashion show and a tea out on the side lawn. The FFA guys were planning a big show they were putting out on the field near their building. The guys in the woodshop were getting their projects all finished to have them out in front of their building to show off. Daniel and all the smart kids in the science and math department were setting up some big experiments.

Friday, there was going to be a big rally in the gym. The cheerleaders and the band were preparing a big show for everyone. The whole school was buzzing with anticipation.

Joan and the cheerleaders came rushing over to Mari and Jenny where they were standing outside the library.

"Did you see us? We were great! Well, we thought we were— don't mean to sound that way," Joan said as she bounced around with her friends.

"Mari, still friends?" Joan and the others bounced off toward the gym.

"Well, I told you she wouldn't have the time of day for us once she made cheerleader!" Jenny said scathingly.

"I guess I have been so busy with other things I haven't had time to notice." Mari brushed it all off.

The fall festival was a big deal on campus. The teachers wanted to show off the good start to the school year, the academic achievements being made and the future of things to come in the school year. By this time in October, everyone was in the swing of things, and harvest was winding down. The smell of change in the air was at hand, and everyone was setting up for a show of the harvest, even with the impending Christmas ball and the concerts the music department had planned for the Christmas season.

"My brother is on the committee now to help plan for the ball. Are you going?" Mari asked Jenny.

"I don't know yet," she said as she changed the subject. "Your new sister Beth seems to be doing well for herself."

"What do you mean by that?" Mari turned and looked sternly at her.

"I mean she seems to be doing all right with those town kids," Jenny said, a little bit snooty.

Mari replied, "She knows Steven's family, that's all, and those kids he knows. What of it?"

"Well, I don't see us with that sort, do you? We're country kids, and they are town kids." Jenny was rather indignant.

Mari looked around. "I don't like that kind of talk from anyone. I don't see the difference. So just quit it." She walked away to go on to her other class, leaving Jenny on her own.

On the way home on the bus, Jenny sat closer to Mari. "I'm sorry about earlier, Mari. I don't mean anything by it." They rolled past the place where Elzbeth used to live.

"I wonder what ever happened to that girl and those awful people who lived there?" Jenny said.

"Yeah, I wonder?" Beth said, smiling inside. Mari looked back as they passed.

"Sure is quiet there now, isn't it? I wonder if my dad knows what is happening with that ranch. Maybe it will be for sale sometime if no one lives there now," Mari mused to herself out loud.

Mark overheard Jenny's question and replied, "I heard those men were put in jail for something. I would like to have that place for myself. I could make something of that vineyard. It has good stock on it."

One of the immigrant boys spoke up, "My dad was over there looking at that place the other week, and I think he is going to buy it."

"Hi, my name is Mark Rogers. What is yours? I'm sorry we haven't met yet."

In a heavy Italian accent, he spoke his name. "Call me Alanso, Alanso Martin. My brother Dante, he is the younger one. We come from Italy just in January. Our father is a vintner from Italy. We hope to make fine wine here in Napa Valley."

Mark went on, "We have the ranch up the road from the big white gate. Come up any time to see our vineyard. We have Mountain Zinfandel grapes. Only one of three vineyards in the valley like it," Mark said with pride.

The bus rolled to a quick stop for Jenny to get off. She looked at Mari and gave an expression of *whoa...looking...at him!* Mari smiled and nodded her head. Beth was almost laughing out loud. The boys continued to talk as Mari and Beth snickered and jabbed at each other knowingly.

"See you, fellas. I mean it. Come on up the road anytime, and I'll show you around and introduce you to our dad, R. G. Rogers."

"Yeah, we already know about him. Like to really meet him."

Mark, Daniel, Robin, Annie, Mari, and Beth pilled off the bus. Dante lowered the window and shouted, "Bye, bye Beth."

"How did he know my name?" Beth asked Annie.

"He must have heard Jenny say it on the bus. Come on."

They all waved and went on their way. Annie and Robin got in the door and found their mother in tears again.

"What's the matter, Mom?" Robin put her arms around her in a big hug.

"Your father is off to Texas again for another dog show, leaving us alone again. There is so much to do around here, and now I am so big and fat I can hardly get anything done."

Annie spoke up, "Grandma will give us money, and we can hire someone to help out at the kennel."

Robin turned. "We can't always ask grandma for money. She always does everything for us. I think we should just go to San Francisco and spend the weekend to see her anyway. That should cheer you up, Mama."

Annie jumped up and down. "That would be so much fun, Mommy. Please let us? We can go shopping, and Robin can get a dress for the ball."

Robin scolded her, "Who said I was going to the ball anyway?"

"Well, didn't Mark ask you? I saw you two talking. I just guessed he did. Didn't he? Well?" Annie said, whining a bit.

"Oh, you two. Stop it right now." Mrs. Moore started into the kitchen.

"Let's have something really special to eat. I will call your grandmother tonight and see what she says," Mrs. Moore said cheerfully.

That weekend, they did go into the City. Their grandfather was a merchant marine, captain of a big merchant ship that sailed all over the world. He was gone all the time just like their dad. Grandma loved it when they came. She loved indulging them in anything they wanted. Shopping was the best. They went to Sacks Fifth Avenue, Neiman Marcus, Macys, Blum's Candy, the Top of the Mark, and all the best restaurants in town. They loved going down to the pier to watch all the big ships come into the bay. Maybe it would be grandpa's ship.

Grandma took them to the de Young museum and Golden Gate Park. They were able to get into the Presidio and drive around the beautiful houses where the officers lived.

"I will marry one of these officers someday," Annie said dreamily.

"Oh, sure you will. And he will be gone all the time too," Robin said strongly. "I will marry a rich rancher and have a big house with lots of kids. I'll have a big barn and horses too," Robin added, dreaming.

They shopped all day Saturday and Sunday. When they returned home, things were just the same. Grandma had given them permission to hire a couple of hands to look after things on the place. Their mother seemed a little happier and busier now that she had to manage the men and see to it that things were under control again.

"Where have you been all weekend, Robin? I came down to see you Saturday," Mark said while they waited for the bus.

"We went into the City to see our grandma. My mother needed some help. Our dad is in Texas at a dog show. We hope he comes home with some big trophies. That will make his dogs worth a lot of money when he has puppies."

"My dad said I could go to the ball. Are you going to go with me?" Mark was filled with hope.

"I bought a pink dress. I was hoping we would get to go. It will be great!" she replied, really excited.

Mark leaned in and kissed her on the cheek. Daniel kept his mouth shut for once. He just watched his big brother in a special moment. They all piled on the bus and sat down in strategic places for the best social advantage.

Alanso and Dante boarded the bus. The girls all watched closely to see where they would sit now. Dante moved toward Beth and sat one seat away.

"Hi, Beth. It's Beth, right? I heard your name the other day. I am Dante. I think we're in the same classes?"

Beth was taken by surprise. "I think I have seen you around. We saw your place when you moved in a while back. We all wondered who the new people were who took over the place. It was empty for a long time. Do you think your dad will really buy that place on the Oakville Road? I think the place must need a lot of work," Beth said.

Mari looked on with amazement at how well she handled herself. She was a completely new person with such confidence now. She mused to herself, *I think this little bird can fly by herself now.*

"Look at that," Jenny said, poking Mari on the arm. "She gets in with just anybody, doesn't she?"

"Be careful. You just might turn completely green," Mari said with great pride. "Know if you're going to the ball yet?" Mari took this opportunity to be a bit petty.

"Haven't decided yet," Jen replied with the turn of her head.

Margot got on the bus and sat close to Alanso and Mark, taking up a conversation with them both. They were all close in age and had a lot in common.

"Alanso, think you might get to the ball?" Mark asked.

"I don't know about a ball. What is that all about?" Alanso asked.

"Well, you and Margot could go together and dance and have a great time of it. Everyone dresses up in their best suit, and the girls wear fancy dresses. We dance and eat and just have a great time. Think about it and see what you think."

Alanso looked at Margot. "You want to go to ball?"

"Every girl wants to go to the ball," she said with a smile.

"Well, then you and I will go to this ball, okay?" Alanso smiled.

The bus turned into the drive, in front of the gray stone building and rolled to a stop.

"That's us. See you guys later." Alanso stood up with his books under his left arm and waved Margot to go ahead of him as they left the bus together.

"Did you see that?" Jenny said in amazement. "Just that easy, she got a date to the ball. Can you get that?"

"I think it's really wonderful for her. Like she said, every girl wants to go to the ball." Mari laughed out loud as they left the bus.

There was Steven, waiting at the corner of the gray stone.

"I don't see Robb anywhere, Mari. What has happened with him?" Jen leaned over to Mari quietly.

"I think you know. Don't be that way about it. I don't care anyway. If he wants to be like that, what difference does it make to me?" Mari went ahead. "Hi, Steven. You wouldn't believe what just happened on the bus. Alanso and Margot are going to the ball together. My brother set it up, right in front of everybody."

They both laughed and walked into the building.

Robb was coming in behind them. "Mari, wait up. I want to see you." He rushed up. "Hi, Steven. What's up with you?" He pushed in and got nearer to Mari. "You and I are going to the ball, right?"

Steven stood in closer to Mari. "I don't think so. She's going with me."

"I don't think so. She's promised to me." Robb was acting really tough. "We made a pact last summer, and she is my girl."

Mari got really angry. "How is it if I'm your girl you're seeing Jenny? Steven asked me to the ball, and you never did! Steven is a real gentleman, and you're not. Steven and I will be going to the ball!"

"Oh, that. She isn't anything. I just went out there one time." Robb tried to brush it off.

"That doesn't work for me. You don't even come around with me since then or walk me to class or hardly talk to me. You never even told the guys that we were going together. If you liked me, you would be there for me and be my friend in front of everybody. Don't come around and take my sandwich anymore. You are a creep!" She walked away quickly. Tears ran down her face as she went to class.

"Mari, I need to talk to you." Jenny rushed up behind her. "What? What do you want now?" Mari said impatiently.

"I have to tell you something," Jen whispered.

"Well, it will have to wait. I'll see you at lunch." Mari could hardly keep her mind on her classes all morning. Lunchtime seemed to be a century away.

"Mari, there you are. I need to see you." Jenny caught up with her at the lockers.

They walked out to the lawn where they always sat. No one was there yet.

"I missed my period a few months," Jenny started.

"What? What do you mean you missed your period? How is that?" Mari was almost angry. "What have you gone and done? Who have you been with anyway? I didn't know you were seeing anyone special. You been sneaking around?"

Jenny started to cry. "Well, it's like this. You know Robb came out to my place that Saturday… We were out in our barn, and before I knew it he came on…I wanted…he kissed me and…I just loved it, so…before I knew it…it felt so good, and I couldn't stop. I just wanted him to love me and be the one for me." She put her hands over her face. "He doesn't even talk to me anymore like before. What am I going to do?"

Mari put her hand on her arm. "You better straighten up before everyone gets here."

Joan and the cheerleaders all came bouncing up. "You guys want to see our routine?" They all jumped out on the lawn in front of them and started in. The guys were walking up at that point. Robb reached down to take Mari's sandwich.

"Buzz off, jerk! I told you. You've had your last sandwich from me. Bring your own lunch." Mari covered her lunch with her skirt.

"Oh, don't be like that, Blondie. You know you don't mean it," Robb tried to appeal to her kindness.

"Push off, Robb! I mean it! Get off with you. We're watching Joan and the cheerleaders," Mari insisted.

Steven and Zack sat close to the girls while the other guys were a bit farther away.

"Did you hear about Alanso and Margot? They're going to the ball together." Zack snickered.

"Why is that so funny?" Mari said.

Zack sheepishly replied, "Oh, I don't know. It just is?"

Steven interjected an idea, "Well, those boys are Catholic, and she is a Protestant."

"Well, who are you taking, anyway?" Jenny said with an air about her.

Zack shyly replied, "Nobody would go with me. I can't dance. I just would go for the food anyway. I bet your mom will make some of her pies."

Jenny spoke up, "I *will* go with you. If you want. My folks will be helping out anyway. I could come into town with them. We could meet at the door."

Zack looked at her. "Seriously? That isn't how I think it would go for me. I think a guy has to pick a girl up and take her in his car. That way, after we get out on our own for a while, you know…get some stuff?" He motioned with his hand as if to be drinking.

Jenney put her head down. "Yeah, I know. I don't think I would like that. You better find someone else to take."

Steven punched him. "What do you mean 'get some stuff'? You don't even smoke or drink. You tryin' to sound like a big shot?"

Zack pushed back. "Well, isn't that what everyone does when they go to a dance?"

"No, not everyone. I plan to dance a lot, eat a lot, laugh a lot, and dance with the prettiest girl in school." He poked at him and nodded to Mari.

"You and Mari? You and Mari? You never—"

"Yeah, me and Mari," he said with pride.

Mari almost cried and laughed. "Yeah, me and Steven!"

The cheerleaders finished their routine and were bouncing all over. Joan bounced over. "Did you like it?" Three of them jumped all around with Joan. Joan sat near Zack. "Did you like it?"

"Ah, sure. You like pie? There's going to be a lot of pie at the ball," Zack said shyly.

"You asking me to the ball, Zack?"

"Well, if you ain't goin' with anyone else?" He pulled back and looked at her, smiling.

"Sure. We can dance the night away. See ya! Talk to you later." Off she ran with the other girls.

"Did you see that? She said she would go with me to the ball! Just like that! I'm goin' to have pie and dance with the prettiest girl in school," Zack shouted. "Yahoo!"

"I don't think so." Steven motioned to Mari. "Me and Mari, remember?"

They all got up and started for the lockers. Everyone was laughing and pushing Zack about his lucky day.

"Me and Joan!" Zack bounced as he walked backward, facing the guys.

"Mari, I still have to talk to you," Jen said quietly.

"I'll see you later!" Mari brushed her off. "Sure," she said as she pushed what was left of her lunch into her locker since Robb hadn't eaten it. The girls rushed into home economics. The class was really fun today. They were planning the tea and the fashion show for the fall festival.

The bus ride was long and slow on the way home that day. Mari didn't know what to tell Jenny. Her heart was heavy with it all—Annie and her mother, now Jenny. Everyone was chatting and laughing as the bus rumbled along, stopping and letting kids off and starting up with a jerk. Mari strained to look at the ranch where Elzbeth used to live, wondering about what happened there. Jenny got off at her place and waved bye.

Robin and Annie pushed her to get her attention. "We're here, Mari."

Mark leaned back and said, "Off you go!"

"Oh, thanks." Mari got the mail and got through the big white gate, waving to Annie. Robin and Mark were talking at the fence near the horse barn up the road across from the kennel. Mari and Beth passed by.

"Hi, you guys." Mark waved her on.

Beth and Mari got to the gate on the road where Jenny's property line came in the road up to the ranch.

"What are you doing here, Jenny? How did you get up here anyway?" Beth said in surprise.

"You go on ahead, Beth. I need to talk with Jenny about something," Mari said.

"You sure?" Beth stumbled as she turned around and walked backward up the road, then turned and went on by herself.

"What am I going to do, Mari?" Jen started.

"First of all, have you told your mom?" Mari said anxiously.

"My dad will beat me. He beats me for just about anything now. What will he do this time?" She started to cry.

"I know. I've seen the belt marks on you in the showers in gym. Let it go for a while and see if you get your period anyway. You may just be late," Mari tried to encourage her.

"No, I know I'm not just late. It's two months now."

"Oh God! Robb! What will his family say and do?" Mari was getting really upset.

"No one can know. Not now!" Jenny wailed.

Mari raised her voice a little. "What do you mean no one can know? You will show, and everyone will know!"

Jenny spoke through her tears, "By the time I start to show, it will be Christmas vacation, and no one will see me."

Mari put her stuff on the ground and took Jenny's hands. "It will be almost June when the baby is due. What will you do about school? You can't go to school like that."

"Maybe I'll fall down the hill and lose the baby, and everything will just go away," she wailed.

"That is stupid. You could just kill yourself doing that," Mari said, starting to cry now.

All of a sudden, they heard a truck coming up the road.

"I bet that's my dad!" Mari said anxiously. "Get home now. You need to tell your mother."

RG pulled up and stopped. "What the hell. What are you girls doing here?"

Mari waved bye to Jen as she slipped down into the brush to get down to her ranch below. Mari threw her stuff on the seat and sat down, shutting the door hard.

"Save the door, Brat! What the hell you mad about?" RG said gruffly.

"Oh, Daddy, Jenny is in trouble. Her dad is going to beat the hell out of her. He will really hurt her this time," she wailed.

"What now? That man really has a temper. Do I need to talk to him?" her dad suggested.

Mari started to cry. "I'm not sure. I have to talk to Mama about this one."

"What kind of trouble? Girl trouble?"

"The worst!" Mari said through her tears.

"Son of a bitch! What the hell! When did all this happen? Who did this to her?" he shouted as he pushed on the gas pedal.

"It isn't as if she didn't want to do it, Daddy. She knew what she was doing. She just made a mistake. She just wanted him to like her. She said it felt good, and she liked it."

"Jesus Christ, girl! What the hell! She isn't going to like it now!" He was yelling now. They were approaching the fork in the road. "Straighten up before you get to the house. Don't let on around the boys. We'll talk to your mother later when no one is around. I'll talk to her myself and let you know what we decide to do. You stay out of trouble, you hear! Goddamn it! Don't you get yourself into any trouble!" He was still shouting in his anger, having heard this trouble.

Mari wiped her face with the bottom of her skirt. "Oh, Daddy, I know better than that. You know that!"

They pulled up in front of the barn. Mari picked up her stuff and the mail and jumped out of the truck. She hurried down the path to the house. Beth was in the kitchen already helping her mom. That was so nice to have her. It gave her a break from all the things she had to do. She quickly went up to her room and changed her clothes. She went across the hall to the bathroom and washed her hands and face. She stopped and went to the toilet.

Oh, darn, I started my period! Well, lucky me! Daddy should be pleased, she mused to herself in a funny way.

"Got some aspirin, Mama? I could use some," Mari said as she bounced into the kitchen.

"You all right?" Beth asked.

"Yeah, period!" she replied without seeming to care. *Never to worry about me*, she thought to herself. *I wouldn't have a chance of that happening to me. Who would want to do that with me anyway?*

Mari started in on the things she knew she was to do. "When I get done here, I'm going up to the barn and get the dogs fed. I'll see if Daniel needs any help with the rabbits after I feed the chickens and ducks. See ya!" Out the door she scooted and up the path, glad to be out of the kitchen. Beth was a real godsend.

Thank You, Jesus, in all things today, she pondered. *All things?*

Suddenly Daniel charged toward her and shouted, "I'm having babies! Mari, come and look at the doe. She's pulled all her hair and made a bed for them."

"Well, look at that. Everyone is having babies," Mari said out loud, thinking about Mrs. Moore and Jenny.

"No, just this one. See?" Daniel yelled.

"Did you look anywhere else? I bet you missed something." Mari started down the row. They looked around at the other cages and saw three others who were ready.

Daniel changed his attitude and seemed to soften as he took special care now. Mari laughed out loud and went on with her jobs.

CHAPTER 7

Fred and Sarah

MARI WAS LOOKING FORWARD TO the weekend. She had had enough drama at school to last a lifetime. The ranch was so beautiful this time of year. The grape harvest was almost over, and all the workers were still camping out behind the corral. The vineyard was changing colors and was so beautiful. The walnut trees were dropping their fruit to be harvested. The mornings were still fresh and crisp with dew. Things were going well for Elzbeth. Daniel had settled down and was kept really busy with the math and English departments and their projects for the fall festival. Mark was at the top of his class in school and sports. The Rutherford 4-H club was winning everything. What more could she want?

"Mama, you know I need a new dress to go to the ball. When are we going to look for a dress?"

Mama reached over to the end table next to the big overstuffed chair. "Here, take a look in the Sears catalog."

"Oh, Mama, you don't really mean it? I couldn't! Robin got her dress in the ity. Why can't we go to the City and get one for me?" Mari begged.

RG laid his paper down on his lap and looked over. "I think you could go into San Francisco and have a look. What do you think, Mama?" He smiled at mama and went back to reading his paper.

"I think you and Beth can have a trip into the City. We will make it a weekend. Where should we stay? The Franciscan Hotel at the top of the hill from Union Square? That would keep us close to all the stores where we would want to go," Mama said as she scooted up to the edge of her chair and took the catalog from Mari.

"I think I'll hire a man to drive you. Fred Bender and his wife have been recommended to me a while back. I think I'll have them come up and live in the little house across the creek from the clothesline. How's that, Mama? Fred's wife can help around the house too." He put his paper down. "Off to bed, everyone." He held mama's hand as they left the room.

"Did you hear that, Elzbeth?" Mari said excitedly.

"Don't call me that anymore, Mari! You might slip at school, and someone will hear you!" She was close to tears. "I am not that girl anymore!" She rose from her seat and ran out of the room.

"I'm sorry, Beth!" Mari ran after her. "I'm sorry!"

The girls were getting ready for bed quietly.

"I know Mama will get you a new dress too, Beth, even if you don't have a date," Mari started.

Beth said sharply, "I've never been to the City like you. I've never stayed in a hotel like you. I've never…" Tears were coming down her face.

"I'm sorry, Beth. I just forgot. Everything is so wonderful and seems just so normal. I just forget about things." Mari touched her arm.

Beth pushed away and got into her bed. "I still have dreams about it all. That's all. It never leaves me. Everything here doesn't seem normal," Beth said through her tears.

"I'm sorry, Beth. We just don't want to bring any of it up. Whenever you want to talk about it…," Mari said quietly.

"I don't really want to talk about it!" Beth said as she rolled over and turned her back to Mari. They both lay silently.

"You would look great in a pink dress, Beth," Mari whispered.

It seemed to take forever to get to sleep. Mari listened at the night sounds. She could hear the dogs out in the vineyard howling as they chased something. Morning came too soon. She was tired now and could only think of the trip to the City and a new dress.

Blue, that is what I want. Beth will have pink, and I will have blue. Thoughts of the trip to the city were running through her head as she ran through the morning routine. Beth stayed with mama in the kitchen. She found the barn and all the animals too much and preferred learning how to do the cooking.

"What is that, Mrs. Rogers? What are you making today?" Beth was excited.

"I thought we could make some cinnamon rolls today. I just take some of the bread dough here and make it sweet. Here, see?"

She went on and showed her how she was doing it. "Set it aside from the other dough. This other we put into loaves." She cut the dough into chunks the size of each loaf. "Now take this and roll it out on the board. Put a little flour on the board so it won't stick. See? Like this." She slapped the dough on the board and rolled it out. "Now take some of the butter here in the crock and spread it all over the dough like this." She quickly spread the butter all over the dough. "Hand me that tin of brown sugar, dear."

She waved her hand to show her. She opened it and took a big scoop from the sugar and scooped up the soft dark-brown sugar and spread it all over the buttered dough. "Sprinkle as much cinnamon as you like all over like this." She was generous with the cinnamon. She walked into the pantry and took a large bag of walnuts down. "Get one of those large knives out of the drawer, dear." She pointed to the drawer.

Beth searched through the drawer. "This one?" She handed her one of the knives.

"No. Take this one." Helen reached into the drawer and took out the one she wanted. "This will do the job we want." She took the bag of nuts, opened it quickly, and spread handfuls all over the cutting board. She quickly took the knife and chopped the nuts, her hands quickly moving in rhythm.

Beth said in amazement, "How do you do that so smoothly?"

"I will teach you some other time. It takes practice." Helen took the nuts up in both her hands and sprinkled them all over the dough. "See? Like this." She ran her hands over the nuts to smooth them out over the sugar and dough. "Hand me that tin of raisins. We will sprinkle some on here too. Now take the edge of the dough and roll it up like this." She grabbed the edge of the dough and rolled it up

91

carefully. "Take this big knife and cut about an inch or less to make each roll. Oh, I forgot to get the pan ready."

She stopped and wiped her hands on a towel. "Take this pan. This one will do. We need some cream too. Get the cream, dear." She waved her hand again.

Beth got the cream quickly. "Here, Mrs. Rogers." She watched with intent as Helen smeared butter all over the bottom of the pan. She sprinkled some brown sugar over it all and then poured cream in the pan.

"Now! back to the dough. Take each one of the cut pieces and place them in the cream. Like this." She carefully laid each one row by row. "There. Now sprinkle some more of the cinnamon and a little more of the brown sugar on the top like this." Her hands moved quickly and smoothly as she demonstrated the procedure to Beth. "Let the dough rise for a while, and then we will bake it at 350 degrees for about twenty-five or thirty minutes." Helen set the pan off to the side and wiped her hands on the towel she was using. "Next time you can do it. How about that?"

Beth replied, "I don't know if I could do it yet."

"I'm sure you can if you tried. There isn't anything you can't do when you make up your mind to it." Helen gave her a big hug. "Now, set the table and get things ready for breakfast. They'll all be down here after they get done with their chores."

"Mari said you might buy me a dress too when you go to the City. Am I going with you?" Beth said as she started out to the dining room.

Helen raised her voice as Beth walked away. "Of course, you will come, and you will have a new dress too." Helen hummed to herself as she went on with preparing breakfast. She too was looking forward to the trip to the City. It had been several months since she had been shopping.

Later in the morning, Fred Bender and his wife, Sarah, drove up to the house. They pulled up under the big oak tree in front of the barn. They were alone.

"Mama!" Who are those people up at the barn?" Mari shouted from the living room.

"Oh, quick, get your father. That must be Fred Bender and Sarah." Mama had excitement in her voice.

Mari ran up to the library where her father was and spoke loudly, "Daddy, there are some people up at the barn. Mama says it's Fred Bender and his wife, Sarah. Were you expecting them today?"

RG set his book down quickly and almost ran up to the barn. Mari followed. The boys seemed to come out of nowhere to see the people who were standing out under the big oak tree now. RG walked up and shook Fred's hand firmly.

"Great to have you. Sarah, is it? I'll show you to the house. Come on down and meet Mama. We'll get you settled in as soon as you're ready." RG guided them down the path to the house. "Come this way." Meeting mama at the veranda, he introduced them. "This is Sarah, Mama. She is here to give you a hand around the house. She'll do whatever you need." RG was not as stern as usual.

Mama greeted Sarah, "I am so pleased to have you. We'll get on just fine. First, let's take you out to the little house where we can set you up. You can drive your car down around to park over near the creak, where we can cross over the little bridge. Come with me." They walked down the veranda past the kitchen and over to the clothesline near the creek. "Here is the little house where you can settle in. It will be quite cozy for you and very private. Take this path and over this little bridge with me."

Sarah followed quickly behind mama. Fred followed behind them, looking around with amazement.

"What a nice setup. We'll do just fine, won't we, Sarah?" he said as he followed.

They got to the little house, and mama opened the door. "It isn't really ready for you as RG didn't let us know you were coming today. We'll get this cleaned up and set you up now."

Sarah went in and stood in the middle of the main room. "It will be very nice once we settle in. Do you think we can come back tomorrow and bring our things then?"

Mama seemed surprised. "Of course. Whatever you need, we can take care of you."

Sarah went into the other part of the little house and looked around. "We can get it cleaned up in no time and be ready for work by Monday. Will that be all right with you? We can sit down, and you can set out what you have in mind for me to do on a daily basis." Sarah already had a take-charge tone and confidence about her.

Fred was looking the place over and seemed pleased. "This is going to be great. We'll love it here! Thanks a lot, Mrs. Rogers. We'll get our things and stay tonight and be off tomorrow to get what we need to get settled in."

They left and went back across the little bridge to the house. RG was talking to the boys and filling them in on the plans.

"They gunna help us with our chores?" Daniel said with anticipation.

RG replied in a slightly sarcastic tone, "I don't think so. Don't get any ideas you'll get out of any work of your own. Fred is here to help me, and Sarah is here to help your mother. Get on with you both now!"

They ran off up to the barn. The dogs followed.

Mari nudged Beth. "That sure is a surprise! Never knew about that."

Beth whispered, "What are they going to do here? Who are they anyway?"

"I guess my dad hired them as extra hands to help around the ranch and help Mama. Things are just too much for my mom. She needs help around the house so she can do 4-H and other stuff she wants to do."

Mari seemed a bit perplexed by it all. "Mama? Are we still going to get to go to the City?" Mari inquired, a bit worried.

"Oh yes. This is going to be wonderful. Now we can go next weekend," mama said with a spark and some excitement Mari had not seen before.

The week passed by slowly for both the girls. Friday after school, they boarded the bus as usual.

Margot scooted close to the girls. "I already have my dress for the ball. How about you?"

Mari leaned in close to her. "Not yet. I think we're going to the City this weekend to shop. Where did you get yours?"

Margot was very excited. "We found one at Sax. It's pink. I went strapless! What you think?" she spoke with a bit of her German accent.

Mari said, a bit surprised, "Strapless?"

"Yes! I have a piece of netting as a stole to keep my shoulders warm. It's beautiful." The girls all giggled.

"My mother said Beth could have a new dress too, even if she doesn't get a date," Mari said quietly.

"Oh, someone will ask her. She is so nice," Margot said with confidence.

Jenny moved closer to the girls. "What's the big secret?"

Mari turned. "No secret. We're just talking about our dresses for the Ball. Do you have yours yet?"

Jenny turned her face toward the window. "Not yet."

The bus pulled up to her stop, and she rushed to get off the bus. "Bye, see ya!" Off she quickly walked up the drive to the house, not turning back. The bus pulled away as Mari and Beth watched her walk up to her house.

Beth spoke softly, "What's the matter with her?"

Mari whispered, "*Oh*, I don't think she has a date. I'm thinking she isn't going to the Ball."

The bus pulled up to the big white gate and stopped. They all piled off. Mari got the mail while everyone was rushing through the gate. Mark spent time with Robin before she went up to her house.

Annie ran on up ahead without her. "Bye, Beth. See you later."

Beth waved as she waited for Mari. "Can I take some of your stuff?" She reached out to lighten the load.

"Thanks." She juggled the load between them.

"There's something with Jenny, isn't there? What's going on?" Beth asked as they walked together.

"Oh, I think she wishes Robb would ask her to the ball, and he hasn't," Mari said, trying to avoid telling her the truth.

"Well, I think Robb is a real jerk! He thinks because he is so hot at sports he's a big shot," Beth said firmly.

"Yeah, I think so too. I might talk to him and see if he will take her. I think he should take her," Mari said as they walked up the road.

They trudged up the road quietly. The weather was getting colder, and lizards were running across the road, giving them a start each time.

"Oh, I hate those things," Mari said loudly.

"They aren't going to hurt you," Beth said with a smile.

"Yeah, I know. You are so brave!" Mari walked quickly past the place where the lizards were.

"You think we'll go to the City this weekend, Mari?" Beth yelled as Mari was ahead of her now.

"I think so. That's what Mama said last week," Mari shouted, turning around. Beth caught up with her. They picked up the pace and ran together.

They got up to the house, rushed up to their room, changed, then got out to the barn to take care of their chores. Daniel was already working with his rabbits.

"You going to the ball, Daniel?" Beth said as they worked together.

"Maybe. I don't dance. My friends and I don't dance. We take care of the refreshments. We're the barkeepers." Daniel was avoiding her.

"Barkeepers? We don't have a bar!" Beth was astonished.

"Not booze, stupid! Just the soda and punch." Daniel laughed at her.

"Oh." Beth put her head down, feeling a bit silly. Just then, Mari rushed in.

"I'm done. I'll see you at the house." She ran down to the house quickly to see her mother. Popping into the kitchen, she stopped short. Sarah was in the kitchen preparing dinner, and mama was nowhere in sight.

"Where's my mother, Sarah?" Mari said in surprise.

"I think she is up in her room getting ready to go to the City tomorrow."

Mari turned quickly to leave. "Really? Going to the City?" Out the door she went and up the veranda to the bedroom wing of the house. She leaped up the stairs and through the door, down the hall to her mother's room. She stood just inside the door as she watched her mother laying out several dresses on the bed.

"We going to the City?" Mari said breathlessly.

"Yes, tomorrow. You, Beth, and I will go early in the morning, so you will have to get yourselves ready. I'll come in and help you pick out what to wear. We have to look good in the City."

"Oh, Mama, I want a blue dress. We have to find a blue one. Margot has a pink one. Robin has a pink one. I have to have a blue one. Steven will like me in a blue dress." Mari was getting really excited.

"Now, calm down. This is a big deal for Beth. She has never been to the City before," mama spoke softly.

"Well, I haven't been that often either," Mari said, a bit indignantly.

Just then, Beth came in. "What's happening?"

"We have to get our stuff packed and ready to go to San Francisco tomorrow!" Mari spoke with great enthusiasm.

Beth became upset. "I've never been. What would I wear?"

Mama stopped and walked over to them both. "Now, you girls don't worry. I will take care of everything and pick out your clothes tonight. I will make sure you take the right things," mama reassured them.

They all went down together to the living room. By then, RG and the boys were there.

"Dinner ready, dear?" RG said as he looked over his paper.

"I think so. I'll check with Sarah," mama replied.

Just then Sarah came out of the kitchen. "We're ready to serve, Mrs. Rogers." Fred and Sarah were in the kitchen together now, and they worked quickly to have it all brought to the table.

"Thank you, Sarah," mama spoke as Sarah and Fred brought everything out.

Everyone sat down.

"What a great day, Mama!" RG slapped his napkin on his lap. "Thank the Lord for all his greatness. Pass the squash, will you, son?"

Everyone passed the dishes around and served themselves.

"Off to the big city tomorrow, is it? I can remember when I was a boy the first time I went. There were still horses and buggies. The hills are so steep I thought they would never make it up." RG laughed.

"We going?" Daniel spoke up. "No, fellas. This is a trip just for the woman. Dresses! Dresses! This trip. Woman need dresses! You need a dress?"

Everyone laughed.

"I'll take you fellas into St. Helena to the men's store and get you whatever you need if you're going to the ball," RG assured the boys.

Beth spoke up quickly, "Mark is taking Robin, and she has a pink dress. Daniel said he wasn't thinking about going."

RG mused, "I think he will go. It's time he went and put himself out there."

Mari smiled and said snidely, "Who would go with him any-way? You're such a geek!"

Mama said abruptly, "That is enough of that. That isn't kind. Daniel, you get out there and find someone to take to the ball. All the girls at school want to go. You find someone and make them happy. This is a happy time of year at the school. You have to be a part of it."

Everyone grew silent for the moment.

"I want to get Robin a corsage. Where do I get one, Mama?" Mark stopped eating for a moment.

"I know," Beth jumped in with excitement. "The little flower shop on Main Street. They have the best. They even have other stuff to put in the yard or in the house."

"How do you know that?" Daniel spoke up.

"Mari and I were in town when she was selling her eggs, and I saw it," she said quickly.

"That's right. We were in town and walked around and looked in all the stores. It was fun," Mari replied.

"Next time you get into town, son, you drop in and order what you want and put it on my bill," RG said assuredly. "Daniel, you do the same when you're ready."

"Thanks, Dad," Mark spoke up quickly.

"Yeah, thanks, Dad," Daniel said with a mouth full of food.

They all finished dinner and went about their normal evening routine. Mari, Beth, and mama went up to their room and laid out the things they were going to take to the city. Sarah came up and helped them pack.

"Thank you, Sarah. We'll see you in the morning," mama said as they finished. "Now, you girls get some sleep as we'll leave early in the morning." Mama shut the door behind them.

CHAPTER 8

The City

MARI AND BETH QUICKLY RAN down for breakfast where Sarah and Fred had everything set out. Everyone rushed through breakfast and quickly left the table. Beth and Mari rushed up to their room to finish packing their luggage. They pushed into the bathroom together to brush their teeth and throw the last of their personal things in their bags. They grabbed their luggage and rushed down to the veranda.

"What's that!" Beth shouted. "I never!" The girls stood on the veranda just outside the kitchen door looking out on the drive. Fred was standing there next to a big black car. He had a black suit on and a hat.

"Ready when you are, ladies," he said, very dignified.

Mama and Sarah were walking down the veranda with their luggage. "Come on, girls, get in. Fred is waiting."

Mari and Beth piled down the stairs and set their luggage down. Fred took each case, opened the trunk of the big black car, and stacked them in carefully.

"Here, Mrs. Rogers. I'll take those for you." He took her cases and carefully placed them in the trunk and opened the back door. "Here you go, ladies."

Mama and the girls climbed into the back seat. Fred opened the side door for Sarah to get in as he carefully shut the door once she was seated. He almost skipped around the front of the car as he rushed to get in the driver's seat. "Everybody ready?" He turned slightly to look in the back. "Off we go!" He started the engine and slowly moved away down the road so as not to make too much dust.

RG and the boys were standing on the veranda now, watching the whole thing. "Come on now, let's get to it, boys."

As they turned to get on with their chores, Mark said, "I wish we could go."

RG put his hand on his shoulder and said assuredly, "We will. We'll make it a man's weekend sometime."

The trip was exciting for them all as they drove in the big black car. "When did we get this car?" Mari asked as they drove down the Silverado Trail.

"Last week," mama said as if it weren't anything special.

"Where has it been? I didn't see it until today," Mari said, surprised.

"Your dad kept it in the barn out of sight to make it a surprise. The boys knew all about it," her mother said with a smile.

Beth jumped in, "I'm surprised Daniel didn't tell anyone. He's such a spoilsport."

The whole time they were on their way, the girls looked out the windows at everything they passed, asking questions about where they were and what was this or what was that.

They drove past Vallejo and on to the Carquinez Bridge, passing all the oil refineries and the big huge storage tanks.

Mari held her nose and blurted out, "What's that smell?"

"Oh, that's the smell of the oil refineries," Beth said quietly.

"How do you know so much?" Mari said as she turned and looked at her.

"I used to live around here, I think. I just remembered." Beth strained to look out the window. Everyone was quiet as they drove on.

They drove across the Bay Bridge and into the city, up the hills and down in the big black car. Fred at the wheel was so smart and proud with Sarah by his side. Mama was quietly excited as they arrived at the Top of the Mark. They drove into the huge entrance where they were met with several young men in uniforms. When the big black car came to a stop, they rushed to the doors and opened them.

"Welcome to the Top of the Mark, ladies."

The girls giggled and climbed out, looking all around at the beauty of the hotel.

"I never!" Sarah said quietly.

"Shhhh," Fred said as he assisted mama, "don't let on."

Sarah came to assist Mrs. Rogers. "Come with me, Mrs. Rogers. I will take care of everything for you."

As they approached the great doors, two men in uniform opened them and greeted them with a smile. Mama went up to the front desk. "I am Mrs. Rogers. I have reservations for my party."

The man behind the desk replied, "Yes, we have been expecting you. Everything is ready." He waved at someone to the side. "Take Mrs. Rogers and her family to their rooms please."

A handsome man came up and motioned to two young men in uniform. "Bring their luggage along now." They all followed the man to the elevator. Fred, with Sarah in tow, also carried some luggage.

Sarah stood close to mama in the elevator. "I'll take care of anything you need, Mrs. Rogers," she whispered quietly.

"You don't have to talk like that here. Just be the same as if we were home," Helen replied.

Mari and Beth giggled a little. Fred looked very straight and important in his uniform. They got to the tenth floor, and the doors opened. They didn't go far and came to the end of the hall where the doors were quite large.

"Your suites are here, madam," the handsome man said. He opened them, and the two young men entered with all the bags. They all went in together.

"These are your rooms. Where do you want your bags?" the one man said.

Mama went close and directed them to each room. "The girls will take this room. Fred and Sarah will take that room. This will be my room here. Thank you."

She seemed to have done this all before and was very much at ease. The young men quickly placed the luggage and hurried out. The handsome man stood near the door, and mama went over and thanked him.

"Will that be all, Mrs. Rogers? Just call me, and I will take care of anything you need. The car will be in the garage when you need it. Just let us know ahead of time. The valet will bring it up for you."

Mama said, "Thank you, Gordon. You know I can count on you."

He left and shut both the big doors.

The girls were in their rooms looking out the big windows with amazement. "Have you ever?" Beth started to say.

"Not since I was really little. We have been so busy at the ranch with 4-H and stuff we just haven't taken a break," Mari said as she started to open her luggage. "I think we should unpack our stuff now. Look here. Put your stuff in these drawers, and I'll take the one over here." Mari was trying to show her confidence as she started to put her things in a drawer.

"I'll take this bed. You want that one?" She pointed.

"Sure. Whatever you say." Beth started to unpack her things.

Sarah was with mama, getting her settled, while Fred unpacked their things in their room. Fred came out and announced to the girls, "When you're ready, we'll go down and look around, okay?"

The girls ran into the room where Sarah and mama were.

"We're going down with Fred, Mama," Mari said excitedly.

"You girls stay close by Fred and don't stray away," Sarah spoke with authority.

"Do as you are told now!" Mama added as she sat down in a big chair near the window.

Fred and the girls left the big room through the big doors, down the elevator, and out into the lobby of the hotel.

"Come with me, girls. I'll show you something. Would you like something to drink?"

They followed quickly and went out toward the back of the lobby, out through some huge glass doors draped with soft white sheer fabric that seemed to move gently with the slightest breeze from the outside. They went out through the big doors that reached high to the ceiling and into a beautiful patio garden that was really not outside, nor was it really inside. The chairs and tables had white tablecloths with little vases of flowers. Each table was exquisitely set and ready for guests.

A man in a suit came up. "How many will there be, sir?" he asked Fred.

"Three. Thank you." They followed the man to a table across the room. The girls followed. The man pulled a chair out for Mari to sit as Fred pulled a chair out for Beth.

"Nice to see you again, sir," the man said to Fred. "What can we get for these ladies today? Take a look at the menu for a moment."

Before the girls could even notice, a very tall handsome young man placed glasses of ice water at each place.

"Henry, the girls are in the city to buy new dresses for their Christmas ball. Let's show them a good time. They just want something to drink." Fred flipped his napkin and put it on his lap.

"Yes, sir. We have just the thing. Soda, pink lemonade, Italian ice in many flavors—"

"Oh, I think I'll have that," Beth said. "I've never had that before." She looked up at the man.

"And what flavor would you like, sweetheart? We have raspberry, blackberry, strawberry—"

Beth interrupted, "Raspberry! Please. That sounds really great."

"I'll have the same," Mari said as she set her menu down.

"Wonderful. Wonderful choice." The young man took the menus in his arm and left quickly.

Thanks, Henry," Fred said.

Others were coming in the room while they were sitting and looking around at the hanging ferns and baskets of flowers all around the room. Everyone was all dressed up in fine clothes.

"Do you think we look all right?" Beth whispered to Mari.

"What do we care? Fred is with us." Just then, the tall handsome young man came up and set their drinks down.

"Oh, how pretty they look. Whipped cream on the top and a cherry too," Beth said as she just sat and admired it.

"Almost too pretty to drink?" Fred said as he laughed a little. The girls took their straws and dove into the adventure with delight. Fred and the girls talked and laughed as they enjoyed their drinks.

"All done, girls? Are you ready to go? Let's see if your mother is ready now." Fred stood up and held Beth's chair as she got up. The handsome young man held Mari's chair as she got up. They walked around the tables and out through the big doors back into the lobby of the hotel.

Mari said to Beth, "Let's not look like bumpkins and look around as if we never saw anything like this before."

Beth laughed quietly. "As if?"

They giggled and walked behind Fred. He looked so different in his smart uniform. Once back up at the suite, the girls bounced into the room telling mama all about the indoor patio where they had "Italian ice."

"Will you girls be ready to have your dinner soon? Or are you too full from your drinks now?" Mama smiled.

"I think reservations are at six-thirty, Mrs. Rogers," Fred announced. "You and the girls are expected in the Fireside Room. Sarah and I will dine in the lounge and meet with you later."

"Thank you, Fred," she replied. "Mari, you and Beth go into your room and settle down for a while and watch some television. Sarah will let you know when you need to change your clothes for dinner."

Mari stood in the middle of the room. "What should we wear for dinner?"

"Sarah will set out your dresses and shoes for you. She knows what you should wear," her mother assured her.

The girls rushed into their room and shut the door. Mari skipped over to her bed and plopped down on it. "Isn't this dreamy? Everything is so beautiful. We don't even have to do any chores!"

Beth sat on the end of her bed. "I never...I never saw such a place. You seem to think this is all so normal," she said sharply. "I don't want to ever think this is normal. This is so grand and so special. Everyone waits on us."

Mari sat up on the end of her bed. "I think this is grand and special too. I just am really enjoying it all. My dad works hard for all this, and my mother deserves special treatment once in a while, after all she does for all of us all the time up at the ranch. She works really hard every day. We all work really hard. I don't take any of this for granted. When I grow up, who knows what kind of life I will have." Mari got up and turned on the television.

"What's on? Let's see what's on." She stood in front of the tele-vision, turning the dials. There are only three channels to pick from. "Oh, look. *Howdy Doody Time* with Wild Buffalo Bill."

"Hi, kids. It's Howdy Doody Time," shouted Wild Buffalo Bill to the music.

Mari ran back to her bed and lay down facing the television with hands holding her chin up. She sang along, "It's Howdy Doody Time, it's Howdy Doody Time."

Beth started to laugh as Mari sang along.

"What a silly show!" Mari laughed also. "It's really so silly and wonderful. Look at all those kids having such a great time."

They lay on their beds and watched for a while, laughing and singing along. Mari looked over and saw that Beth had fallen asleep. She lay quietly on her back looking up at the ceiling. She wondered what kind of dress she would find and if Steven would like it. He was tall and thin. Very handsome the way he walked with such con-fidence. He had manners and was really smart in school. Mari won-dered why he even asked her to the ball. He could have asked anyone else, and they would have jumped at the chance to go with him. Her heart skipped a beat thinking about him. She closed her eyes and fell asleep as the music played on the television.

Sarah opened the door and quietly entered the room. "It's time for you girls to get yourselves ready for dinner. Wake up now."

They both sat up with a start.

"Oh, it's dark out already," Beth said. "Dinner now? I don't think I could eat much."

"Oh, I can always eat," Mari said as she jumped up.

Sarah was getting their dresses out and laying them out on the bed. "You girls go now and wash up a bit and get these dresses on. Your mother will be in the front room waiting for you."

The girls rushed around and quickly put themselves together. Mari stood in front of the big mirror and looked at herself. "Not a bumpkin tonight!" She twirled around and saw Beth. "You look great! How you have changed in all this time. I love you so. I always wanted a sister." Mari went over and took both her hands and held them tight. "Sisters?"

"Sisters!" Beth said with a smile.

They went out into the room where mama was sitting in the big chair. She stood up and smiled. "You both look wonderful. Hope you are hungry. I certainly am. I am looking forward to this since I didn't have to prepare it."

Fred opened the door. "After you, ladies."

They went down the elevator and out into the lobby. Fred and Sarah walked them to the Fireside Room and made sure Mrs. Rogers was taken care of by Alfred.

"Thank you, Alfred. It's nice to see you again," mama said as they entered the room and were taken to their seats.

The girls followed as if they knew what they were doing now. Mari and Beth looked at each other with little smiles as they tried not to look as if they didn't know what they were doing. They sat down just as they had that afternoon and took their napkins just as if it were nothing.

The handsome young man from the patio was there again. This time, he had on a different uniform. He stood near mama.

"May I bring you ladies something to drink tonight?"

"Oh, Mama, may we have a soda?" Mari pleaded.

Mama spoke up softly, "I'll have a glass of Sauvignon Blanc by Mondavi. The girls will have a soda."

"Thank you, madam." The young man turned away and left quickly.

The waiter came up and said, "Your dinners will be right up very soon, Mrs. Rogers. Will there be anything else you would like?"

"No, thank you. The girls and I are all settled."

"What are we having, Mother?" Mari asked.

"I thought you both would like some Cornish game hens with some brown rice mixed with wild rice and some mixed vegetables. The chef is a friend of mine, and he has them all ready for us."

Mari was a bit put out to think she couldn't choose her own dinner. The waiters came with big trays and set their plates before them.

"This looks wonderful!" Mari said with surprise and pleasure. "What do you think, Beth?"

Beth sat back in her chair in amazement. "I think we could make this at home. Don't you think, Mrs. Rogers?"

"Yes, it really is quite simple. But when someone else does it, it's so much more special. Don't you think? It's all about the sauce."

Beth took special interest in looking it all over, figuring out how she could do the same thing when they got home.

"Where are we going first in the morning, Mama?" Mari said as she cut her hen.

"I think we will start at Saks Fifth Avenue and then wind our way down to Macys. We can have lunch at Blum's. There are some other little dress shops along the way. We'll just see what we find."

"I think Beth should have a pink dress, or even a green one to go with her hair. Don't you think? Beth?"

Beth was busy eating and looked up. "What?" she said.

"Your dress? What color do you want?" Mari said impatiently.

"Oh, when I see one I like, I'll just pick that. Whatever fits, I will be happy," Beth said as she ate with enthusiasm.

"You don't have to just take whatever. My mom and dad want you to have what you really want. That's what this trip is all about. Enjoy…I am." Mari took a big bite and looked at her mother.

"That's right, Beth. We all are here to have a great time and have this very special moment in our lives. The Christmas ball is going to be one of the most special moments in your life, and we all want it to be wonderful. This is special for me as well. I look forward to seeing my girls looking beautiful and having a great time." She smiled at them both. "This is my time too. I want you to know."

"Thanks, Mama, this is really great. I'm loving this!" Mari said with a smile. She nudged Beth. "How's your 'Cornish game hen' and that sauce?"

They both laughed.

The next morning, they were up with the sound of people talking out in the next room.

"What is going on out there?" Mari said to Beth.

"I wouldn't know." She snuck over to the door and cracked it open to look out.

"There's a waiter out there with a table full of stuff. It looks like we're having breakfast here in the suite," she whispered.

"*What?*" Mari jumped out of bed and peeked through the cracked door.

"Get dressed quick before Sarah comes in here to get us up," Beth said to Mari.

"We don't have to get dressed. We can just put on our robes and eat in our PJs," Mari said as she quickly put on her robe. "Come on! I could eat a horse."

"After that dinner last night?" Beth was astounded. Out the door they rushed.

"Well, look who's up?" Fred said. "Come on, everyone. Look what someone else cooked up for all of us. A king's feast!" They all sat down around the table and enjoyed the beautiful breakfast mama had ordered.

"Ready? Everyone ready?" mama said as she knocked on the door. "Fred is waiting with the car downstairs. Don't keep him waiting."

The girls piled out of their rooms all dressed up for the big-city life. Down to the lobby they went and out to the car port where Fred was standing next to the big black car.

"Off you go, girls," he said as he opened the door.

Sarah sat in the front with Fred, Mama and the girls in the back. They drove up to the front door of Saks Fifth Avenue. Fred got out, opened the door, and assisted Mrs. Rogers first, then the girls. Sarah and Mrs. Rogers walked together with the girls following. Fred drove off.

"Where is he going? He can't just leave us here?" Mari said, a bit surprised.

"He's only taking the car to the parking garage. He'll meet us in the store," Sarah said quietly.

Mari and Beth looked around with amazement at all the beautiful displays of merchandise. They went right upstairs to the evening-gown department. There they met a lady who walked up to Sarah.

"I am Sarah, Mrs. Rogers's personal assistant. We have an appointment this morning to see some gowns for our girls for their Christmas ball."

The lady waved them on to the area where there were some beautiful chairs which she suggested they could sit down. "I will have Harriet assist you shortly."

The girls stood there for a moment and looked around. "I don't see any dresses, Mama. Where are they?"

"Shhh, sit down, and you will see."

A very thin little lady came out of the side where there was a large arched door. She had on a black skirt and a white blouse with some very smart black shoes. Her hair was done up in a bun on the top of her head.

"How nice to see you again, Helen. Are these your girls? How wonderful. What will we be looking for today?"

"Well, Harriet, it's time for their Christmas ball. We need some nice dresses for Mari and Beth. They already have some ideas of their own. We're hoping you can show them something no one else will have in St. Helena. Beth has this pretty strawberry-blonde hair, and Mari is fair and blonde. She wants a blue dress. You will have to take special care with Beth. She said she didn't know just what she thought she wanted," mama explained.

Harriet took Mari by both hands and held out her arms, looking her figure over. "I am sure we will find something special for you." Then she turned to Beth, took her by the hands, and twirled her around. "You will be easy. I am sure I'll find something you'll just love." Harriet turned away. "I need some help out here."

Two ladies came out, and Harriet gave them instructions. Then they went back through the arched doors. A few moments later, some pretty girls came out wearing dresses. They walked out and stood in front of the girls, turning first to the left and then to the right. Then they twirled around and stood facing the girls.

Mama said, "What do you think of these?"

Mari and Beth almost dropped their mouths. They couldn't contain themselves.

"Whoa!" Mari said with excitement.

Beth was speechless. Harriet stood aside and waved the models out. Then two more models walked out with even more lovely dresses on. Before the girls knew it, a young girl walked up in a black dress with a white apron on, wearing a cute little hat. She had a tray of glasses with punch in them.

"Would you like a drink?" she asked as she leaned down with the tray in between Mari and Beth.

"Oh, thank you," Mari said as she took a glass.

"No, thanks," Beth said as she continued to watch the models parade around in the dresses. "Are these dresses used when you buy them, Mrs. Rogers?" Beth asked quietly.

"No, dear. When you choose one, they make one up just for you in your size."

"How long does that take? We can't take our dress home today?" Beth seemed annoyed.

"Now, Beth, relax. Just take your time and look at what they have available here. We have other places to look today. If you see something you like here, we can have them set it aside, and we can call back later," mama said quietly.

Mari set her glass down on the tray on the table next to her. "I think these dresses are a bit old for us. I saw some pictures in *Seventeen* magazine that showed what we're looking for. Where will we find those dresses?"

Harriet quickly rushed the models out. "Just wait. I will get something I know you will just love." A few minutes later, four younger girls came out wearing some other dresses.

"Now that is what I am talking about!" Mari said with a little more enthusiasm. "What do you think, Beth?"

Beth stood up and walked over to one of the models. "May I feel the fabric?"

Harriet walked over. "Yes. This is a fine tool laid over satin. The two spaghetti straps add a youthful charm with a simple smooth strapless-looking bodes with the zipper on the side to give the back a smooth, seamless look. The gathered skirt flows gently just to the ankles in a ballerina length for dancing. It comes in several colors to choose from." She waved her hand, and one of the other ladies handed her a pallet with samples of the colors of fabric the dresses came in.

"We can use a satin or velvet ribbon around the waste and tie it in a soft bow in the back. We have one that comes with an iridescent shine to it also. It gives it a bit of sparkle in the evening light when you are dancing." Harriet took the fabric of the skirt the model was wearing and swished it a little.

Beth was intent as she examined the fabric and the design of the dress the model was wearing. Mari was now standing behind admiring her as Beth carefully examined the fabric.

"Don't you just love it?" Mari said with excitement.

"Let her be, Mari. This is her moment. She has to think and decide for herself." Mama waved her hand to motion Mari away.

Mari walked around and looked at the other models with no interest at all. She took another glass of punch. "Do you have a ladies' room?" she whispered to the maid with the tray.

"Oh yes, come with me."

Just then, Sarah stepped up and said, "I'll go with you." They left the room together.

"Beth might like that dress, ya think?" Mari said to Sarah, a little excited. "First thing out of the gate!"

Sarah looked at her. "This is all new to her, and she is easily pleased. Besides, that dress really suits her. It's as sweet as she is. Don't act like a snob."

When they returned, Beth and mama were huddled together by the chairs.

"Harriet, I think Beth really likes this dress. We have not finished our shopping today. I would like to come back later after lunch and see it again. That way, Beth will know for sure if this is what she really wants."

Harriet smiled. "I will be glad to save this and keep it out for her. Call me if you change your mind."

"We will. Thank you, Harriet. I'll see you later," Mama replied.

Mari and Sarah joined them, and they all went out where Fred was waiting for them by the car.

"How did he know we were ready?" Beth said in surprise.

Sarah replied, "Harriet called the garage and told him we were coming down."

"What a life!" Beth exclaimed.

CHAPTER 9

The Dresses

"Where are we off to now?" Mari said, a little impatient.

"Well, there are some shops along the way around the square we might pop into," her mother said just a little sharply. "Why not take a look as we work our way around before we get to Blum's for lunch?"

Mari leaned forward to speak to Fred, "Please, let us out in the next block. I see some interesting places." He pulled over, and they all jumped out with Mari in the lead. She headed for a little shop with some French name. "I'll try this place, okay?" She rushed in before anyone could even return a reply.

"May I assist you, my dear?" a soft voice with a little French accent came from behind a glass counter. The lady was slight in build and very beautiful.

"Yes, I am looking for a dress to wear to our school's Christmas ball in St. Helena. Would you have anything I could look at?" Mari said in a very confident manner.

Just then, mama, Beth, and Sarah came in the door.

"Oh, there you are. You almost got away from us!" Sarah exclaimed.

"Good morning, ladies. How may I assist you today?" The lady stepped out from behind the counter and walked up to mama.

"I am here with my girls to find some dresses for the ball. Mari saw your shop and thought it was beautiful and decided you might have just the right thing for her dress. I am sorry she has been rude," Mama said with some embarrassment.

"That is quite all right, madam. I am sure we will find something she will find to meet her impeccable taste. Come with me. I will show you what we have." The lady guided them to the back of the store where she invited them to have a seat.

She asked Mari, "Now, you, my dear, come with me, and I will show you some dresses you have never seen before in your life."

The lady walked up to the dresses hanging on the rack against the back wall. She swiftly and elegantly pulled a dress off and swung it out in front of herself and let it hang down, pulling the skirt aside to swish it around as if to dance.

Mari stood with surprise. "It's blue! Just what I wanted!"

The lady explained with her French accent the detail of the dress as she moved around. "You will see the detail for the design is strapless if you desire or not. The bodice of the dress has gentle folds that fall across the bust all the way to the waist at an angle. It fits smoothly across the back with the side zipper to accent your figure. The skirt has two pleats to create the smooth front with smaller pleats continuing along the waist that create fullness to the back of the skirt. It falls to the floor to create an elegant smooth flow as you walk. You will find the fabric is French silk, peau de soie." She spoke it in her delightful French accent.

Mari stood breathless. "I love it! May I touch it?"

"Why, yes. You may even try it on if you like. Come with me." She guided Mari to a large fitting room.

Mama followed and interjected, "I can help you with that, Mari."

As the saleslady hung up the dress, she commented, "I will look in after you in a moment. When you are ready, come out and show us how you look." She slipped out the door.

"Mama, this is just the one. What do you think?" Mari stood and looked at the dress as it hung on the hanger.

"Quite frankly, I am impressed you have chosen the first dress you looked at," her mother said in surprise.

She took the dress off the hanger and suggested, "Well, get your dress off and get this thing on."

Mari slipped her dress off in a flash. The dress went on smoothly. "It's a bit big. Oh no!" Mari exclaimed.

"It can be altered, dear. Don't worry about that," her mother said quietly. "Now go out and show it to Beth and Sarah."

Mari tiptoed out the door. "Well, what do you think?"

Beth took a breath. "Wow, you sure can pick 'um! The color is your blue. That's for sure."

Mari spun around holding up the top of the dress so as not to let it fall down. "It has to be fitted. It's too big for me!"

The saleslady came up and pulled the back of the dress with her hands to show how it would look once it had been tailored. "See, you are beautiful!"

"Mama, may I have it? Oh please?" Mari stood looking in the big mirror.

Mama walked up and asked the lady quietly, "And how much is this gown?"

"Oh, for you today, madam, it will only be $100. I will not charge for the fitting and the tailoring."

Without a pause, Mama asked, "How soon could it be ready? We will be returning to St. Helena on Sunday afternoon."

The saleslady replied, "Let me get my seamstress for you, and we shall see." She quickly left the room and disappeared through a small door. Very quickly, she and another lady came out. The lady was a short, stout woman with gray hair. A long measuring tape hung around her neck. On her wrist was a pincushion. She was dressed in a long black skirt with a white silk blouse.

"Now, let me see, young lady." She grabbed the back of the dress and drew it up tight. "This is nothing. I can have this ready this afternoon, if you like. So you want the little straps, or will it be strapless?"

Mari, standing with the seamstress holding tightly to the dress, said breathlessly, "Oh, strapless please. But if I wanted to change it, could I have the straps to take home?"

"Sure, if it pleases you. Please take it off, my dear, and I shall get right to it." She quickly left the room.

The saleslady stepped up and asked, "If you like, we can take care of that for you today, madam. Shall we?"

Mama paused. "Let me speak to my daughter for a moment."

The saleslady excused herself and quickly disappeared.

"Do you really think I should spend a hundred dollars on a dress you will only wear once?" she whispered.

"Oh, Mother, please, I will wear it for everything. I will never get tired of this dress. I promise," Mari whispered, pleading.

Beth jumped in, "It really is the perfect dress for her."

Sarah sat silently. Mama stepped back and looked at the dress again. "It's your blue, isn't it? You promise?" She turned and asked the lady to come out. "We will take it. Now, Mari, get that thing off so we can get a dress for Beth."

Mari quickly ducked into the dressing room and took the dress off. The dressmaker came in and took the dress with great haste.

"I will have it ready for you by four o'clock this afternoon, my child."

"Oh, thank you, thank you so much," Mari said breathlessly.

Mari came out of the dressing room all smiles. Beth took both her hands in hers. "You did it! You really did it! We'll have so much fun! You and Steven will look grand together."

Mama was at the counter settling up the bill with the French lady. They were smiling and chatting, very happy that one dress was taken care of so quickly.

"Now, let's go to Blum's for lunch. I'm all ready for something to drink. What about you, Sarah?"

They left the store and found Fred waiting at the curb. Fred was excited to see them all. "That didn't take as long as I thought it would. How did you make out?"

"One down and one to go," Sarah said as they got in the car.

When Fred pulled up to the valet at Blum's, they all piled out of the car as a young man took the information from Fred.

"You will love this place, Sarah. I have loved coming here for years. We have taken the children here every time we get into the city." Mama took Sarah's elbow.

"Oh, I remember this. It has been a long time since I was here, Mother," Mari said as she walked behind them. "You wait, Beth, you will just love this place! The food is great, and they have all kinds of candy."

They walked in and stood at the desk where the hostess asked how many were in their party. "Come right this way." They all followed to a large round table.

"The smell is wonderful! I am really hungry now," Beth exclaimed. "Just look at this place. It's like an old-fashioned ice-cream parlor right out of the movies."

Mrs. Rogers leaned over and said, "It has been like this all my life. We love coming here."

Fred, Sarah, Beth, Mari, and Mama spent a lengthy time at Blum's for lunch. They left with their arms full of bags of goodies.

"Don't eat all that in one sitting, girls," Sarah said as they got in the car. Fred handed Sarah three bags of goodies he had.

"Oh, you devil, what have you gone and done?" They laughed.

"Shall we go on to Macy's and see what they have, Beth?" Mama asked gently.

"What do you think, Mari?" Beth said with excitement.

"I always like to see what Macy's has. The building is really beautiful and huge," Mari replied.

"Then that's our next stop!" Fred drove down the street.

Beth looked at the tall buildings and all the people on the sidewalks. "There are some really beautiful people here, but I see some really sad people sitting on the sidewalks. Who are they?"

"Those poor people are homeless, dear," Sarah said quietly.

"Oh." Beth sat silently looking out the window as they passed by.

Once at Macy's, they walked through the expanse of the huge store admiring the building.

"What a place!" Beth said as they made their way up the elevator to the third floor. There was a lady in a uniform sitting on a stool in the elevator who announced each floor and what you could expect to find there. When she closed the door, she announced, "Going up." Beth and Mari stood silently and smiled at each other. The lady announced, "Third floor, ladies' dresses and formal wear."

They left the elevator and saw and expanse of endless racks of beautiful dresses. Mama guided them to the right and said, "This is where we will find dresses for a young girl. Let's see what we can find here."

Fred found a nice chair where he could watch all the people coming and going. Sarah and Mari headed to the racks of formals and started to look at the dresses.

"Beth wants a pink dress, I think," Mari whispered to Sarah. Beth and Mama were off to another rack.

"May I assist you today, my dear?" A saleslady came up to Beth.

"Oh, I need a dress to wear to the school Christmas ball in St. Helena," Beth replied.

"Exactly what do you think you would like? We have so many to choose from. Here, take a look at these over here. These are just right for a young lady like yourself," the saleslady said kindly.

They walked over to another area. The lady pulled out a fluffy yellow dress made of lace.

Mari came up and laughed. "Nothing like that!"

The lady quickly put it back on the rack. "How about this one? This is pretty and pink to go with your lovely hair."

"I don't think so," Beth said, turning to mama. "I think I really like the first one I saw this morning. Can we go back there?"

"Why, yes, dear, whatever you want."

Beth had a tear in her eyes. "I don't want to be any trouble. I don't want to make everyone go to a lot of trouble just for that dress."

Mari jumped right in, "I got what I wanted. You should have what you want too. Isn't that right, Mama?"

"Of course. Let's go and find Fred and see if we can get there in time. We still have to pick up Mari's dress at four o'clock."

Sarah jumped in and reminded them that Fred could go and pick up the dress, or they could call the store and have it sent to the hotel.

"That's right, Sarah. I wasn't thinking. Let's hurry," mama encouraged the girls.

"Going down," the elevator lady said. Beth and Mari smiled at each other. Fred was already ahead getting the valet to bring the car around. They all waited impatiently as they saw other cars pull up and other people driving off.

"How long does it take?" Mari asked impatiently.

"Hush! Don't act like that!" mama whispered as she leaned over to her. Just then, the valet drove up with the car. Fred jumped right up and opened the doors as everyone jumped right in.

"Off we go!" Fred said with enthusiasm. "One last stop for my ladies!"

"Oh, silly, stop it." Sarah laughed. They all laughed.

"This is hard work, shopping!" Beth said out loud.

"That's why we only do it once a year or so," Mari said as she looked out at the crowds on the street.

Fred pulled up to Saks Fifth Avenue where he had dropped the ladies off the first time. "Here you are, ladies." He opened the door for everyone and then drove off as he had done the first time.

"I know where he is going this time," Beth said with a laugh. They rushed into the store where mama met Harriet as they returned to the formal wear.

"I knew we would see you again, Helen. I saved the little dress for your little girl. It's just perfect for her. Wait here, and I will get it." Harriet turned quickly to get the dress.

They all sat down but Beth. She was so excited she was holding her breath. Harriet came out holding the dress high on the hanger. "Now I should have you put this one on and see what you think. Come with me, dear."

Mama followed along to help. Beth slipped out of her dress as Harriet helped put the new dress over her head.

"Now this one is only a sample and is only close to your size. We will have to choose what size and color you want."

Beth spun around and looked in the mirror, tilting her head and looking carefully, turning side to side. "I think this is wonderful. I know some other girls are going to have pink dresses. I saw a pretty green in the fabric swatches when we were here this morning. What do you think, Mrs. Rogers?"

"Whatever you want, sweetheart," she replied quietly.

Beth darted out where Mari and Sarah were. "What do you think?"

Mari stood up. "Perfect! What color are you getting?"

"Everyone else is getting pink. I think I should have the green in the book. Take a look." They both went over to the book where they had left it that morning. "See. What do you think of green?" Beth said with excitement.

Mama was standing behind her now. "What a great choice. With your hair now strawberry blonde, it will be perfect!"

"Then that's it. A velvet ribbon around the waist and the spaghetti straps. May I have it, Mrs. Rogers?" Beth pleaded.

"Of course, you may. Harriet, Beth wants this dress with the green and a velvet ribbon. Can you put some extra ribbon in the box for her hair when you send the dress?"

Beth stood in front of the mirror thinking how the green would look. She spun around a few times looking left and right. She stood and held her arm out, taking Mari's arm. "Yes, Dante, you may dance with me."

Mari stood and laughed at her. "You silly! You have to wear this dress to everything just like I will have to wear mine."

They laughed as they ran into the dressing room to take it off. Mama made arrangements for payment and when the dress would be ready. The dressmaker came in and measured Beth and said the dress would be ready in a week.

"A week? I can't take it home this weekend?" Beth exclaimed in alarm.

Mari touched her arm. "Take it easy. Don't forget they have to make your dress from scratch. It isn't like mine, already made."

"Oh, that's right. I'm so excited!" Beth squealed.

They got to the hotel and up to their rooms. The girls just plopped down on their beds and laughed and laughed. Helen and Sarah made arrangement for Mari's dress to be delivered and relaxed in the big chairs.

"What a day! We really accomplished a lot with those two. I have really had a wonderful time with Mari and Beth today. I find it so wonderful having them both. I won't want to give her up."

"What do you mean Helen?" Sarah said, rather amazed.

"Oh, you don't know. Beth is only with is for a while until… well, next summer…we'll see." She got up and went to her room.

"Well, that's interesting," Sarah said to Fred as they went to their rooms.

The next morning was Sunday. Mama insisted everyone get up and go to church. They piled into the big car and drove several blocks away to a big Lutheran church. It was grand and huge with a big pipe organ playing loudly as they walked in. The music filled the church. The pastor greeted the congregation and instructed them all to open their hymnals and sing hymn 244, "Glory Be to God the Father."

Mari loved the whole thing—the big church, the choir, the pastor, the hymns. "I think I will be a Lutheran!" Mari said breathlessly as they left the church. Everyone else was quiet as they got in the big black car.

The ride home to the ranch was quiet with a little rain as they all thought about the wonderful time they had had.

Mari strained to look more closely as they passed Vallejo, wondering about Beth's comment made earlier on the trip. Who would lose a child and abandon it? Why was Elzbeth with those men? How did she ever get in that position? She was such a wonderful person and so smart and pretty. How could her family ever give her up?

CHAPTER 10

The Fall Festival

IT HAD RAINED SOME THE night before, and Mari, Beth, and the boys hurried to get the chores done quickly. Daniel was exited to look in on his does to see if they had delivered yet.

"Nothing!" he said impatiently. They all ran down to breakfast, rushed to clean up, and change for school. It sprinkled rain on them as they hurried down the road.

Mari was miserable in the cold, complaining to Beth, "Why do we have to walk in the rain? It isn't fair when Fred could drive us in the big black car!"

Beth sneered back. "We're just so spoiled now!"

Daniel and Mark were far ahead of them now.

"How do they do it? We walk fast too. Look at them. They don't even get wet!" Mari wailed. They got to the bus just in time as it rolled up to the big white gate. Everyone climbed on the bus.

Jenny, anxious to see them, asked, "Did you get a new dress when you went shopping?"

Beth jumped right in, "It was dreamy, and we had so much fun."

Mari chimed in, "We both got just what we wanted. It will be a surprise for everyone. We're not telling." She sat down smugly and didn't say another word. Jenny huffed, grabbed her books tightly, and sat looking out the window.

The Italian boys got on the bus next. Dante got on first. He quickly found Beth and sat next to her. "You and I will go to the

Christmas ball? I think we should. Alanso will be with Margot, and I will be with you. We will dance and eat and have a good time, no?" He looked anxiously at her.

"Are you telling me we're going to the Christmas ball? Not asking me? I don't know, Dante. That isn't how we do it here. You ask me nicely," Beth said calmly and sweetly.

Dante replied, "Well, will you be my dance partner and wear your pretty new dress for me?"

"Oh, silly, yes. You and I will go and dance and eat pie, cake, or cookies and drink punch together. You have to come up to the ranch and get me. I am not going in an old pickup truck with R. G. Rogers! I was really hoping you and I would go together. Thank you," she said with a giggle.

All day everyone talked about Beth going with Dante to the Christmas ball. He was a junior, and she was only a freshman. All her friends were ablaze about it. How lucky she was to get a chance to go to the Christmas ball.

At dinner that night, RG announced, "I understand Beth has been invited to the Christmas ball by Dante Martin." Everyone was silent and looked around the table at one another.

"Yes, I was going to talk to you about that soon, sir. I just haven't had a chance to…" Beth paused and looked at Mari.

"Yes, Dad, what a nice young man he is too. I think you should go and see his dad and have them tell you about their plans to buy that place on the Oakville Road," Mari commented.

"Really?" Mark chimed in. "I heard Alanso say they were talking about it. I didn't know they were serious."

Daniel jumped in, "Did you know I have four does ready to have babies?"

Mama interrupted, "Did you see the pie Beth made for tonight?"

"Look here, everyone! I am talking about this Dante kid who wants to take Beth to the Christmas ball! Did you ask your mother?" RG spoke up sharply.

Beth put her fork down. "I don't have a mother to ask."

"Yes, you do. Ask her now!" RG said softly. Everyone put their forks down and looked at him.

"Well?" Beth looked at mama. "May I go to the ball with Dante, Mother?"

Mari, Mark, and Daniel all shouted, "Yes! We're all going! Right?"

Mama nodded and quietly said, "Yes, dear, you are all going to the Christmas ball, and so are RG and I. Now, Daniel, get a date and do it soon. The girls at school all want to go to the ball with someone. You and your friends step up to the plate."

They all laughed and finished dinner with great conversation and anticipation of the Fall Festival and the Christmas ball.

That week, everyone was getting things ready for the Fall Festival on Friday 19. The stores downtown all had fall leaves in the windows and special events planned. All the wineries had special plans for the harvest. Tables were set out with food and wine for everyone to enjoy.

Everyone in town came to the high school to see the fashion show and attend the tea the girls prepared. The freshmen sewing class had a fashion show; the FFA displayed all the things they had been learning. The woodshop class displayed the projects they had made. The music department had concerts. Some of the kids performed quartets, duets, and tap dances. The choir sang, and the band played. The football team walked around in their uniforms strutting their stuff. The cheerleaders bounced around everywhere they went all day.

Steven looked all around for Mari. He finally spotted her at the FFA exhibit. "Did you find anything you wanted to buy, madam?" he asked as he snuck up behind her.

"Oh, you! I love this stuff. Did you make anything?" she said coyly.

"Well, no. I'm not in FFA. Remember, my dad is directing me academically and not into agriculture. I do have a great respect for all these guys and what they are learning. Sometimes I wish I was a part of it too. If you want anything here they made, I'll buy it for you."

Mari spoke softly, "Oh well, everyone has their strengths. Let's go and see what the music department has. I didn't look at the schedule. Did you?"

"Here, how about this wall key holder? You can hang the key to my heart on it," he said, being silly. He held it up to her face, wiggled it, and danced around in front of her.

"I thought they were preforming at one o'clock in the auditorium. I think Zack and some of the guys were going to put on a thing." Mari tried to ignore him, even as she laughed at him.

He put the wall key holder down and grabbed her hand, tugged her, and they both started to run together. They arrived out of breath at the door of the auditorium.

"Tickets please." Margot was at the door.

"We didn't know we had to have tickets. Where do we get them?" Steven said, surprised.

Margot laughed and said with her German accent, "You don't need tickets. Just go right in. I'm just waiting for Alanso. We're going to see Zack and the guys put on their thing. We can sit together."

They waited around for a bit and saw Alanso running from the gym waving his arm. "Wait for me." He was out of breath as he stopped and gave Margot a kiss on the cheek. "I am here, my sweet."

"Don't be silly." Margot grabbed his hand, and they went into the auditorium together swinging and looking at each other.

"How sweet. I really didn't know they were all that connected. I thought they were just going to go to the ball together as friends," Steven said quietly to Mari.

"They have a real connection, don't they? I wonder what their parents think of it?" Mari said, wondering.

She and Steven hurried to get caught up with them. They grabbed a seat close to the front. Everyone was pilling in, excited to see the show.

There were quartets and duets from the choir. Marcella Banks and Tammy Masters did a tap dance wearing little sailor suits. Manuel Rodriquez, Brian Benesch, Charles Chambers, and some other guys formed a mariachi band. They played several numbers and brought the house to a standing ovation.

Zack Chandler, George Hansen, Charlie Ashe, and Bill Lambert came out on the stage with instruments. The crowd went wild cheering and applauding when they came out. The guys stood on one side of the stage for a moment and began to move their instruments up and down. Nothing happened! They stopped and looked at each other and shrugged their shoulders and raised their hands in wonderment. Then they started up again, and all of a sudden, the music played, and they walked all around the stage as if they were playing. George hopped and skipped, raising his knees as he raised his saxophone up and down. Charlie raised his trumpet in the air as if blowing. Bill swung a guitar as if he were Elvis, and Zack had a clarinet swinging wildly. Everyone screamed with laughter and clapped their hands. They went on and on as if they were playing the music. When the music stopped, they bowed and bowed and ran off the stage. Everyone stomped their feet and clapped their hands for more. They came back and started to perform again. It was hilarious! Everyone was bursting with laughter and had such a great time. It was the hit of the day.

No one expected it. The guys had not told anyone they were going to do it.

Mari, Steven, Margot, and Alanso went back stage to see the guys. It had been a thrill. Everyone had loved it! What a surprise! Mari and Margot were jumping all around. "Come on, you guys, let's go and get some ice cream over at the Home Economics Department." Zack and the guys put their instruments in a pile and led the way.

"Do you think Joan saw us?" Zack asked Mari.

"Didn't see her," Mari said as they rushed over to the gray stone building.

"Zack! Zack!"

He turned and saw Joan running.

"What a performance! You were great! I never knew you were going to do that!" She ran up to him and threw her arms around him and gave him a big hug. "We were late to the show, but we got there just in time to see your bit. What a scream!"

They all got to the Home Economics Department. Rushing in the door, they saw hardly anyone was there.

"Where is everyone?" Margot said.

Miss Radcliff was there. "Everyone is still coming over from the show. Did you see it? Everyone was screaming about something."

"That was us! That was us! We brought the house down!" Zack shouted. "We came over for some of the girls' homemade ice cream."

"Well, who would have guessed it would be you boys? Just have a seat, and we will get you some ice cream. On the house!" Miss Radcliff said.

Just then, the rest of the girls came in screaming. "Did you hear them? They were wild! It was crazy! Oh, there you are! You guys were great!" The girls all gathered around the table where Zack and the boys were sitting.

"We came over to get some of your homemade ice cream. Where is it? I'm a star now!" Everyone laughed and patted the guys on the back.

"We're the greatest air band ever! This stuff is great! Who made it?" George shouted.

Beth stepped out and bowed. "I did!"

Mari clapped her hands and said, "That's my sister!"

Everyone stopped and looked.

"Well, not really, but since we have her at our house, I feel like she's my sister. I always wanted one. Isn't she a great cook?"

Everyone applauded.

Daniel and Mark walked in and joined in to get some ice cream.

"Where is all this ice cream our sister made?" Mark yelled.

Steven shouted, "There isn't any left for you. We ate it all!"

They all laughed. Everyone sat around and recounted the activities of the day.

"I saw your parents walking around the buildings, George," Mark pointed to him with his bowl of ice cream.

"There were a lot of parents. I saw the Lamberts too," Joan added. "They rarely get out from working. I think everyone makes a special effort after the harvest, don't you?"

Alanso raised his bowl in the air. "Here's to us!"

Everyone laughed and raised their bowls. "Here's to us!"

"I think we all had better start cleaning up and putting things away. This has been a surprising day and too much fun," Miss Radcliff said. They all pitched in and hugged and laughed.

"I'll see you at church, Mari," Zack shouted.

"You'll see me first, buster," shouted Joan.

"You bet! You're my best girl, Joan." They both left together holding hands and looking at each other.

Mari looked at Steven. "They really make a great couple, don't they?"

Steven smiled. "Not as good as we are." They finished up and walked out together. "I think I have something I have to do. See you in a few minutes." He ran off quickly but returned in a little bit with something behind his back. "Here! I think you need this." He pulled a key out of his pocket and hung it on a hook on the wooden key holder from the woodshop.

Mari laughed. "Now, just how do you think you'll get in your house if you leave that on the hook?" She laughed hard as she took the wall key hanger. "Who made it anyway? They might not want us to have it."

"Oh, they just want the money. They need it to pay for all their wood and stuff," Steven said enthusiastically. "Actually, it says on the back. Let's see. Well, think of this. Clark Blanchard made it. Think I'll tell him it will hold the key to my heart for you, Mari. Then he'll know you and I are pals."

"Oh, silly! Thank you. Give it here. I have the perfect place in my room to put this." Mari laughed.

"What do you think of Dante taking Beth to the Christmas ball? Everyone is talking about it," Steven asked Mari.

"Well, my parents gave her permission to go, so that must mean it's all right. He is older in the junior class, but I think he's honorable and will take good care of her. Besides, you and I will be close at hand to keep an eye on them, right?" she assured him.

He squeezed her hand. "Sure. What do her parents think of it?"

Mari stopped short next to a big redwood tree near the new buildings. "They are so far away they really don't have anything to say about it."

"Don't get all head up about it. I only asked." Steven was surprised and puzzled at her response.

"I'm sorry. I think it's really hard for her not having her own parents around to share in all her fun and happiness. Just look at all the other kids and all the fun they are having. We're all so lucky to be in this school and have every one of us being friends. Really friends!" She looked at Steven. "We're really friends, aren't we? Trust and everything?" She was a little emotional.

"Why? What makes you think I don't trust you or you trust me?" He put his arms around her.

"Everything is so new and different. I just want everything to stay this way forever. You are the best ever, Steven. You are the best ever! You do know how much I care about you! Don't you?" She held on tightly to him.

"Well, I do now! I care about you too, Mari. You are the best ever too. Pals forever? Pals forever! Okay?" He looked down into her face.

She pulled away and looked straight at him. "Pals forever! I think Fred is going to come and get us in the big black car."

"When did your dad get that?" Steven said, surprised.

"Oh, Dad hired Fred and his wife last month to help out at the ranch. He drove us to the city to get our dresses for the ball," Mari said. "Come on, I'll introduce you to Fred and Sarah. They are wonderful and help out a lot. That's why I have been able to get my homework done lately."

They ran over to the parking lot where they found the big black car and Fred waiting. "Want a ride, kid? We can go your way before heading home."

"Yes, sir!" Steven said with excitement.

"Jump right in. Where are the rest of the kids? Hope they'll be along soon," Fred said with a smile.

Steven and Mari sat in the back seat holding hands as they waited for Mark, Daniel, and Beth to get there.

"Hurry up, you kids. RG is waiting for us at the pizza place in town. Who wants pizza?" They all piled in and agreed that Steven needed to stop by his house and tell his parents they were all going out for pizza.

Fred suggested that Steven's parents should come along too. They said they would meet everyone there. Steven's brother came along also.

It was a special day and evening. The moon was orange and full, the leaves full of color, and the smell of harvest all over the valley.

That night it rained. Mari woke up to the fresh smell of rain and wet leaves. She stayed in bed for a bit, thinking of what a wonderful day it had been. She couldn't have wished it to be better.

Beth turned over and looked at her. "I suppose we have to come to reality and do the chores."

"Spoilsport."

Up they went with smiles on their faces.

CHAPTER 11

Jenny

FALL FESTIVAL WAS OVER, ANOTHER day and down the hill in the cold, rainy weather. Mari and Beth stood at the top of the hill on the flats and looked over the valley in awe.

"You can almost see the old place over there, Mari," Beth said rather solemnly.

"A lifetime ago now," Mari said as she pushed her arm to get on down the road.

"I try not to think about it, Mari, but it comes back to me often. Your family seems so wonderful. It does bother me how Daniel beats on you in the barn, and no one does anything about it."

"Oh well, it could be worse. I know other girls who have it a lot worse than I do. Daniel will get his someday. You wait and see." Mari brushed a tear away as they got past the gate in the road where Jenny's property line was. "Stupid gate! Why do they want it here anyway?" Mari muttered.

Cold and wet, they waited impatiently for the bus. "Here it comes!" shouted Daniel, placing himself strategically so he could be the first one on. Robin and Mark were together talking and lingered behind to be last on. Mari and Beth hopped on with Annie.

"Hi, Jen, how are you today?" Mari slid in next to her toward the back of the bus.

"Oh, all right, I guess." She pulled her books close and looked out the window. The bus rolled on, and Dante and Alanso jumped in.

"Hi Beth!" Dante slid in next to her. They whispered to each other, smiling and keeping to themselves.

"Come on, Jen, what is going on with you today?" Mari pleaded, encouraging her.

"Oh, just leave it alone!" Jen whispered strongly.

Margot was on next, and she and Alanso sat close and talked the whole time the bus rambled in to the school.

Everyone piled off the bus. Jenny scooted off quickly to the girls' bathroom and disappeared. Mari and Steven went on to their classes.

That morning when the girls were dressing for PE, Mari saw Jenny dressing in a different spot away from everyone.

"Jenny, look at yourself!" Mari took a towel and held it up to hide her. "What has happened to you?" Mari looked all over her back and side.

"He did it this time, Mari. He did it this time." Jenny was crying quietly.

"Who?" Mari whispered.

"You know! My dad! He beat me because he found out. He found out," she whispered.

Mari was anxious now. "Cover up quickly before anyone else sees these bruises. You have to tell the teacher. You have to report this."

Jenny whispered, "Then everyone else will know."

"Well, everyone else is going to know soon anyway because you've gained weight," Mari said, rushing to help her get dressed.

"I feel sick. I just can't play this morning. Tell the teacher I just can't make it. Will you, Mari?" Jenny sat down on the bench in front of the lockers.

"Okay, I'll cover for you." Mari ran upstairs quickly to see the teacher.

All the rest of the girls were running upstairs to the gym by now, and the locker room was almost empty. Joan came over and whispered, "You feeling bad today, Jen? Period?"

Jenny looked up. "Yeah, feeling bad. Not going to make it today."

Joan ran off quickly. Jenny dressed back in her clothes and went up to the gym with the rest of the girls for roll call. She was late and stood in front of her number just as Mrs. LaBelle called her name.

"Just made it in time, dear?"

"Yes, ma'am. Not up to it today. All right?" Jenny said politely.

"Well, sit in the bleachers and take it easy." Mrs. LaBelle passed on to the rest of the girls and gave instructions on the activity for the day.

Jenny lay down across the seats and fell asleep.

"Come on, Jen. You have to get to your next class." Mari pushed her shoulder after class was over.

"Oh, I don't think I am going to make it. I have cramps, and I feel really bad." She stood up and nearly lost her balance. "Oh, my head!" Jen held her hand up to her head.

Mari took her arm. "You have blood all over your skirt," Mari said in alarm.

"Oh God! Oh God! What's happening?" Jenny started to cry.

"Come on with me to the locker room. We can take care of things there." Mari pulled her to hurry. They rushed down through the bleachers to the locker room.

Mrs. LaBelle saw them and rushed to help. "What's the matter, girls? What is going on?"

Mari whispered, "I think she's having a miscarriage. We need a doctor or something."

"What?" Mrs. LaBelle almost shouted.

"Be quiet," Mari insisted. "No one knows anything about this. Please! Please! Keep it down!"

Mrs. LaBelle rushed with the two girls to the locker room. "Lie here on this bench. I'll get some help and be right back in a minute." She ran quickly to her office. Grabbing the phone, she dialed the operator. "I need an ambulance at the high school gym right away! Please hurry! I think I have a girl who's having a miscarriage! Yes, that's right. Just get here fast!" She hung up the phone and dialed the office. "Get me the principal, Lillian. I need him down in the girls' locker room. It's an emergency. He needs to run, run fast!" She hung up the phone and ran back down to the locker room. "How are you, dear?"

By then, Jenny was in tears and in a great deal of pain. "Let's take your slips off and get some towels," Mrs. LaBelle said quietly. "Mari, get some wet washcloths for her face. Let's roll up some towels and make her more comfortable."

Mari rushed to get the towels wet in the shower and ran back with them and wiped Jenny's face. "You'll be all right, Jen. You will be all right," Mari spoke softly.

After a bit, the men from the ambulance came running down with the principal. "What's happening here? What is your name, child?" one man took her hand and felt her pulse.

The principal took Mari aside. "What do you know about this?"

"Well, I know everything. It has been a secret. My dad and mother know. Now her dad knows, and he beat her and bruised her all over her back and ribs. He beats her a lot for no good reason." Mari was really upset by now and trying not to cry.

By this time, the ambulance men were putting Jenny on the gurney and taking her out to the ambulance. Mari, Mrs. LaBelle, and the principal followed. Mrs. LaBelle held Mari close as the ambulance drove away.

"Will you call her parents? What will they do to her now?" Mari whispered to Mrs. LaBelle.

"I don't know, dear. We'll keep her secret. It won't do anyone any good to know what has happened," Mrs. LaBelle said, a bit anxious.

The bell rang for classes to let out for lunch. Mrs. LaBelle suggested that Mari call her parents and go home for the day since she had already missed her other morning classes.

"I think I can make it. I'll get my lunch and meet everyone out on the front lawn. Thanks anyway." Mari turned and walked backward as she waved. "Thanks! Thanks a bunch!" Mari ran quickly and got her lunch. Everyone was already out on the lawn.

"Did you see the ambulance? Did you see? Who was it? Do you know?" Joan and the cheerleaders were all there with Robb, Steven, Zack, and the rest of the gang.

Mari spoke quietly, "It was Jenny. She fell and hurt herself, and Mrs. LaBelle and the principal had to call an ambulance. I'm pretty sure they are just taking precautions to be sure she's okay. She wasn't feeling very good in gym class. I think she just was dizzy or something. Maybe she didn't eat breakfast or something."

Joan jumped in, "Oh, just that time, you know."

Steven came over to Mari. "Here, let's sit here. I have an apple in my lunch. Want a bite?" He held the apple out to her.

"Oh, silly. Thanks." Mari choked up to hold back tears.

Zack jumped over and said, "Should the guys and I play our band at the pep rally? We could do it again. We know all sorts of numbers!" Everyone laughed.

"Yeah, all sorts. There wouldn't be a thing you couldn't play," Robb chided. "What's for lunch, Mari?" he asked as he grabbed for hers.

"Bug off, jerk face. I told you, you had your last free lunch from me. Now bug off." Mari held tight to her lunch bag.

Steven held his hand up. "Yeah, bug off! Mari isn't feeding you anymore, jerk face!"

Joan and the cheerleaders bounced off giggling and jumping around. "Bye, Mari, see you later." All the rest of the gang waved. The warning bell rang, and they all got up. Mari brushed off her skirt, looking herself over.

"You're fine. Nothing is out of place. You don't have to worry. Do you?" Steven said with concern.

"No, not to worry. I take good care of myself when I need to." They walked briskly to the gray stone building to the lockers.

"I have to get upstairs to class. See you in study hall?" Steven said as he brushed her arm with his hand.

Mari was still shaken with the events concerning Jenny, but she knew it would end well. There wouldn't be any baby, and no one would know a thing about it. It was just another secret to keep.

Mari waited alone for her dad at the big white gate after sending Beth on up the hill. She heard the big truck coming around the bend in the road and already had the gate open for him.

"Well, what the hell are you doing down here this time of day, Brat?" RG was perplexed to see her. She climbed into the truck after she closed the big gate.

"I have some bad news to tell you. Well, maybe it can be good news. Jenny went to the hospital while we were at school today. Her dad had beat her and bruised her pretty badly. I think she had a miscarriage. I still really don't know for sure. Mrs. LaBelle helped me in the gym."

"What do you mean helped you in the gym?" RG insisted.

"Well, Jenny wasn't feeling well when we first started to get ready for PE. Mrs. LaBelle excused her from class and sent her to sit up in the bleachers and rest. She fell asleep, and when I went up to get her after class, she had blood all over her skirt. Anyway, from there, Mrs. LaBelle took care of us and called the ambulance and the principal. No one at school knows what happened. They were all in class. So no one knows what happened. It's still a secret. Daddy, it's still a secret. We don't want anyone to know," Mari was in tears at this point.

"Okay, Brat, settle down. I will talk to your mother and see what to do. We'll let you know after we talk to some people." He reached over and patted her on her arm.

"Did you see the ambulance, Mari?" Beth inquired eagerly after RG and Mari came into the house.

"Yes. I happened to be with Jenny in the gym when it all happened. She will be fine. I think she just fell and was dizzy. They just had to take precautions, that's all." Mari set all her stuff down. "I really need to go to the bathroom. See you in a minute." She ran up to her room and to the bathroom. Running water in the sink, she filled her hands with water, leaned down, and splashed her face several times.

She looked in the mirror and spoke out loud, "Oh, I know, Mother. Oh, but for the grace of God, therefore go I."

"I never! Daddy scares the hell out of me. Stay away from those sexy boys in the vineyard! Yes, Daddy, I will be an old maid and stay away from those boys." She grabbed a towel and dried her face.

"You all right in there, girl?" Her mother was at the door.

Mari stepped out. "Oh, Mama, it was awful. Jenny was miserable. I really was scared for her. What is going to happen to her? Her parents are really so awful to her."

Mama held her in her arms. "Now, now, your dad will talk to some people and sort it all out." Her mother held her for a moment. "Now let's go down and take care of dinner. The boys and Beth have done all the chores. Just pull yourself together and come down. Fred and Sarah have everything ready. All we have to do is sit for dinner." They turned and walked down together.

"You got out of all your work today, snot face." Daniel sneered at Mari.

"Oh, shut up!" Mark blurted out. "Everyone has a bad day. Leave her alone. Mind your manners once in your life. What is wrong with you, Daniel?"

Beth slammed her fork on the table in disgust in the way Daniel was behaving.

"Now look at this. I have made a new dish for dinner, everyone. Let me know what you think of it." Sarah held a large serving dish out.

"Well, doesn't that smell good?" RG exclaimed. "Let's all say a word. Thank you, God, for all good things."

"What is that anyway?" Daniel asked impertinently.

"It's a tamale pie. I learned it from a chef in San Francisco. I made a big salad, some salsa, and some shredded cheese to put on the top," explained Sarah.

Fred came out with some bottles of beer. "Here, sir, you will want this to go with this meal."

"Don't say, I wouldn't mind. Thanks," RG said with gusto.

Mama spoke up softly, "Why don't you and Sarah sit down with us tonight and join us. We need some cheering up tonight." They all sat down and made light conversation.

"I think I will just go right up to bed, Mama," Mari said as she excused herself from the table. No one said a word.

"Well then, good night, dear. See you in the morning," Mama said as Mari left the room.

The days were rainy now, and everyone was in the lunchroom out of the weather. Jenny missed school for several days. Everyone whispered about her and missed her.

"Wonder when Jen will get back to school?" Joan said at lunch a couple days later. "I haven't heard."

Mari spoke up, "My mother said she was home now and that she will be back in school next week. Nothing to worry about." She brushed it off and changed the subject. "Zack? Are you and the guys going to play your air band at the rally? We love it."

"Yeah, we have a whole repertoire of songs we know." Everyone laughed.

"I bet it takes a lot of practice," Robb chimed in. Robb and his pals stood up and pretended to be an air band with instruments. The bell rang, and everyone gathered up their stuff and went out to their lockers and off to class.

"See you in study hall, Mari," Steven shouted as they went off.

"Yeah!" She smiled at him and tipped her nose up and nodded.

On the way home, Mari got off the bus at Jenny's and walked up the road to the house. The house sat perched on the edge of the hill with a beautiful huge veranda all across the front. A porch swing hung off on the left, moving slightly. The house was painted yellow with white trim. There were big hay barns out in the back with tractors and equipment all standing around.

She knocked on the door and waited.

"Well, look here! Hello, Mari. Come on in. The kids are all watching television. Would you like some hot chocolate?" Mrs. Hayward was very welcoming and gracious.

"Sure, thanks. Hi, Jenny." Mari walked across the room where all the kids were watching the television. It was one they called a console in a big beautiful wood piece of furniture. Mari had not seen many televisions, and this one was really nice. They were watching a Western movie: *Hopalong Cassidy*.

The girls went into the kitchen with Mrs. Hayward. They sat at the table watching her as she made the chocolate.

"How was school, dear?" Mrs. Hayward asked quietly as she brought the cups to the table.

"Everyone misses Jenny. That's for sure. They all wonder how she is," Mari said in between sips.

"I'll be back on Monday. I feel really great now. Huh, Mama?" Jenny said assuredly.

"Yes. She is all back to her old self. We're all happy things turned out so well. I am sure we have a lot to thank you for, Mari!" Mrs. Hayward said as she came close and patted her on the shoulder.

"Well, I must say, I have been worried and concerned how things turned out," Mari said, putting her cup down.

"Your dad came down and talked to my dad last week. Did you know?" Jenny inquired.

"Actually, I didn't know. He did say he planned to stop in some-time." Mari tried to stay casual about it.

"He really had a nice talk with my dad, and since then, things are really much better between us," Jenny said.

"Yes, thank you, Mari. We really appreciate how much you have helped," Mrs. Hayward spoke softly.

"Well, I really should stand out on the driveway and wait for my dad to come by. I wouldn't want to have to climb up the vineyard through the brush to the road if I missed him." Mari got up from the table. "I really am glad everything has worked out well for you, Jen. Maybe you will get to go to the Christmas ball, after all." Mari hugged her and left the kitchen in a rush to catch her dad.

"Bye, you kids. Have fun watching television!" Mari slipped down the porch stairs and hurried down to the Trail. She was lucky and saw her dad's big green truck coming up from the south. She waved him down and hopped in.

CHAPTER 12

The Competition

THE SUN HAD COME OUT, and the valley was beautiful. The leaves had almost completely fallen from the vineyards. The end of October and grape harvest was over, and all the workers had left the ranch for the season. The air was fresh and clean. Nothing dramatic had happened, and routine had fallen into place over the past weeks.

Mari and Beth caught the church bus on Sunday as usual. They waited at the big gate and glad it wasn't too cold. Mari had a new jacket and wanted to show it off to Jenny. The bus rumbled down the road and screeched to a halt at the big gate. Mari jumped in, looking for Jenny.

"Oh, there you are! We were hoping to see you today." Beth jumped right next to her seat.

Mari scooted in. "How are you lately?"

"I am really good. Things are better at home, and my dad has changed. So we just don't talk," she said quietly.

Dante and Alanso got on the bus. Everyone started to sing songs and clap their hands. Margot got in, and everyone cheered. It was a happy time.

"We're singing at the Baptist church today. I'm so happy they started a choir now," Mari said, all excited. "Beth is singing a solo. She is so beautiful."

Jenny reached over and tapped Beth on the shoulder. "Does your friend Dante come and hear you sing? Or does he go over to the Presbyterian church?"

Beth turned sharply. "Actually, the boys are Catholic! They walk over to their church. Everyone here is really nice about everyone getting to their own church. What's the difference to you?" Beth spoke a bit sharply.

"Oh, I am sorry!" Jenny replied.

"I see you are your old self now. Glad to see it, Jen," Mari quipped.

They jumped off the bus, and everyone went their own way.

Mari and Beth sang and clapped their hands and had a great time in church.

"Hi, Beth, ready to go home?" Dante walked up while everyone was waiting for the pastor to come and drive the bus home. Dante questioned, "What would we all do if we didn't have the bus? We need to give them some money to help out, don't you think?"

Beth spoke up with surprise, "I'll ask RG about it. We always have money for things we really need."

Mari interrupted, "Well, don't be rushing in with something until you ask first, Beth."

"Oh, I am sorry. I shouldn't have spoken out. But I am going to ask when we get home." She swung around and boarded the bus, sitting down in a bit of a huff for the rest of the trip home.

"RG, we had a discussion about the Baptist bus today. Dante suggested we needed to contribute to the church since we all use the bus. The pastor is always so nice to let everyone ride it even if they don't come to his church. What do you think?" Beth spoke with a mouthful of food at the dinner table.

RG sat back in his chair, placing his napkin on the table. "Well, Thanksgiving is coming up. We should be thankful for all we have and what people do for us. Mother and I will take it under advisement and let you know. How is that?"

Mari spoke up, "I think it's a bit presumptuous of Beth to ask for such a thing, don't you think?"

Mark jumped in, "She is a part of the family now, and you consider her as your sister. Why shouldn't she ask for something important to her? You didn't think of it to ask. Don't be jealous."

"I'm not!" Mari said indignantly. She got up from the table and went into the kitchen with Sarah. "Did you hear that? I am not jealous!" Mari stood at the kitchen table stiff in her anger.

"I think it sounds like it, dear. Sisters do have their moments. Go back out there and behave." Sarah turned to her work. "Look at that, Fred. Sisters! They really are into it. How wonderful. We're part of a real family now." Sarah smiled to herself.

"Yes, dear." He reached over and kissed her on the cheek and patted her on the butt and went out the door.

Monday morning, everyone was up and out getting the chores done early. The weather was nice, even a bit warm. The does had their babies, and Daniel was caring for them as if he were the father. "See, they're all hopping around, and the doe will let me pick them up." Daniel showed Mari and Beth. "Here, take some like this." He took two and stuffed them into his shirt. "Here, you take some. They are really soft."

Beth took one and held it close to her face. "How wonderful. They are so precious."

"Oh, don't get too soft on them. Daniel is going to kill them all and sell them to the butcher in St. Helena. He makes a lot of money with his rabbits," Mari said a bit sharply.

"Oh no. How could you? You meanie!" Beth wailed.

"That's reality, Beth. That's how we make a living. We live well, and you seem to enjoy the rabbit when we have it for dinner," Daniel said strongly.

"Oh, you're right. How thankful we all are. We have rabbit, duck, chicken, beef, fish, and all sorts of great food here. I have already been so spoiled since I have been here. I almost forget my life before this."

Mark walked in, overhearing what they were saying. "We all are spoiled and forget that we live a great life here on the ranch. We complain when we have to get up and do all the chores in the cold mornings and then catch the bus for school. We should all find some of our own money to put for the Baptist bus you and Mari ride on."

Daniel chimed in, "I can give some of my rabbit money, and Mark can give some from the sale of one of his calves."

Mari jumped in, "I can give some from the sale of my eggs from my chickens."

Beth started to cry, "I have nothing to sell or give. What do I have?"

Mark suggested, "Well, you can take some of the ducks to the butcher and sell them."

Beth wailed, "You mean I have to kill them and dress them?"

Mark replied without thinking, "Of course! That's life on the ranch."

"Well, I never!" Beth handed back the bunnies. She walked out of the barn and stood by the corral where the ducks were nesting.

"You! You ducks! We'll see about you!" She stormed down to the house, barging into the kitchen. "Sarah, do you know how to kill a duck? I have to kill some ducks!"

"What do you mean you have to kill some ducks?" Sarah said in surprise, holding some pie dough in her hand.

"Mark said I had to kill some ducks if I wanted to contribute money for the bus." She was wailing at this point.

"Now settle down. Let's talk about this a little." Sarah put the dough down. "Why do you need to raise money for the bus?"

Beth stopped wailing. "Those kids all have some project, and I don't have one to call my own. They can raise money and put it in their bank accounts. I don't have any bank account or any money of my own. If they want to help with the bus, they have money. I don't! Mark said I could have the ducks. But that means I have to kill them. I never...I never..." She put her hands over her face.

Fred walked in. "What is all this fuss about? I heard something about killing ducks?"

Sarah picked up the dough and started to work on it. "Yes, Mark said she could have charge of the ducks and sell them to the butcher in St. Helena. That means she has to kill them."

"Well, not to worry. I can do it for you, and no one will have to be the wiser. How would that be?" Fred said cheerfully.

Beth rushed over and grabbed him by the waist and hugged him hard. "Oh, thank you. Will you help me make arrangements with the butcher too and take them in with me?"

"Sure, not to worry." He smiled at Sarah. "That will be our secret."

Mama came in and asked, "What is all the fuss about? All you kids have to get down the hill to school. You'll miss the bus. Fred, take them down the hill today so they don't miss that bus." She was a bit annoyed to see everyone had taken so long doing their chores

That day, Fred got on the phone to the butcher. "Hey, Mr. Charley, can you use some duck for Thanksgiving? We got some ducks up here we want to get rid of." He paused a moment. "Well, thanks anyway." He turned to Sarah. "I couldn't make a deal. What am I going to tell Beth?"

Sarah paused. "Why not call the butcher at the Oakville Grocery Store?"

"Good idea!" He turned and picked up the phone. "Hey, Adalfo. You got a need for some duck for Thanksgiving? We got some ducks we want to get rid of. The kid up here wants to make some money to give for the Baptist bus." He paused. "Great! How much will you give her for them?" He paused again. "Great! When do you want 'um?" He paused. "We'll get 'um right over by Tuesday afternoon." He turned to Sarah. "That is how it's done!"

"I guess I better talk to RG and let him know what those kids are up to. You think, Sarah?"

She smiled. "Get on it before they get ahead of you."

He rushed out the door. "Come on, Dagwood, we have a mission to accomplish." They headed out to the walnut trees where RG was working.

"Hey, Fred! Give me a hand here." RG was shaking the walnuts and raking them up.

"I need to let you in on a secret the kids are up to. They all plan to sell rabbits, eggs, a calf, and some ducks so they can contribute for the Baptist bus. I thought you ought to know about it. I promised Beth I would kill the ducks for her since she was squeamish about it."

RG stopped and paused. "How admirable! What the hell. Let them do it. That should keep them busy. You let me know when I need to take them into town to deliver all this stuff. Mark going to kill that calf or just sell it?"

Fred paused. "He never said. I guess we have to figure on that one." The men laughed.

"RG, I think they have themselves a real project," Fred said as he raked up some walnuts.

Everyone was excited at dinner that night as conversation was lively. No one revealed their plans and the secrets they were up to.

RG sat back in his chair and slapped his napkin on the table. "I think I have to go into town on Saturday to put the walnuts into the dryer. Anyone need to go to town for anything?"

All three chimed in, "I do!"

Mark spoke up, "I already made arrangements with Fred for what I have to do. Thanks anyway, Dad."

Daniel interrupted, "I need to get to the butcher. I'll go with you."

Mari joined in, "I have an appointment to sell my eggs at the farmers' market as usual."

Beth added, "I made arrangements with Fred too. Thanks anyway."

RG said with satisfaction, "Well then, it will just be Daniel and Mari. I'll be ready early. You can tool around town and get some candy at the Sweet Shop. We might even get an ice-cream soda."

Beth dug in a little sportingly, "Fred might take us to the Sweet Shop too. You might just see us there!"

Mama spoke softly, "Now, everyone, settle down. Get off with you all. Everyone has their things to do. Help Sarah and Fred and get cleaned up for bed."

"You think you're so smart now, don't you? We'll see who brings in the most money. You and your ducks!" Mari said scathingly.

She went into the bathroom and brushed her teeth and washed up. Humming a bit, she came back into the bedroom and flounced into her bed. She pulled up the covers and rolled over to ignore Beth.

"Good night, Mari." Beth left the room to brush her teeth and washed up for bed. She snuck quietly back and crawled into bed without a word.

Beth woke with a start that Saturday morning. She jumped up and rushed to get ready. Down she went to the kitchen in a rush.

"Sarah, where's Fred? He promised to help me today."

"Well, get your breakfast first, dear. You can find him afterward. Here, have one of these sweet rolls and some milk."

Beth took a plate and served herself. "Helen—I mean, Mama and I made these together. They're really wonderful and gooey. I really love chocolate milk with them too." She poured some chocolate syrup in her glass. She quickly ate and excused herself. "I'll look for Fred up at the barn. See ya later!" She was out the door in a flash, and up the path she flew.

"Where are you off to in such a rush?" a loud voice from the other end of the veranda boomed.

She turned back. "Oh, hi, Mark. I have to find Fred. He promised to help me with the...*shhhh*. You know..."

"Oh, that's right. You'll find him in the back of the corral in one of the little side barns."

She ran quickly around the corral. "Fred, Fred, where are you?" she said in a loud whisper.

"Hey, kid. I'm here," came a voice behind the little barn.

Beth came around the corner. "Oh, my! What have you done? What a mess! What should I do?" She put her hands over her nose. Walking closer, she watched Fred as he cut the head off a duck. Its wings flopped around. There were three others already lying off to the side.

"What do I do now?" Beth said, quite squeamish.

"Well, I already put a fire in that big pit you see over there. See that big pot? Fill it with water, and we will put it on to get the water boiling hot. Then we will dip the ducks in the water, and the feathers will be easy to pull off."

Beth got the pot and went to the faucet by the barn and filled it. She hauled it over. "Okay, I can't lift it over the fire. Please, can you do it for me?" She was struggling to try and carry it. Fred wiped his hands on his pants. He took the big pot and put it on the hook over the fire.

"There. Now it will take a while to get hot. Meanwhile, go get a big pot or something from Sarah to put these guys in. And get some butcher paper too. While you do that, I will build a table out of some sawhorses and planks where we can work," Fred instructed her.

Beth left quickly with intent. She snuck around the little barn quietly so as not to be noticed by Daniel or Mari in the big barn. Flying by the milk house, past the cellar and up the stairs to the kitchen, she spoke out loudly, "Sarah? Fred wants… oh! Hi RG, good Morning."

"What the hell, kid! What are you doing up and around so early today?"

She replied anxiously, "Fred and I have a project…and…"

"Well, go on with you. I won't keep you." He quickly left the room.

Sarah put her finger to her lips. "You almost let the cat out of the bag. What does Fred need?"

Beth said breathlessly, "Some butcher paper and something to put them in like a big pot or tray or something."

Sarah went to the pantry and came out with all she needed. "Go on with you now and don't let anybody catch you."

Beth grabbed it all and went out the door and back the way she came, looking around to be sure no one would see her.

"Oh, Dagwood! Go away! Git, shoo, git," she whispered loudly. He followed her to the little barn.

The water was steaming hot now. Fred had the planks set up on the saw horses. Pointing, Fred said, "Put that on the table, kid."

She set everything down. "Now what?" She stood with her hands on her hips.

"Well, see how I tied this twine around the legs? Watch." He took a duck and dipped it into the hot water. Dipping up and down, he pulled the duck out and slapped it on the planks. "Let her cool to the touch. Now start pulling the feathers off like this."

"Oh! What a stink!" She turned her head.

"Come on now, kid. You want to make some money, don't you?" Fred said encouragingly.

"Well, I didn't know it would be like this. But I am going to win. Mari thinks she is so hot with her eggs. All she has to do is grab them out of the nest and put them in a basket and clean them and put them in a carton."

Fred put another duck in the water, then lapped it on the plank table. He pulled and pulled. Wet feathers flew all over the place.

"See, we will win. I think you will make more money with your ducks than eggs," Fred said as he worked.

Beth really got into it with enthusiasm. They got the ducks all cleaned up and packaged in butcher paper.

"Now, doesn't that look professional?" stated Fred, standing back as he wiped his forehead with his handkerchief. Beth wiped her head with the back of her hand as she stood and admired their handiwork, feathers all over her hair, shirt, jeans, and all over the table and the ground.

"I don't believe I just did that! I just don't believe I just did that!" She went over and gave Fred a big hug around the waist.

"Go and get cleaned up. Take a bath or something and put on some nice clean jeans and a blouse. We can take these over to the Oakville grocery meat market right away. You can collect your money today." Fred was glad they were done.

Beth took off with a flash, sneaking around and up the veranda to the bathroom to take a bath and humming to herself. She put on her best jeans and a shirt with flowers on it. She pulled a sweatshirt over her shirt and flashed down to the kitchen where mama and Sarah were working.

"Seen Fred? We're out of here! Be back later!" She grabbed another sweet roll with a napkin. Out the door to the veranda, she saw Fred coming across the little bridge all cleaned up. The truck was out on the drive in front of the kitchen. Mark was sitting up front waiting.

Fred waved to Sarah. "Be back later. On a secret mission." They pulled away. No one had seen them. They had done it all before ten o'clock.

"Where is Fred going, Mama?" Daniel asked as he came in from the barn. "I have to get my rabbits ready for the butcher today. Do you think Dad will be ready to go this afternoon? He said he was going in to take the walnuts to the dryer."

Sarah motioned to the sweet rolls. "Have a roll and some milk, Daniel, and then get on with your job. I know your dad is expecting to help you. Just find him out in the walnut trees." Daniel was intent and scarfed down the milk and rolls.

Rushing out the door looking for his dad in the trees, he shouted, "Hey, Dad? Hey, Dad? I am ready for the rabbits!"

"Over here, boy!" His dad stopped raking and leaned the rake against the tree.

"Come on!" Daniel started for the barn. "Let's get to it. I think Mari already has her eggs ready to go. We're the last ones. I overheard Mark on the phone this morning making some kind of deal about selling his calves. You know anything about that?"

"What's this? I am not sure I am up with you on what is going on?" RG put his hand on Daniel's shoulder as they walked up the road to the barn.

"I guess I let the cat out of the bag, Dad. Mark and us, we all decided the other day to pitch in and put some money to the Baptist bus for Mari and her friends on Sundays. Mari is selling some of her eggs, Mark said he could sell one of his calves, I can sell some of my rabbits, and Mark said Beth could sell some of the ducks to the butcher," Daniel said breathlessly.

"Well, fancy that! You all are a bunch of schemers. I thought we were just doing the usual rabbits for the butcher today. How many are you giving up for the bus?" RG pretended he didn't know a thing.

"Oh, I don't know. Depends on how much everyone else gives. They can't beat me out," Daniel said competitively.

They got to the barn, and RG paused. "You think that is the right attitude when you're giving for a charity? I think you have to give from your heart. Do you really think the bus is important?"

Daniel shrugged his shoulders. They set up and got ready for killing the rabbits. Daniel went around and counted them all.

"I have sixty-four, not counting the babies we just had. I need to keep enough to have my usual order of eight for the butcher every two weeks. I bet he would take six more for Thanksgiving this week. That would give me twelve dollars for the bus. What do you think, Dad?"

They were well into their work skinning and preparing the rabbits. They were wrapping them and stacking them, ready to load up.

"I think that's a very generous offer, son. Whatever you can make a deal with the butcher, don't brag about what you are doing with the extra rabbits. That would spoil the whole purpose on what you are doing," RG spoke softly but strongly in his manner.

"Okay, Dad," Daniel replied.

They went down to the house and cleaned up. Daniel barged his way into the kitchen where he found his dad and mother. RG had his arms around Helen, kissing her.

"Woo! Sorry. I didn't mean to interrupt," Daniel said smartly.

"You'll be so fortunate to find a woman as great as your mom someday, son." RG patted her on the butt, turned, and quickly went out the door to the veranda.

"Come on, son. Off we go to make a big deal with the butcher." They went up to the barn and loaded the rabbits in a big box.

"Where is Mari?" Daniel yelled impatiently.

"I haven't seen her around all morning," RG replied.

"I think I heard her yowling at the piano up in the library," replied Daniel snidely.

They jumped in the truck and drove down to the house. RG laid hard on the horn. Mari came running out with her basket of eggs.

"I'm ready, Daddy. You gunna let us have something at the Sweet Shop when we're done?" she said breathlessly as she set her eggs in the back of the truck and piled in next to Daniel. "Scoot over, please."

Off they went barreling down the road. The sun was shining, and the clouds were white and fluffy.

"I think I'll have an ice-cream soda at the Sweet Shop," remarked Daniel, lifting his head as if he were the high and mighty.

"That really sounds good. I am getting hungry now," RG joined in. "I think we should find some real food too, don't you?"

Mari joined in, "Oh yes, I think so. Maybe I could look around the shops for a minute."

"I think that could work out too, Brat," RG said, smiling.

The trip down the Silverado Trail seemed long with anticipation. They pulled up to the butcher first. Mari scooted out of the truck to let Daniel out. He rushed in without the rabbits.

"Hey, you forgot your rabbits!" Mari shouted.

"No, he has to make a deal first. Let him go," RG said quietly.

"Oh, then I will take care of my eggs while he's doing that." Mari grabbed her basket, and off she went down the street to the market. RG stood near the truck and waited. Pretty soon Daniel came out grinning ear to ear.

"Okay, Dad, unload 'um. Mr. Charlie said he would take them all since it's Thanksgiving. What a deal! And he gave me extra too. I can put more than I thought towards the bus."

Daniel went in and unloaded his rabbits. He came out with cash in his hand. "Look, look! What a haul!"

Mari came running up just then. "What do you mean?"

"Look how much I made on the rabbits this week! I'm really in business now!" Daniel said, bragging.

"Good for you, Daniel. How wonderful!" She and Daniel jumped around.

"All right, you kids. Let's get over to the Sweet Shop like we planned." They jumped in the truck and parked it closer in town.

They walked into the warm building and smelled the sweetness of the fountain in the air. The shop always felt warm and friendly.

"Hey, look! There's Beth and Fred!" Daniel ran over quickly to where they were sitting. "What are you doing here?" he demanded.

Mari and RG walked up. "May we join you, Fred? My treat?"

"Sure, let's take the big round table in the back," RG directed. They all went over to the big round oak table in the back. Just then, Mark walked in with a package under his arm.

"Hey! Look everyone is here. How did that happen? What are all you guys doing in town?" Sitting down next to Beth, he winked as he set his package down on the floor next to his chair.

RG quipped, "I think the gig is up, you kids. A little bird told on all of you. So what are we all going to eat? I am hungry as a bear."

Everyone laughed as they picked up the menus.

"So…give it up. What did you get for your eggs, Mari?" Beth said coyly.

"Oh, not much," Mari replied slyly.

"Okay, Daniel? How did you do?" she said smartly.

"I'll let you know," he said as he held the menu high in front of his face.

"Mark? How's bout you?" She looked over the top of her menu.

Fred interrupted, "I think I'll have a hamburger and a beer."

"Same here!" RG joined in with enthusiasm.

Diane, the waitress, came up to the table. "May I take your order, RG?"

"They all may have whatever they want. Put it on my tab today," he said with great gusto.

She took everyone's order all round.

Beth started in again, "Well?"

"Well what, Beth?" Mari said slyly.

"You know. Everyone, give it up. How well did we do? I just have to know right now!"

Daniel laughed. "You are so impatient! I made a killing! I sold six extra rabbits over the eight I usually sell. Besides, Mr. Charlie gave me a bonus too!"

Beth spoke impatiently, "That doesn't tell how well you did for the bus!"

Mark jumped in, "Everyone, take this pencil and write down what you got, and we'll see. Deal?" He handed the pencil to Daniel and a napkin. Daniel wrote something down. "No, you take your own napkin and write your own numbers on it, and then we'll show at the same time."

Daniel passed the pencil to Mari. She wrote hers down and passed the pencil to Mark. Mark wrote his down and passed the pencil to Beth.

"Here, let me have the pencil." RG reached for the pencil. He wrote something on a napkin. Fred reached for the pencil. He wrote something.

"Okay, everyone, at the count of three, put your napkins out in the middle of the table," Beth demanded. "One, two, three!" They all slapped their napkins on the table in all seriousness.

RG reached out and scooped them up quickly. "Well now, let's see. A-huh, a-huh, a-huh, a-huh. Sixty dollars…forty dollars…one hundred dollars! I think you kids won!" He put the napkins in his pocket. "Now, wasn't that fun?"

Daniel sat back in his chair. "Aren't gunna tell, are you?"

"Nope!" RG sat back in his chair and smiled.

"Happy Thanksgiving, kids!" Fred said with pride.

Chapter 13

Making Amends

Beth still felt not quite a part of the family and yet wanted to be. The time with Sarah and Helen in the kitchen was a true treasure and so much to learn about cooking.

The family always had such a grand way of sitting at the table with a formality to it and yet a casual relaxed time for conversation. Everyone had a time to talk about their plans or projects, even some harmless gossip. RG and Helen always had comments about politics and other people in the valley and their opinions. 4-H was always a big topic of conversation. Mark was taking on more and more of the responsibilities of the vineyard, and Daniel always had his growing rabbit business. Mari played the piano and sang while playing. She always took care of the chickens and the dogs.

Beth now took on the ducks. Oh, the ducks.

Adalfo had called Mrs. Rogers and wondered if Beth had any more ducks before Thanksgiving. He had sold them all out and had more requests than ever before.

Walking back down the road the next week to get on the bus for school, Mari and Beth shivered in the cold. They walked quickly to keep warm.

"I had a great weekend, Mari, didn't you?" Beth said, a bit out of breath.

"Oh, I'm sure you did. Still, you did do well with your ducks." Mari laughed.

"Not mad anymore?" Beth looked over as they walked on.

"No, not mad. Just put out a little that my contribution was such a pittance compared to everyone else's. Honestly!" she said in frustration.

They arrived at the big white gate. Mari pulled the latch and swung it open just far enough for the two of them to get through. They were the last to arrive.

"What took you lazy butts so long?" Daniel sneered.

"Well, I see you're back to your old self!" Mari sharply replied.

Mark interjected, "Oh, shut up, you two, and knock it off."

The bus rumbled down to a halt, and they all piled in. Everyone found their strategic places for the best social advantage.

Mari looked for Jenny toward the back of the bus. "Hey. How are you feeling?" she whispered as she scooted in next to her.

"I really feel just fine. No one has beat me up lately. We had my mom's brother and three bratty kids over for the weekend. Their mom let them get away with anything they wanted to. I will never—" She paused.

Mari interrupted, "Yes, you will. We have a great future ahead of us."

Just then, Dante and Alanso got on. Dante smoothly got to the seat nearest Beth. "Happy to see you today, pretty girl." Dante winked at her.

"You may sit with me if you like." Beth patted the seat by her side. "I missed you. We had a contest to see who would make the most money selling our stuff. I did pretty good, if I don't say so myself."

"And what stuff did you sell?" Dante inquired.

"I was in charge of killing the ducks and taking them to the butcher," she said smugly.

"You kill ducks all by yourself and take them to butcher?" Dante turned sideways, looking at her intently.

"Well, I did have help. But I did a lot. It was a real mess, let me tell you!" She squirmed in her seat and smiled slyly.

They talked and laughed without even noticing anyone else on the bus.

Margot got on and quickly sat with Alanso. They sat close and chatted quietly until they arrived at the gray stone building. Everyone piled off, rushing to get to the building out of the cold.

"Hey, good-looken'? What you got cooken'?" came a voice behind the big redwood tree. Steven stepped out with a single-stem daisy. "For you, Your Highness."

"Oh, you silly person! Where did you get that?" Mari said as she took the flower and leaned in to hug him. They walked close as they hurried into the building to their lockers.

"See you in the lunch room," Mari whispered as she closed her locker, carefully holding her flower close to her books.

"See ya!" Steven stood and watched her walk away.

"Pretty nice! You lucky dude!" Bill came up behind him and patted him on the back. "I wish I had something like that."

"It just worked out for me at the right time, I guess." Steven turned and started up the west stairway to class. "We hit it off one night after a game at a dance. I kept after her until she caved," he said as they approached the classroom.

"That's how it's done?" Bill said as they entered the classroom.

Everyone was rushing into the room to get seated.

Robb entered last. Making a big show, he stated, "I'm here. We can all get started now!" He bowed and tossed his book on his desk.

"You think you're so hot, Mr. Muscles! That's all you are!" Charlie sneered.

Mr. Brown entered the room, talking as he walked in. "Does anyone recall where we left off on Friday?" He opened his book and placed it on the lectern in front of his desk.

Robb stood up with his chest out. "The settlers came out on the Oregon Trail, from about 1811 to 1840. Fur traders and trappers laid out the first of the trails. The trail was only traveled by horseback or on foot. In 1836, I think in May, some one thousand migrants formed a wagon train in Independence, Missouri, and reached Fort Hall, Idaho. They eventually made it to Oregon, making it possible for many of our families to be here in California today."

Mr. Brown continued, "The trail was about two thousand miles and took people about four to six months to get out here. They all had dreams of owning land and farming. Just think of the disease, food poisoning, typhoid, and especially cholera that killed a lot of the people on the way here."

Robb sat down while Mr. Brown spoke. They all sat quietly the whole time. They all had a great discussion about it all. The bell rang and they all got up and filed out.

"Well done, dude! Sorry about that thing before." Charlie patted him on the back. They all piled down the stairs and out to the ag building.

"Going to the ball, Robb?" George walked backward in front of the others. "Got a hot date?"

"No, not yet. Can't make up my mind what I want to do. Maybe I won't even go," Robb tried to brush it off. "I have other plans at Christmas with family. I might be too busy."

"Oh, everyone goes to the ball. No one ever misses the Christmas ball. Even guys without a date go and pick up some girl who comes alone," George chided him.

They reached the Quonset hut out in the back, barely making it on time. "About time you boys showed up. We have a lot to get to today," Mr. Collins yelled. "Now, where did we leave off before Thanksgiving?" Everyone laughed and looked at Robb.

"I'll let George handle this one, sir," Robb said, pushing his friend forward.

The class was ending, and Bill motioned to the guys. "See you in the lunch room?" They all nodded. The bell rang, and they all rushed out, waving to Mr. Collins. "Thanks, sir," Bill shouted.

By the time they got in the lunch room it was very crowded. The girls were already there. Robb, Bill, George, and Charlie pushed up to the counter to order some food.

"No sandwich from Mari today?" George sneered.

"Not for a while. She is totally mad at me over something I did," Robb said in a rather humble way.

The guys all returned to the table where the girls were sitting.

"I think it's too crowded here. Let's go over to the gym," Joan urged. "The other cheerleaders want to meet over there to practice some new stuff. You all should come and watch us. Just eat your lunch in the bleachers."

"That's a great idea!" Jenny stood up and followed Joan as they started to leave. Mari and the rest picked up their lunch and followed out the door.

"Hey, wait up, Jen." Robb ran and grabbed her elbow. "I want to talk to you about something."

She pulled her arm away. "I can't imagine you would have anything to talk to me about!"

"You know I do. I think it's my fault that you were sick before. I had a lot to think about last weekend while I was at home. We had company for a few days, and my aunt had a baby with her. I just couldn't get it out of my mind what you went through because of me. I'm sorry, Jenny. I really am sorry! I didn't mean anything bad to happen to you. Please…"

She paused and looked at him. "Can you really tell me you truly care one little bit! My dad beat me. I had bruises all over my body. He killed our baby! Mari was the only one I could go to. How many other people know now? How did you find out?" She was almost shouting it out. Tears were down her cheeks.

"I just figured it out. No one told me. I knew what we had done that Saturday last summer. I am sorry, Jen. I'm sorry. Can you forgive me? I figured you really mean something to me, and I want us to be friends, more than friends. You are really a terrific person. I think I really care about you. Please…" He was emotional at this point.

"I just wanted you to love me and like me, Robb. I didn't want Mari to have you. I think you are really smart and…well, someday you will be somebody and…and well, I want to be with you," she cried, wiping her face.

The other kids were in the gym by now, and they were alone in front of the gym. Robb took both her hands. "Please, Jen, come to the Christmas ball with me, and we can make everything up. I swear! I won't do any more stupid stuff. We'll just dance and eat sandwiches you make." He reached down and kissed her.

"Oh, I'll think about it. My dad is really mad. I don't know if he will let me go now. I think everyone is waiting for us, and it's cold out here." They went inside and climbed the bleachers together holding hands.

Zack raised his arm. "Over here, Robb. The cheerleaders are doing a new routine."

George yelled out, "Go, Babs! Go, Babs!" He whistled with his fingers between his teeth as he stood, waving his arms at the girls.

"You idiot! What the heck? What you doin'?" Parker reached over to get him to sit down.

"No, that's the one I want. She's the one. I want to take her to the ball. Ya think she would even notice me?" George sat down and pushed Parker on the shoulder.

"Oh, she might. Hard to tell." Parker pointed to Pauline Banks. "That Pauline! I talk to her out on the lawn a lot. I just didn't think she would want to go with a farm boy like me," Parker said modestly.

"Give them a chance, you guys. Jenny and I made up, and if her dad will let her, I'm taking her to the ball. All the girls want to go. That's what I heard. It's our job to take 'um," Robb said with a bit of pride.

"You're such a jock, and we're just FFA guys. You town kids have it all wrapped up," Charlie interjected. "I'm going it alone so I can eat my fill and have a good time."

Jenny and Mari were sitting close, whispering quietly.

"Robb came to me and said he was sorry and wants to take me to the Christmas ball. I don't know how he found out. He said he just figured it out on his own. He said his aunt was at their place for the weekend with a baby, and it just came to him why I was sick and in the hospital. What do you think my dad will do? What will he say?"

Mari touched her arm. "I don't know about your mom and dad. They confuse me. I think I'll talk to my parents and see what they think, and maybe my dad can talk to your dad about it. He talked to him before about hitting you. He's really good at sorting things out with people."

"They know? How many people in the valley know about me?" Jenny was angry and fearful.

"What do you think? I was going to keep this all to myself? I was the one with you through the whole time. Give me a break!" Mari was a bit annoyed now.

"Oh, Mari, I am sorry. I'm still confused about the whole thing. My dad is weird, and my mom is weird. I don't think my brother knows what happened to me. He just stays out of the way of my dad."

The bell rang. They all got up and started to climb down the bleachers to leave. George hopped down the bleachers, yelling, "Babs! Babs! Great job!"

"You like the new routine?" she said as she walked over with here pompoms. She shook one toward his face. "I thought it up this time!"

"Walk with me?" George said quietly. "I wondered if you might want to go to the Christmas ball with me?" He was apprehensive.

"Why, yes. I thought you would never ask. We always had such a nice time at lunch out on the lawn. I already bought a dress, hoping you would ask. My parents already said I could go if you asked."

"Really? You already asked them?" he said in surprise.

"Well, silly, who else would I go with?" She bounced a bit as they walked to the new building for class.

"Look at that. George snared a date to the ball." Parker pushed Charlie as they walked in the door.

Everyone rushed out to get to their next class. As they walked across campus to the new buildings, Parker strategically walked up near Pauline. "Think I could talk to you after class, Pauline?"

"Sure, talk to me now," she quickly replied as they walked together.

"Well, well, I was wondering if you had any plans about the Christmas ball?" he said quietly.

"What do you mean?" she replied.

"You know, is anyone taking you?" His face was getting red now.

"Not so far. I figured I would go it alone if I had to. Why?" She knew what he was up to and wouldn't make it easy for him. "You want to go with me? I mean, we could go together. You think?"

They were at the door by now. She went in first, "I would love to! Talk to you later, okay?"

They sat down in their seats. Parker was stunned and now couldn't concentrate on class. He opened his math book and turned the pages.

"Parker? I think we're in English class now," George whispered.

"Oh yeah." He quickly changed books. He pulled out his homework and rushed to hand it in with the rest of the class. The whole time, he was watching the back of Pauline's head. Her hair was honey-colored and had a silk blue ribbon that tied part of it to the back of her head in a long curl. The bell finally rang to his relief. He again strategically worked his way around her so he could walk down the sidewalk to the next class with her.

"So do you have to ask your parents if you can go with me? I can talk to your dad if I have to," he said quietly.

"I'm sure he will approve of you. I already told them we talk at lunch out on the front lawn," she said with confidence. They parted to go to their own classes.

"See you later." Parker waved.

She smiled and waved her hand as she held her books. "Yeah! See ya!"

Charlie walked alongside Parker. "Snared one? What a dude? Well done, pal!" He slapped Parker on the back.

"Oh, shut up! You should work at it. It isn't hard at all. Just jump in and find one and have as much fun as the rest of us." Parker pushed him back.

Spirits were high now. Things were falling into place. Everyone was finding their match and looking forward to the ball.

Jenny was worried and hopeful about Robb. Could she trust him now? Was this going to be as wonderful as she dreamed it would be? How would her father take the news? Would he beat her again?

She found her dad in the hay barn when she got home that afternoon. She had changed her school clothes into her work jeans. As she approached him with dread in her heart, he spoke up, "Need something, kid?" His tone was not harsh.

"As a matter of fact, I need to talk to you about something. I know I have been a big disappointment to you lately. I want you to know I have learned my lesson and know how blessed I am." She started to cry now. "I really want you to know I was really stupid. I promise I will never get into trouble again, Daddy. Really! I promise!"

He walked over close to her. "I am sorry too, kid. I am sorry too. I am trying to make things better around here too. I'm going to give it a try too. Now what is it you want?" He touched her on the shoulder.

"I want to go to the Christmas ball with Robb."

"What the hell? With Robb? After…," he shouted.

She flinched and stepped back.

"What the hell! I don't—" He stopped. "I promised I would do better too. What makes you think this boy will make it up to you now?" he demanded.

Jenny stood straight now and resolute. "He came to me and said he guessed what had happened, and he is sorry. I believe him. He wants to take me to the ball and be friends. This is important to me, Daddy. Everyone else has a date. I need to have this date. It will be the best ever. I promise. I promise we won't do anything again. *We* will just dance and eat and be with the gang. Besides that, Mr. and Mrs. Rogers will be there, and you and the other parents can have a good time too. No one else knows what happened to me anyway. So don't worry about that, Daddy," she wailed.

He rushed over to her and hugged her. "We'll keep our promise now and have a new start, okay, Jenny?"

Jenny stood still. "Need any help out here, Daddy? I can help. The other kids help out around their ranches. I can help too."

"Come on, kid. I'll show you how this twine gets on the bailing machine." They went to work, and she had great hope in the future.

As she was working with her dad, it occurred to her she needed to see Mrs. Rogers. "I need to go and see Mrs. Rogers, Dad. I think I'll run up to the ranch real fast before dinner. Is that all right with you?

Her father stood firmly and looked at her. "I think I will drive you up there and have a talk with RG myself," he said thoughtfully.

She and her dad got in the truck, took off, and quickly barreled up to the ranch.

"Hi, Mrs. Rogers," Jenny said breathlessly as she came into the kitchen. "I wanted to come up and see you. I know you are busy and it's late, but my dad wanted to see RG too."

Helen stopped in her tracks in surprise. She put her towel down and walked over and gave her a hug. "I am so pleased to see you. How are things at home now?"

Jenny hugged her back. "That is why I am here. I wanted to thank you and everyone here for what you have done for me. My dad and I have made amends, and we think we will have a new start now. I have learned my lesson, and I know I have to behave." She started to cry.

"Oh, now, that's all right. We're all on your side. We're glad things turned out for you in the end."

"I wanted to tell you I'm going to the ball with Robb, after all."

Helen turned sharply and looked surprised. "Really? How in the world? What do your parents have to say about that?"

With an impassioned plea, Jenny went on, "Things have worked out. That's why I'm here. To tell you, Robb came to me and made amends and apologized and said he was sorry he put me through everything. He guessed what happened to me when he was home during Thanksgiving week and said he was really sorry and wants to be friends. Ever since he said that, he has been really swell and treats me really nice." Jenny was pleading with her.

"Well, I am surely surprised. And I am glad too. No one can be more surprised than I am, dear." Helen wiped her hands with a towel.

Just then, RG and Mr. Hayward walked into the kitchen. "We had a great talk, Helen. Frank and I have a good understanding, and I think things are going well for them. I agree, Robb should take Jenny to the ball. Frank and Hazel will attend the ball with us."

Mr. Hayward shook hands with RG. "We'll be off now. Thank you, thank you very much for all you have done for us." He wiped his face with his handkerchief, turned, took Jenny by the hand, and walked out to the truck.

Chapter 14

Anticipation

Preparation for the ball was closing in on the committee. Four weeks away, and so much had to be done. Mark and Robin were on the committee. Bill Lambert and Harper Collins headed it up. The decoration theme was a secret as usual.

"I want Mark to get a subcommittee together and make sure all the tables and chairs are in good order. You have to go and find them in storage wherever they got to. Ask the maintenance people out at their shed, okay?" Bill spelled out at the meeting.

"Harper, you and Robin make sure all the tablecloths and stuff we need are found and washed up and ready. Get anyone you need to help you," Bill ordered. "I'll see my dad about electrical stuff we'll need for lighting. This year will be spectacular!" he said with pride.

"I'm making a list of all the details so we don't forget anything," Robin said with her pencil and pad in her secretarial attitude.

Harper started, "Now about the theme. Blue lighting to go with it. Lots of blue and white tablecloths. Blue lights. We can hang silver stars from the rafters. We need to get some people to help make the stars."

"We'll meet every day at lunchtime in the science lab. No one goes there and will not hear what we're up to. Don't let on to too many people what our theme is, or the cat will be out of the bag and spoil the whole surprise," Mark said with confidence.

Robin offered to see to arranging a small group from the Home Economics Department to arrange for people to provide all the different cakes, cookies, and what not, punch, soda, and water.

"See everyone tomorrow?" Bill said.

"Mum's the word!" Robin whispered.

That night, Mark was excited to share at the dinner table and yet kept quiet about all the details of the ball.

"I need to get into town this week, Dad. Bill Lambert and I have to meet with his dad about lighting for the gym for the Christmas ball. We want to have blue lighting all over. We'll need a spotlight that isn't too bright but will show up when we highlight a couple dancing," Mark explained.

"I'm going up to St. Helena Wednesday. Think you boys could get into town on your own and meet at the electrical shop to meet with Mr. Lambert after school? I'll drive you home," RG replied.

"That would be swell, Dad. May I call Bill on the phone tonight?" Mark asked politely.

"Make it quick and don't hang on too long. It cost too much money to call into St. Helena, ya know?" RG said strongly.

"Sure, Dad, no chitchat!" Mark assured him.

"Did you here that, Mari? Mark gets to use the phone!" Beth whispered in astonishment.

"I never get to use the phone. Never!" Mari whispered back.

After dinner, everyone left the table and went their own way.

"Hey, Bill?" Mark said a bit loudly as he held the phone up to his ear. "Oh, Mr. Lambert, sir. This is Mark Rogers. My dad is R. G. Rogers. Bill and I need to talk to you about some lighting for the Christmas ball. My dad said he would meet me in town on Wednesday so Bill and I could meet with you. And talk to you, Sir. Think you would be around on Wednesday after school so we could talk to you, sir?" Mark said awkwardly. "Bill is heading up the committee. Harper Collins, Robin Moore, and I are on the main committee. We have to keep everything a secret, the theme and all. The lighting will be the main thing with the theme this year. We hoped you would help us, sir," Mark stumbled.

"Hold on, kid. Who you say you are? I know your dad, RG. Sure, I can make it a point to be here for you and Bill on Wednesday after school. I'll be looking forward to seeing your dad again," Mr. Lambert said with gusto and a bit of a laugh in his tone of voice.

"Thanks, Mr. Lambert. Tell Bill I called. Goodbye," Mark said with a bit of haste in his voice. He hung up the phone and whispered to himself, "That wasn't so hard now, was it?"

"Say, Dad, Mr. Lambert said he would meet with us on Wednesday. Looking forward to seeing you again!" Mark shouted out in the air, not quite sure where his dad was. He quickly went up to his room, filled with excitement.

Mari, Beth, and Daniel were already up in the library waiting to see Mark before they went to bed. Mari and Beth were huddled in the big green chair with a book. Daniel was on the floor next to the shelves with a book.

"How'd it go?" Mari sang out slyly.

"He's a great guy, that Lambert. Knows our dad, ya know," Mark said as he stood in the middle of the room.

"I think he does business with Dad in town on some of the houses Dad's building in Napa," Daniel pipped up from behind his book without looking up.

"It's about time you kids went to bed. Daniel, did you make it up to Beth yet?" Mark said with authority.

"We just wanted to know what happened on the phone," Beth said as she scooted out of the big green chair. "I never got to talk on a phone. Can you hear? Does it sound far away?" she said sincerely.

"Oh yeah. Sounds pretty normal to me," Mark said as he was leaving the room going to his room.

They all picked up and left for their rooms.

Beth and Mari lay in their beds facing each other. "I can't wait for the ball. It will be so dreamy. I never got to go to a ball. Ever!" Beth said in a whisper.

"This is my first ball. I've only been to the dances after the games. Never to the Christmas ball. Every year I hear about it, and it always sounds dreamy," Mari whispered.

"Have to ask Mark who is selling the tickets so the guys get them on time," Beth said as she rolled over and pulled her blankets around her.

"I heard Mark say he met with the committee yesterday," Mari said as she rolled over. "Night."

Everyone was talking about who was going to the ball with whom. Thursday and Friday, tickets went on sale for the ball.

"Oh, look! The committee has set up a table in the lunch room for the tickets." Beth came up to Mari quickly. "Do you think the guys know they have to get the tickets? Or do we have to buy our own?" she said with a bit of excitement in her voice.

"Oh, I'm pretty sure they know they have to buy the tickets if they asked a girl. That's the deal. They have to get you some flowers and take you out for dinner or something before the dance. At least that is what I heard before," Mari said with confidence.

Bill and Harper were sitting behind the table. Parker and Pauline were standing in front talking. Beth stood and watched.

Bill pulled out his wallet and handed over a ten-dollar bill. Harper handed him two light-blue envelopes with silver glitter all over it. "Show this at the door when you arrive, Parker. You will find your date's dance card inside. Be sure you give it to Pauline before the dance so you can fill in your name for all her dances. You wouldn't want anyone else to cut in," Harper said with a bit of a song and a smile in her voice.

"Thanks, guys! We plan to be there early and have some pie. Someone better make some pie," Parker said seriously.

"Aren't we going out for dinner first?" Harper asked.

"Sure! But I'm savin' room for some of that pie I hear they always have every year," Parker said cheerily.

George and Babs were in line, and others started to line up.

"Did you hear that? Did you see the envelope? It was so beautiful. What is a dance card?" Beth was full of questions.

"Come on. I'll tell you while we eat." Mari pushed her toward the door.

"I can't eat with you guys. I have to go and see my gang out at the music building. See ya!" Beth ran off down the path toward the music building. Mari stood for a moment in amazement watching her.

Mari headed out the door to her locker. Steven was running from the new buildings.

"Mari? What's up? Going for lunch? Sorry I'm late. Had to hand in some homework." Steven caught up with her as she entered the gray stone building. "Already had lunch? Why are you going to your locker?" He held the door for her.

"No and no! It was too crowded in the lunch room, and I wanted to leave," she said a bit impatiently. "Bill and Harper are in there selling tickets to the Christmas ball, that's all."

"Oh, got 'um already. See? Would you like your dance card now or later?" he said as he swung around in front of her, walking backward. He whipped them out of his pocket, waving them in her face. "Got 'um, *See?* Got 'um! Got 'um! Now you have to go with me. Ha-ha!" He leaned in close to her face, looked around, and then kissed her.

"You! I just had a moment! Sorry! This whole thing is so exciting, and I have such expectations." Mari was upset now.

"What expectations? I'm not expecting anything but a good time dancing with the prettiest girl in this school and eating some good treats. Oh, and by the way, we're going to go out to dinner at the best place in town at seven o'clock. Maybe at Shaw's Mercantile," he said as he held her hand and laughed. "Mercantile! Ha-ha!" He tickled her on the cheek. "Olay with you?" He looked into her face now.

She had tears in her eyes now. "Oh, silly! I don't want you to go off with the guys and leave me standing. Like, like…well, you know. Some of the guys do that," she said quietly.

"I promise. We—that is, you and I—are going to have the time of our lives and a night to remember," Steven said strongly.

Zack and Joan came running in the door.

"Got our tickets! You guys want to go to dinner with us? We plan to take in a really nice dinner someplace special. How about it?" Zack waved his blue envelopes in the air.

"We were just talking about that. Have to figure out the best place and make reservations. Everyone will be going someplace, and

I don't want to be left out in the cold. Why don't you and I figure it out and surprise the girls?" Steven said enthusiastically.

"Good idea! What you say, Joan?" Zack asked her politely.

"You guys are in charge! Let us know, and we'll be ready for what every you have in store," Joan said with a giggle.

The bell rang. Mari pulled away from Steven and walked with Joan to class.

"Whatever you have in store?" Mari said sarcastically. "They better not have any really big surprises, that's all!"

"*Oh*, you are so prim and proper! We're not going to be doin' anything! You know what I mean!" Joan said to reassure her.

"Well, you know some people do stuff when there's a dance. I want to dance and have a great time, that's all," Mari said strongly. "If you go with Steven and me, we mean to just have a great time," Mari said again.

"Okay, I get it! I promise! Okay?" Joan said back.

They reached the English classroom and sat down. Everyone was buzzing about getting their blue envelopes.

Andrew Brothers waved his envelope at them and winked. "Me and Hydie Teasdale!"

Mr. Hanford shouted, "Now settle down, everyone! Get your assignments out and be ready for presentations. Mari, you be the first to go. Step up here and read what you have."

Mari sifted through the papers in her hand. "Can someone else start?" she said timidly.

"*No*! You start. Get your brave on and just do it," Mr. Hanford said strongly.

She got it together and walked up to the front of the classroom and presented her paper, then sat down nervously.

"Loved it! Loved it! Great job, Mari," Joan whispered. "Didn't know you were such a public speaker."

"4-H training, I guess." She brightened up.

Everyone else presented their work one by one. The bell rang.

"Glad that's over!" Mari said sarcastically. She gathered up her stuff and walked out and headed to the library for study hall. She looked for Steven and hoped he would get there in time to sit close by.

"Hey, Blondie!" Robb slid in across the table from her. "All ready to go to the ball? I heard you gave a great presentation in Mr. Hanford's class," he teased her.

"Are you ready? Did you get your tickets already?" Mari asked.

"I have to wait for my dad to give me the money. You know how he is about handing over any money," Robb said seriously. "I have to make it a good night for Jenny. I owe it to her," he said humbly.

"I'll say you do!" Mari said, a little snippy. "Steven, Zack, and Joan and I are going together. You going with anybody?"

"Hadn't thought that far. I guess it would be the safest thing to do. I have to ask George and see if he and Babs will hook up with us," he replied thoughtfully.

By then, Steven walked over to the table and sat next to Robb across the table from Mari. He winked at her. "You guys okay? I have to get some serious studying in. Have some work at home to get done when I get there." Steven opened his books and went to it.

They all settled in and worked hard during the hour. The bell rang, and everyone got up.

"Walk with me?" Steven walked close to Mari. "You and Robb okay?"

"Yeah, we're swell now. He and Jenny are good now, and her parents are letting him take her to the ball. I think that is really wonderful, don't you?" Mari said as they walked to their lockers.

"I didn't know how things were, that's all," Steven said, a little jealous.

"Hey? You don't have anything to worry about me and Robb. It's just you and me. I'm so happy I could just burst! You and me, Steven! That's what I want. Got it?" Mari looked at him seriously.

"You and me," Steve replied.

"Have to get to the bus. See you tomorrow." Mari rushed off.

Steven stood near the big redwood tree and watched her get on the bus. He waved and turned as he started to walk to town.

The bus ride was long as Mari sat thoughtfully. Jenny sat quietly today. Beth and Dante sat together, chatting. Alanso and Margot sat together as they did now. Mark and Robin sat together now. Everyone seemed comfortable with one another. No secrets about that.

"Daniel? Did you ever ask anyone to the ball yet?" Beth prodded as they walked up the road close by.

"Don't start something now, Beth!" Mari shouted at her.

"I'm just asking! Mama said he needed to choose someone pretty soon. After all, tickets are ready. He will have to get his and let some lucky girl know she *gets* to go with *him*!" Beth said snidely.

Daniel was walking backward now, yelling at the girls. "I think I'll ask Nadene Weston. She is the pretty little red-headed girl. Yes! I think Nadene Weston!" he said with confidence.

"Who says she doesn't have a date already?" Mari said, a bit snotty. "She's really nice, and everyone likes her," she added.

"Oh, she'll go with me, all right! I checked it out already. No one asked her. Everyone is too afraid to ask her. Her dad owns the men's clothier in town. Mark and I were already in there getting a new suit with Dad. You missed out! Ha-ha!" He turned around and started to run up the road.

"Well, we'll see how that goes!" Mari said to Beth as they walked to the bridge and up the hill.

"You think she would really go with *him*?" Beth said snidely.

"I bet she would. They run in the same gang at lunch," Mari said assuredly.

They walked briskly in the cold. "I still think Fred should come down and pick us up. I don't see why we have to walk in this weather. My good shoes get all dirty and worn," Mari said in disgust.

"I agree. We're special now. Since we're sisters now, we have to make a stand together and demand our right to be driven and not have to walk. Look at us, packing all this stuff like a pair of pack-horses!" Beth said with her head up in the air as if she was somebody.

"I'll watch as you make the demands. See how that goes! I think, since you're the favorite lately, you'll carry more weight than I will," Mari said, prodding her.

"What do you mean 'favorite lately'?" Beth said as she stopped in her tracks.

"It's true! Dad whooped Daniel for the way he spoke to *you*! He never does a thing about what Daniel does to me!" Mari said indignantly.

They walked on in silence. Dagwood was at the fork in the road. "Hey, Daggie! Hey, boy. You love me! Come on. You and me pal." Mari ran as she brushed his back and urged him to run along with her.

Beth watched with a tug in her heart. She whispered to herself, "You don't know what you have."

Chores were done as usual. Beth took care of her new little ducklings, Daniel his new bunnies. Mark came down from checking after the calves up at the pasture and hollered, "Better get down to the house. Sarah has dinner almost on the table by now! Better get washed up quick!"

Mari sauntered down the path to the veranda. "You think Daniel will get Nadene Weston to go to the ball with him?" Mari asked Mark as they washed up at the wash station on the veranda.

"Nadene? Got to be kidding! What guts! Have to see him pull that one off!" Mark said as he dried his arms and face. They walked into the dining room together.

"The kids are on their way. Saw them up at the barn when we came down." Mark sat down in his chair and looked over the table. "I could eat a whole chicken by myself." Mark sat back in his chair, looking at Mari.

"My chickens are too busy laying eggs and not for eating!" she chided back with her head in the air.

By then, everyone was at the table, and Sarah had everything set out. RG said some words to God and thanked Him for everything good.

"Dad, I'm going to take Nadene Weston to the Christmas ball. Can I have some money?" Daniel said as they passed the potatoes around.

"Nadene?" RG mused. "Nadene who?" He paused to think. "Oh yeah. The little red-headed girl at the clothiers. Have a chance she will say yes? Did you already ask her?" RG said, knowing already he hadn't.

"Nope. She will say yes when I show her the tickets," Daniel said, rather puffed up.

"I really think this stinks!" Mari said impatiently. "You have no manners! You think so much of yourself to think a girl, any girl, let alone Nadene, would just jump at the chance to go to the ball just because you wave a blue envelope in her face and assume she will take you up on a date at the last minute?" Mari was really upset and angry.

"Now, dear," Mama said quietly. "Let it be."

Beth jumped in quickly, "I was wondering if Fred would…ah, could…ah, well, ah…come down and pick us up after school so we wouldn't have to walk in the rain and ruin our shoes in the mud? We have so much stuff to carry…the mail and all our books and stuff." Beth raised her fork up and stuffed her mouth full of potatoes down. "Besides, then we could get home sooner and get our chores done sooner," she added with her mouth full.

"Well, then we could all have a ride," Daniel butted in.

Mama spoke up, "Well, dear, I think that could be arranged. I will ask Fred to take care of that for you."

"See? I told you," Mari leaned over and said quietly.

"That's enough, Mari," Mama said.

"Yeah, Mari!" Daniel sneered.

After dinner, everyone went their way. Mari went to the library and sat in the big green chair to read her history book.

"What's going on with you and Beth, Mari?" Mark commented as he came into the room and sat on the arm of the chair.

"Oh, she sure is the favorite around here, that's all," Mari said as she looked up from her book. "It will work out to my advantage anyway," she sniped.

"Don't let little things get under your skin, okay?" Mark patted her on the shoulder. "Night. See you in the morning."

"No homework?" Mari raised her voice as he walked away.

He waved. "I'm good!"

Mari got up and went in to get ready for bed. She got in bed before Beth came in.

"We'll have clean shoes now. Mari, Mari? Asleep?" Beth looked over. Mari pretended to be asleep already.

The Saturday before Thanksgiving, Mari was worried about Jenny getting a dress for the ball. She met RG in the living room, who was reading the paper after breakfast.

"Can you see if you could talk to Jenny's dad and see if she got a new dress for the ball?" Mari sat on a little stool at her fathers' feet.

"I don't think I can do that. Not for me to say. Don't worry about it. They won't let her down. Not now. You'll see!" He patted her on the head and went back to his paper.

"Can't help but worry." Mari got up and left the room.

Mark was just coming down the path from the barn. "Hey, Mari? Come and help me here!" He stopped and shouted before he got to the veranda.

"With what?" she said, a bit cranky as she came out of the house and went up the path to meet him.

"I have a bunch of things I need to do for the ball, and no one turned out to finish it," Mark said with irritation.

They went into the middle of the barn where the big room with the floor was. There were cardboard stars all over the place, blue paint, and quart jars of glitter on some sawhorse tables.

"See? I need to get all these done. Paint them this light blue and sprinkle glitter all over them. We have to tie string on them so we can hang them from the rafters in the gym." He was waving his arms and pointing at it all.

"Oh my God, at this late hour! No one would help? Why?" Mari said in amazement. "Do you think we need to call some of the kids to come up here and get this done? I'm going to call Robin and tell her to get her butt up here right now. She and her sister can get up here and help. You should make Daniel help. He's such a but-thead. He needs to get in and help too." Mari was wound up by now.

Off down to the house she ran. "Dad, Dad, Dad! I need to call Robin right now and tell her to get her butt up here now to help Mark do something up at the barn for the ball. We can't get this done all by ourselves," she demanded.

"Whoa! Wait just a minute, sprout!" He put his paper down. "Call who? What?"

Mari explained all over again and stood defiant in front of his chair.

"All right, go ahead. Make it quick. No chitchat." RG was amused at it by now.

Mari held the phone close to her ear. "Hi, Mrs. Moore. Is Robin there? Mark and I need her and Anne to get up here right now to help finish the decorations for the ball. No one will help. She is on the committee anyway, and she should do it," Mari said impatiently.

Mrs. Moore was startled and replied, "Now, Mari, calm down. Let me call Robin to the phone. Wait a minute."

Mari could hear Mrs. Moore calling Robin to the phone. "Robin! Robin! Come quickly. Mari is on the phone for you!"

Mari ran through the problem and encouraged Robin to get up to the ranch as soon as possible.

"I think we can get there right away, Mari. We don't have anything left to do around here. See you as soon as we can. Bye."

Robin turned and yelled at Anne, "Get out here, Anne. We have to get up to the Rogers's ranch right now to help with the decorations for the ball. No one else wanted to help." Robin rushed to change her clothes so she would look her best when she saw Mark.

The rest of the day, they all worked together painting and sprinkling glitter all over the stars. Tying string on the corners, they stacked them all in some boxes left over from going to the grocery store.

"These will be beautiful! Who is going to hang them and when?" Mari asked Mark.

"Well, that part we have in hand. Friday night and all day Saturday, the whole committee and some of the helpers will be there with some of the dads to get it all set up. The gym will be closed off to everyone. No basketball that weekend. We have some old parachutes from the air force. One of the dads got them from Brewster's Army Surplus Store," Mark explained.

They all were sitting on the floor, pleased with their work.

"I think we deserve something to drink and eat," Mari said as she got up. "Come on down to the house. I think if we sneak in the kitchen, we can find something."

"Come on, Robin," Mark said as he reached both his hands down to lift her up, holding her in his arms as if to dance.

"I think we should just have a big dance party right here in this big old barn," Robin said wishfully.

They all went down to the veranda and washed up at the wash station. They snuck into the kitchen. No one was there. Mari snooped around and found some cookies. Mark got some milk out. As they sat around, Mark said, "Wait here. I have an idea."

Mark went out and down the veranda over the little bridge past the clothesline to Fred's house. "Hey, Fred? Hey, Fred?" he called out at the door. "Would you drive the girls back down the hill? They have really worked hard and could use a lift," Mark pleaded.

Fred came out wiping his face with a towel. "Sure. Right now?" he inquired.

"Yeah, right now. We're all done, and they have to get home pretty soon," Mark said.

"I'll bring the car around in a minute. See you there." Fred turned and went back into the little house.

Mark ran back across the bridge and up the veranda. "Got a ride for you guys! You won't have to walk. I'll go with you." Mark was excited. They rode down in the big black car together.

Anne snuggled close to Robin. "This is really swell! Thanks a bunch, Mark." Annie giggled.

They drove up to the house, and Mark walked Robin to the door. "Come up next week? I can ask Fred to come and get you," he whispered, giving her a kiss on the cheek. "I'll call you, okay?"

"I would like that. See you then." Robin turned and went inside.

Mark skipped a bit as he got back to the car. He really looked forward to the week off.

CHAPTER 15

Mama's Secret Surprise

THE HOUSE WAS WARM AND COZY. With the chores all done, there seemed a new quiet in the air. The dogs were all sleeping in their boxes on the veranda. The ducks were nestled under the walnut trees up next to the corral fence. Nothing seemed to be in a hurry.

"Ready to hit the road, kids? Already Thanksgiving vacation and Christmas shopping is at hand!" RG announced, flipping his napkin on the table as he sat back in his chair. "Mark, you drive the truck today. I'll ride along. Fred will take the little ones, Mama, and Sarah in the big car. We'll all have a trip into town."

Mari and Beth looked at each other and smiled as if they had a secret.

Daniel piped up, "Why do I have to go with them?"

"Oh, all right! You come along with us men, boy!" RG said, reconsidering the arrangements.

"All aboard, ladies!" Fred opened the door to the car. "Jump in. Sarah and the missus will be right along." He noticed the silence and attitude of the girls. "Now let's not let Daniel spoil our fun," he spoke in a jovial tone.

Mama and Sarah joined them, and off they went down the road, following far enough behind the truck so as not to catch any of their dust. The weather was cold with signs of rain coming. The leaves on the grapevines had fallen off, making the vines look black with the dry branches draping down in a tangle. The walnut trees still had some leaves hanging on, drooping down yellow and brown with spots on them. The ground seemed a mess as Mari watched out the window. It was not the prettiest time of year. Soon they would be out in the vineyard pruning the vines, fingers and the end of their nose turning red from the cold. She wasn't looking forward to it.

"I think Dante and Alanso might be in town," Beth said softly, trying to get Mari's attention.

They got to the gate and waited for Daniel to open it. He stood at attention, saluting as they passed through. He ran quickly, jumping in the truck. Off they went down the Trail to town. They passed the Martin Ranch and saw Alanso and Dante in their truck pulling out. The boys followed all the way into town.

Everyone scattered their own way. Beth looked for Dante. Mari was independent as usual. Mark and Alanso joined up. RG and Daniel were off on their own.

Mrs. Rogers and Sarah went shopping down the street to see what Mrs. Alexander had in her new shop, The Elegant Closet. They came back with big packages in tow.

It was approaching five o'clock, and RG needed to get back to the ranch to milk Baby. "Better close it down here, boys. Baby won't wait." RG reached out and put his hand on Daniel's shoulder. "Good job, boy! Got a lot accomplished!"

The boys huddled close in the truck in the cold. "Wish we had a new truck, Dad," Mark said. "The new ones have a heater in them."

"Maybe later. Have to sell a couple of houses first. Maybe a new car for you too." He patted Mark on the leg.

"Really, Dad? I saw a yellow convertible in St. Helena at the car dealer's when the bus drove by. That would be rich," Mark said wishfully.

"Have to wait, son. Have to wait," RG said firmly.

The ride home was quiet. Everyone seemed to have their thoughts out the window, dreaming of good times past and present. The weather had turned to a cold rain with some hard wind starting to blow. The house was chilly when they got in. Everyone was willing to get the fire bolstered up in the living room and up in the library. The dogs were anxious to see everyone and wanted to be fed. RG drove the truck up to the pasture to milk Baby. The boys quickly made the rounds to check on the rabbits, chickens, and the ducks. They fed the dogs quickly and ran down to the warm kitchen.

Mari and Beth helped Sarah in the kitchen with a light supper for everyone. Mama was nowhere to be seen. "What happened to Mama?" Mari asked Sarah. "I didn't see where she got off to when we got home."

"Last I saw her, she was up in her room with her packages," Mark spoke up casually. "I know you and Mama were shopping at Mrs. Alexander's new shop. She must have bought something new."

"Well, I do know what she bought. Everyone will be surprised," Sarah said rather smugly.

"Do tell! What could she have found at The Elegant Closet?" Beth inquired slyly.

"Yes, do tell! Do tell!" Mari insisted. They both huddled close to Sarah, giggling quietly, and looked at each other, their eyes twinkling with expectation.

"It's not for me to tell," Sarah said smartly.

They all sat round the kitchen table with their light supper. RG came in with a pail of milk to put into the churns to make butter. "What's the big secret? I know something is going on. I see it in your faces."

He poured the milk into the two churns sitting on the counter. "Where's your mother? Did we leave her in town?" he said as he put the bucket in the sink. He was smiling now as he already knew what mama was up to.

Just then, Helen came in the room with two gift boxes wrapped in white tissue paper with curly string ribbon tied around them. There were little cards on each package. She stood in the middle of the kitchen as RG came over to give her a hug and a kiss and a pat on the butt.

"This is for you, Mari. Happy birthday early. I couldn't wait for weeks to give this to you." She put the boxes on the table in front of her.

Mari started to cry. "What did you go and do? You never!" She picked up one of the packages and shook it. "This is just a joke on me. There isn't anything in it, right?" She looked around at everyone.

"*No*! Go ahead open it. No joke," Mark said, encouraging her. "Mama and Sarah did the town."

Everyone was looking at her now. She tore into the paper and pulled the ribbon off. She lifted the lid on the box and set it aside on the table in front of Daniel.

"Oh my! *Oh my!*" She gasped. She pulled an off-white wool skirt with windowpane plaid of blue strips out of the box and held it up. "I love it! I love it!" She held it up to her cheek and felt the soft fabric. "Thank you! Thank you! I never had a straight skirt I didn't have to make myself."

"Now open the other one. Open the other one," Beth urged with excitement. "See what's in the other one."

"Oh, that's right. There is another one," Mari set the skirt on the box lid in front of Daniel. She ripped the white tissue paper and the curly ribbon off the package, tossing the paper on the floor next to her. She lifted the lid. "Oh my! Oh my! It's blue. It's blue!" She pulled a powder-blue sweater out of the box and held it up to her shoulders, laying it against her chest. She felt the soft angora knit with her hand. "This is so soft. I have never. Never! Oh, thank you, Mama. Thank you, Mama. This will be my best outfit ever." Mari got up from the table and went over to her mother and gave her a big hug and a kiss.

Helen held her in her arms for a moment. "Now everyone run along. We have had enough excitement for one day." Helen was containing her emotions as she let Mari go out of her arms.

"Now we will have to have Fred pick us up at the gate after school when it rains. Wouldn't want that outfit to get rained on," Beth chided.

"That's right, Dad," Daniel spoke up with authority.

"Happy birthday, Brat!" RG put his arm around her and gave her a hug and kissed her on her head.

"Happy birthday, Mari," Mark said, smiling. "You will really look swell in that."

Daniel pushed the wrapping paper and the box with the skirt in it over to Mari. "Happy birthday, Mari! Here's your stuff."

Everyone got up and went off to the living room. Fred followed, stoked the fire, and added more wood. Sarah cleaned up the kitchen with Helen. They laughed as they talked about the fun they had shopping that afternoon.

Mari and Beth had already gone up to the bedroom wing. Mari had gathered up the gift boxes, paper, and ribbons in her arms to take it up to her room. She dropped it on her bed and lifted the sweater up to herself again. She looked in the big mirror standing against the wall. "I never! I never!" She danced around in a circle.

Beth sat on her bed watching. "You will really look great in that. Why not put it on now and let's see?" She lay down on her side, holding her head up with one hand. "Come on. Come on. Let's see it. Put it on! I have to see you in it before I go to sleep," she begged.

"Oh, all right!" Mari gave in.

Mari quickly put the outfit on and stood in front of the mirror, turning from one side to the other. "I know Steven will just love this. I will wear my white buck saddle oxfords with this and buy some light-blue angora socks," Mari said with confidence.

The room had warmed up from the fire in the library, making it warm and cozy. They both went to bed that night with big comforters Helen had put on, pleased with the whole day and the trip to town.

CHAPTER 16

Preparation

MARI HAD NEVER EXPECTED ANYTHING for her birthday. Her mother always held it against her for having her birthday on the same day as her wedding anniversary, let alone being only six days before Christmas. As if that was Mari's fault! Often there was nothing special about it. RG and Helen would often go into town to a concert and out to dinner for their anniversary. Mari would get pajamas on her bed, and that would be all that would be said. She would be fifteen now. She did feel older and more like a woman. She had Steven on her mind a lot now. Beth was also a great companion to her. The next day, Mari needed to talk with her mother.

"Mama? What is ever going to happen with Beth?" Mari asked quietly Monday morning while she stood in her mother's room, watching her making the bed. "When is Beth's birthday? Do we know? What are we going to get her for Christmas? I got such a nice outfit. Shouldn't she get one too?" Mari was rather insistent.

Helen straightened up and looked at her in amazement. "I did get something for her also. I was going to wait until Christmas. Do I have to give it to her early to make you happy?"

"Oh, I'm sorry! I don't mean to have you think I want that. I was just worried because I haven't had enough time to shop for presents. We all have been so busy with the ball and all. We barely have had time to make many Christmas cookies, that's all," Mari flashed back at her. "I'm really happy with my new outfit. I just want you to know. I just don't want Beth to feel bad if I'm the only one who got a new outfit."

"I don't want you to worry about it, dear. You take care of yourself, and I will take care of Beth." Helen was a bit sharp.

Mari left the room and went to her room and sat on her bed. She was upset now. Tears swelled up in her eyes. She didn't understand her mother's reaction to her questions. She got up and went to the library and sat down and played the piano for a while.

All she could think of while she played was how her mother reacted about Beth. No one had said any more about her situation for weeks now. What was going to happen in the months to come? Would they have to give Beth up? Who would take her? Where would she go? Where were her parents? Why was she at that place with those men? Mari played fiercely on the piano as she pondered all this.

"Oh, Lord, please don't let Beth be taken away from me. That is my Christmas wish," Mari spoke out loud.

"Who are you talking to, Mari?" a voice came from the hall. She stopped playing and looked. "Oh, Fred! It's you! I was talking to God," Mari said softly as Fred entered the room with an arm full of wood.

"God is listening. He hears all our prayers. He will always answer—yes, no, or wait," Fred reassured her. "All things work together for good for those who love the Lord," Fred said as he stoked the fire. "Even if we don't see His answer as a good thing."

Mari listened quietly. "No one tells me anything. I just wanted to know what was going to happen with Beth. I don't even know when her birthday is. I don't even have a present for her for Christmas. We never get to go into town and shop for stuff and surprise anyone for Christmas or a birthday. Mama got to go shopping and surprise me. I always have to put my egg money in the bank. I want to spend some of it and buy some presents for the boys and everyone." Mari was crying by now. "What would be wrong with that?" she wailed.

"Now, sweetheart, I think we can talk this over with RG and see what he thinks. Sarah and I could take you kids into town to shop today. No one would know what you bought, and we could tuck it under the tree secretly at night when no one would be looking."

Fred was comforting her now. "I bet he would give you permission to spend some of your egg money if you wanted to." He patted her on the shoulder.

Mari stood up and hugged him around the waist. "Oh, that would be wonderful, Fred. It's almost too late. The Ball is next week, and we will only have three weekends to make cookies and get presents. Would you really talk to my dad?" She held on tight.

"Sure, kid. Now let go and get on with you." Fred pulled her away and quickly left the room.

Fred walked up to the barn with purpose and intent. "Say, RG, what would you think if Sarah and I took the Brat and the others into town to do some more Christmas shopping?" Fred stood resolute near the tractor where RG was working.

"Well, I hadn't given it any thought quite frankly." RG stood up and took his handkerchief out of his pocket and wiped his forehead and face. He took the beanie off his head and wiped his hair back, setting the little hat back on his head. "I guess we should go down the canyon and cut a tree. Time just slipped by me," he said regretfully.

"You and I can go now with the boys and be back in an hour if we hurry," Fred insisted. "I'll round them up right away. You get the tools, and I'll be right back." Fred turned and left the barn before RG had a chance to respond.

He and the boys returned in a matter of minutes. They all lit out, up the road to the pasture, through the gate to the milking barn. They cut across the pasture past the barn to the fence ducking over the wire and down the canyon. It didn't take long, and they found a little tree about six feet tall. The trees were growing too close together and needed to be thinned anyway.

"I get to put the star on the top!" Daniel said as they pulled the tree up the hill.

"Oh, all right. This year you can do it," RG reassured him. They got the tree up to the barn within an hour. They got a five-gallon bucket and filled it with sand and some dirt. "This will be solid enough to hold the tree. Daniel, you get some water when we get it in the house. Once we plant this tree in the bucket, you can give it a drink. You will have to keep it watered every day," RG instructed.

"I think the boxes of ornaments are over in the corner in the tack room, Mark. You go and get them. Meet you down at the house in the living room," Fred ordered.

Mark moved swiftly and cut through the barn to the tack room. Daniel followed. "I can carry one box too."

"Sure, take this one. I will get this big one." Mark picked up a large box and headed for the house, Daniel in tow.

RG and Fred were already setting the furniture around to make room for the tree. "How about here?" Fred pointed to the corner farthest from the fireplace.

"Great!" RG pushed the tree into the corner. "There's an outlet here for the lights. Did anyone find the lights?" RG pulled one of the boxes close and opened it. "What the hell!" He flinched. "Got a dead mouse in here!" Everyone laughed. He picked it up and took it outside and tossed it out over the veranda. When he got back in the room, the boys had pulled the lights out of the box.

"I'll plug them in and see if they still work, Dad," Daniel said enthusiastically.

Mark was carefully getting the boxes of ornaments out. "I remember these. I got this one for my tenth birthday. Here, Daniel, this one is yours. This one is Mari's."

RG and Fred stood back and watched as the boys carefully hung the lights and the ornaments on the tree.

"Everyone will be surprised to see this, Dad. Us men do a great job of it, don't we?" Daniel said with pride, standing back and admiring their work.

"Sure, son. Thanks to Fred, we got this thing put up before too late." RG shook Fred's hand. "Clean up all these boxes now and wipe up any needles or dust you made. Sarah will skin us alive if she sees we made a mess of her floor."

RG left the room and went up to the barn to finish his work.

Fred and the boys finished up and went off to the corral to work on the woodpile.

Helen and Sarah knew something was going on in the living room and stayed away until they all left. They snuck in and took a peek. "Look what those rascals have gone and done. I can't believe they did such a great job of it!" Helen said to Sarah. "We can put the finishing touch on it. I have a white sheet we can put under the tree and cover up that old bucket. We will have to get Beth an ornament of her own. You and I will have to make another trip into town soon."

Sarah smiled and agreed. "I will enjoy that. I find it a nice break to get off the hill and into civilization." She wiped her hands on the towel she was holding and returned to the kitchen.

Just then, Mari and Beth came charging into the kitchen. "I think we have to find Fred. Anyone know where he is?" Beth said, out of breath.

Mari added, "We need Fred to help us do something."

"Well, we just saw all the men go up to the barn. You should look there. The boys went to the corral and were working on wood," Sarah replied.

"What are you girls up to anyway? Don't get into anything with the boys. You know you always get into it with them," Helen said sharply.

"Oh, we aren't going to have anything to do with them. We have something else we have to do," Mari said with attitude.

The girls rushed out of the kitchen looking for Fred. They reached the barn out of breath. "Fred! Fred?" Beth shouted. "Oh! There you are! Mari and I have something to ask you."

RG came around from behind the tractor. "What are you up to, Brat? Fred and I are working. Can this wait?"

Beth stood straight. "Actually, *no*! We have something important we need to do, and Fred is the only one who can help us."

"Well, in that case, go to it, Fred. These girls have something *important* that only you can attend to." Smiling, he went back to the tractor.

Fred and the girls went outside the barn and stood talking. "We need to kill some ducks and sell some eggs so we can go shopping. Did you ask Dad if you could take us to town? We could earn some money to spend on Christmas presents if you would help us." Beth was squirming around, begging him.

"I did ask, and he agreed that Sarah and your mother would need to make a trip into town and do some more shopping. I haven't asked when they wanted to go. I think we can arrange a trip this afternoon. Would that be soon enough? We will have to get right on the ducks this morning. Are you prepared to do that, kid?" Fred asked, putting his hand on Beth's shoulder.

"Oh yes. I can do it anytime you're ready. I know what to do now. Mari can help too. Can't you, Mari?" She grabbed Mari's arm. "You will help me this time, won't you? Fred will show you what we did last time," Beth pleaded with her.

"Of course, I will. That stuff doesn't bother me any. I'll go and get the big pots and whatever we need. I think we should keep our pots and stuff out in the tack room so when we need it, we won't have to bother anyone in the house."

They split up and went off to get everything ready. They met in back of the little barn where Fred had set things up before.

Daniel and Mark saw them going back there while they were chopping wood. "What are they up to, Mark?" Daniel said quietly.

"I think they're going to kill some ducks again. They seem to be trying to do it secretly," Mark replied.

"I bet they plan to go into town. We better get in on it," Daniel said slyly. "I think I'll call Charlie King in St. Helena and find out if he needs some more rabbits. Will you help me? I'll share the profits with you, fifty-fifty, okay?" Daniel had a nicer tone than usual.

"You don't have to do that. If you need to get some Christmas money, you keep it. I have plenty from the sale of my calves," Mark said as he stood with the Canadian wood splitter in his hand.

They piled up the wood they had chopped and covered it with a tarp. As they walked over to the house, Mark said quietly, "You go on and use the phone and don't tell anyone. Just be really quiet. I'll cover for you." They snuck into the living room and made the phone call to the butcher in town. Daniel was very professional about it, planning to bring the rabbits in that afternoon.

"I bet Fred will drive us in. Or I could ask Dad if I could drive the truck myself now that I have my license," Mark said confidently. The boys snuck out and up to the barn to work on selecting some rabbits to take to the butcher. They worked quietly on the other side of the barn out of sight from their dad.

By eleven, they had finished and had put the rabbit meat in the big cooler in the tack room. They had kept an eye out for the girls the whole time.

"Those kids have to be done by now, ya think?" Daniel whispered to Mark. "Let's sneak over and see how they are doing," Daniel said slyly.

"If we go through the corral and around the little horse barn, we can see 'um," Mark whispered. They washed their hands and arms quickly and took off out the back door of the tack room and snuck across the corral.

"Look at all those feathers! Gee-whiz, what a mess!" Daniel let out loudly.

"I thought we were going to sneak a peek, stupid! Now they will see us," Mark argued.

"I see you guys! We know you are there. Stay away! We're busy, and it's none of your bee's wax what we're doing!" Beth shouted.

"Oh, let them in. What harm will it be at this point?" Mari said reluctantly. "You guys know now what we're up to." Mari wiped feathers off her shirt. She wiped her face with the back of her hand and pushed her hair back. "This's a really stinking job. We couldn't have done it without Fred. We know you guys were killing rabbits. That's *nothing* compared to this!" She turned to Beth. "We're the best! Thanks, Fred!" She stood firmly.

Mark picked up a towel and handed it to her. "You look great, kid. I have to hand it to you! You too, Beth! What a great job you girls have done. Dad will be proud of you both. Thanks, Fred. We're so lucky to have you here. You and Sarah have been a lifesaver for us all. What can Daniel and I do now to help you?" Mark had crawled through the fence by now, Daniel following.

"What a stinking job! You guys can sure make a mess of it out here!" Daniel remarked, trying to sound nice. "I'll clean up the fire for you and bury the awful for you." He went over to the side of the barn and got a shovel and started at it. "What a stinking job! Rabbit shit, duck shit, feathers, yuck!" he shouted as he worked.

At that, everyone laughed as the girls wrapped the ducks up in butcher paper and put them in a box.

"I'll take them up to the tack-room cooler for you, Beth," Mark said as he picked up the box.

Fred was putting out the fire and tossed the water out in the field. "Better all take a bath after this before you get in to town, or no one will have anything to do with you," Fred said in amusement.

"I'm first!" Beth announced.

"I'm next!" added Mari.

"I think we can wash up in the open shower in the tack room, Daniel," Mark said firmly. "I know it isn't hot water, but maybe a little warm. If we rush, we won't get cold. Then we can use the bathroom when the girls are all done, okay?"

"Gee, what a man has to go through for the woman around here!" Daniel said as he finished cleaning up the area.

Fred was already walking away. "You kids have done a great job of it. I think I can leave you on your own now. Just let me know when you're all ready to go. That way, we can have time to collect your money, eat a late lunch at the Sweet Shop, do your shopping, *and* maybe see some special friends. Ya think?" he spoke in a cheerfully assuring way.

"I think I'll call Steven and see if he can meet us at the Sweet Shop for lunch. Mark will pay," Mari said wishfully.

"You really like him a lot, don't you?" Mark said kindly. "He seems like a really nice kid and does well in school."

"He is pretty smart. But better than that, he is really thoughtful and kind. Besides that, he loves the Lord and likes to go to church like I do," Mari said as they ducked through the fence to get up to the barn. "Why don't you want to go to church with me?" she inquired softly.

"Maybe someday. Maybe someday," Mark spoke a bit seriously.

They got to the tack room and put the ducks in the cooler with the rabbits. "You guys really killed a lot of rabbits this time. The butcher must really figure he has a market for them," she said, surprised.

Daniel and Beth followed behind. Once in the tack room, Daniel started to undress and get the water going in the open shower.

"What do you think you are doing, stupid? There are girls here!" Mark shouted at him.

Daniel paused and shouted, "Get the hell out of here, you guys. Can't you see men have business to take care of here?"

The girls giggled and ran out of the room, screaming, "What a jerk face! Men? Not a man yet!" Beth hollered as they ran through the rabbet hutches. The girls cleaned up in a hurry. They knew the boys still needed to use the bathroom.

Mark had asked to drive the truck into town on a secret mission. RG already knew what was going on as Fred had apprised him earlier.

"I loaded up the bounty, kids. Squeeze in, and we can make it into town in time to get to the Oakville Store and the butcher in St. Helena," Mark said with authority.

"I am *not* sitting with those girls! I'll sit in the back. I brought a big blanket. I can sit on the bench with the boxes," Daniel said strongly.

"Whatever, be that way! We don't have cooties!" Beth said indignantly.

Off they went down the road. Fred and RG stood in front of the barn near the watering trough under the big oak tree, watching as the truck went around the dam.

"Can't believe they are all grown up and on their own, doing business in town and going into partnership with each other." RG wiped his face with his handkerchief.

By the time the kids got to the butcher's and into town, it was late. They stopped by Steven's to pick him up. They all piled into the Sweet Shop and had lunch.

"I don't think we really have time to do any shopping," Mark said as he paid the bill. "Let's plan to come in tomorrow and make a day of it. Mama and Sarah will want to get into town. I heard Sarah tell Fred she needed to get off the hill."

Steven agreed. "I would like to see you again anyway, Mari. That would be a great excuse," he said as he kissed her on the cheek.

They all got up very pleased with the day and the money they had made. Daniel started to brag again. "I bet I made more money than you did!"

"Oh, shut up, stupid! Don't spoil everything. We all worked together and had a great time for a change," Beth spoke up sharply.

"That's right, Beth. This is how I like things. This is exactly what we hear when Pastor Bob talks on Sunday mornings. I just want it like this all the time, Daniel," Mari spoke softly and firmly.

"Aww, come on now, you guys. Cut it out! Thanks for lunch. Nice seeing you all. See you tomorrow?" He punched Daniel on the shoulder. "I'm going to run up to Shaw's Mercantile and have a look around."

They all walked out together. Mark put his hand on the back of Daniel's neck. "Better change your attitude, kid! Or Dad will have your hide again."

Beth and Mari jumped in the truck and pulled the blanket over their legs. Daniel pulled his blanket around and sat on the bench in the back of the truck. Off they went. The ride was quiet as the truck rumbled along up the Trail.

They reached home just in time to take care of their chores and sit down for dinner. After dinner, everyone went into the living room to listen to the radio and read, as usual. Fred and Sarah joined them before they did the dishes and cleaned up from dinner.

"Oh my! Look at this!" Beth exclaimed. "Who did this? When?" She stood in the middle of the room and looked at the Christmas tree.

Daniel was reaching down to plug in the lights. "Now that's a tree! Us men went and got it this morning while you all were duffing around doing nothin'," he said, bragging. "Dad, can I put the star on the top now?" he pleaded.

"Sure, son, now is as good a time as any," RG replied cheerfully.

"Sarah and I will have to finish putting the rest of the ornaments on tomorrow," mama added quietly. "We have some other things that still have to go on the tree," she said, looking at Sarah.

"Yes, that's right. We will finish it up tomorrow," Sarah jumped right in brightly.

"I think everyone has had a day of excitement now, so off to bed with you all. Take some time in the library and relax for a bit.

Sleep tight!" mama ordered. The kids left the room and went up to the library.

"RG, we need to get things arranged for our anniversary and Mari's birthday. What had you planned for us, dear?" Mama set her magazine down on her lap.

"Well, I really had no plans at all this year, what with all the trouble with the Brat and the kid. This year, those kids have really taken on a bunch of plans of their own. I never saw such a flurry of activity. I can't even keep up with the jobs in town, let alone all that is going on around here. Haven't Sarah and Fred been a big help to you and set you free of some of your duties?" he spoke seriously.

"I guess I don't mind this year if we don't go to a concert or out to dinner this week. But sometime when things settle down, just you and I should take a moment for ourselves," she gently persuaded him.

RG rose from his chair and went over to her, took her by her hand, pulled her up, and put his arms around her. "I love you so. You make all the difference around here. We will make plans, I promise." He kissed her and held her tight.

They left the room together and went up to the library. "You kids, off to bed with you. Now!" RG said sternly. "See you all early tomorrow." He and mama went to their room and shut the door.

Mari, Beth, Mark, and Daniel all went to their rooms.

Beth quietly got into her PJs and cuddled under her big comforter. "Your dad is so sweet to your mother. That's the kind of man I want in my life," she said wishfully.

"Oh, he's always like that. Gruff and still a big old bear who hugs you when you need it," Mari said as she rolled over and snuggled her pillow, pulling her comforter up close to her face. "See you in the morning."

Chapter 17

Keeping Secrets

Mari woke with a start. "Beth? Where are you? What time is it anyway?" She looked over to see Beth still asleep. It was still quite dark. She could hear the dogs barking and chasing around out in the vineyard. "Oh, bad dream, I guess," she whispered to herself and cuddled back to her pillow. She lay awake for a while, making plans. She mused to herself, *I think Daniel needs a new shirt and a sweater to go over it. Mark just bought one. He doesn't need a sweater. Maybe a book. Maybe some tickets to the movie theater. Beth. Well, Beth needs everything. No problem there. I think she needs an ornament for the Christmas tree. I think I'll get some fabric and make aprons for Mama and Sarah. Fred. What for Fred?*

She dozed off into a deep sleep.

"Mari, Mari! Wake up! Time to get up!" Beth was shaking her.

"What? What's the matter?" Mari rolled over, barely awake. "Already? I just got to sleep," she said with her eyes barely open.

"The boys are already out and down in the kitchen. We have to hurry, or they will leave without us," Beth whispered anxiously.

Mari rolled over. "They won't leave without us. This whole thing is our idea, and Mama and Sarah will wait for us. Did anyone build a fire in the library for us to get dressed in front of?" she said with more of an urgent tone.

"No, just get up! Hurry up! I want to eat before we go," Beth urged.

"Well, go without me and eat!" Mari swung out of bed and stretched. "Boy! It's cold!" She moaned. She moved quickly now, searching for the best outfit to wear. She wanted to look her best for Steven. She grabbed a pair of cords, a blouse with little pink roses on it, and a pink sweater to go over it. She slipped on some warm socks and into her Western boots before hopping across the hall to the bathroom to wash her face quickly and run down to the kitchen.

"Well, 'bout time you showed up. We're waiting for you," Sarah said as she handed Mari a cup of hot chocolate and a sweet roll.

"Had a bad dream last night and was awake for a while. The dogs were barking at something for some time." She blew on her cup and sipped at it. "Hot!" She reached over for the milk jug and added some cold milk to her cup.

Everyone was out of the kitchen by now waiting for Mari and Sarah. Fred laid on the horn. The boys had already loaded more boxes for the butchers and were gone.

"Did Beth go with them?" Mari asked, surprised. "I guess she needed to get to the Oakville store early with more ducks." Mari gulped the last of her chocolate.

"Yes. Now come on. Your mother is waiting out in the car, and the motor is running," Sarah urged.

"At least there's a heater in the car, and it will be warm," Mari said, grabbing her jacket off the rack by the door as she and Sarah rushed out to the car.

Mari squeezed in, reaching for the blanket mama had on her lap. "Nice and warm in here."

Sarah piled in the front seat with Fred. "RG will meet up with us at the Sweet Shop for lunch for sure. I don't think we will see much of the rest of them while they are about their shopping," Fred said with a high spirit.

"Sarah and I have some things we need to find. I think you are on your own, Mari. You may find Beth around town someplace while you're shopping," Mrs. Rogers instructed Mari.

"That's perfectly all right with me. I have some things planned after I sell my eggs. Fred, you did load my eggs, didn't you?" Mari said anxiously.

"Yes, Brat, all loaded in the trunk. They are in your best basket with a nice towel Sarah put around them. They look very festive." Fred smiled at Sarah.

Fred dropped Mari and her eggs at the farm market and drove off. She quickly sold her eggs and walked briskly to the main street. She counted her money as she walked. "I think I'll have to go to the bank and get some money out of my account," she said out loud as she walked. She knew the bank was open. She slipped into the bank and walked up to the teller. "I need to withdraw some funds from my account today," she spoke with confidence. "I am Mareen Jean Rogers. I will need fifty dollars please."

The teller replied, "Just a moment." The teller walked over to a man at a desk and whispered.

The man came over to the window. "You're R. G. Rogers's daughter. So nice to see you, Miss Rogers. Taking money out today? Not depositing?" he inquired.

"Yes, sir, I am going to shop for Christmas presents today. They will be a surprise. I saved my egg money every week, and now I need fifty dollars please," she spoke up bravely.

"Are you sure your father will approve of this withdrawal?" the man said in a tone.

"It's my money, sir. It's my account, and no one said I had to have permission from anyone to get my money when I needed it." She was a bit indignant at this point.

"Well, all right, Miss Rogers. You may have your money. Have a merry Christmas." The man returned to his desk. The teller counted out fifty dollars—five, ten, twenty, thirty, forty, and fifty. "That is a lot of money for a young lady to spend for Christmas," the teller said with an attitude.

Mari turned quickly without a reply and put her money in her pocket. She was boiling mad. She muttered to herself, "I will take all my money out of this bank and go to the other one and see if they treat me better!" She stood on the corner and looked around, pulling her thoughts together.

She walked briskly down the block to the other bank and walked in resolutely to speak to someone about opening an account.

She found a lady sitting at a desk near the front of the bank. "Hello, my name is Mareen Jean Rogers, and my father is R. G. Rogers. I was wondering about opening an account here at your bank. What would I have to do to open an account here? Do I need my parents' permission? I have my own money that I earn every week and would like to deposit my earnings here. I would also like to be able to withdraw a sum of money once in a while for things I need to buy for my business or for whatever I need," she explained thoughtfully.

"Well, young lady, we can arrange this for you anytime you would like. All you need to do is bring in your money and fill out this card with all your information that we need. You are free to add or take your money anytime you want to without any permission from anyone. We know your father and mother very well. What is your business? Mari, isn't it?

Mari sat down in the chair in front of the desk, relieved. "I sell my eggs at the farm market every week. The other bank almost wouldn't let me have any of my money just now," she said, almost ready to cry. "When I get done with my shopping for Christmas presents, I am going over there and get all my money and bring it over here and deposit it today," she spoke sternly. "I'm going to tell my father about this too! Thank you very much. I will be back later." Mari smiled and got up and hurried out the door.

She first stopped at Goddard's Hardware and Home Décor, and she went right to the fishing department. She stood and looked at all the stuff and studied it all, thinking to herself, *Daniel has a bunch of stuff. I bet he could use this tackle box.*

Just then, a man walked up. "May I be of some assistance, young lady? Oh, it's you, Mari. Nice to see you. All on your own today?"

She replied quickly, "Yes. We're all in town today shopping secretly for Christmas presents. I thought Daniel could use a nice tackle box like this one." She lifted the one she was looking at and showed it to him.

"Let me show you this one over here. I think this would take care of all his needs when he goes fishing at the lake. I know he doesn't have a good box yet," the man said knowingly.

"You know my brother?" Mari said in surprise.

"Yes, I'm Mark Blanchard's dad. Mark and the boys have fished together in the summer. Guess you didn't know about that," he said with a smile.

"How much is it?" Mari asked as she examined it.

"Well, let's see. The price is on this sticker. It's eight dollars. I can have it wrapped up if you like. That way, no one will see what you bought and keep your secret," Mr. Blanchard said as he took the box from Mari. "Would you like this one?"

"Yes, that will be perfect. He would never guess what I got him." They walked up to the counter.

"Are you going to put this on your father's account today?" Mr. Blanchard asked as he started to write on a pad.

"Oh no. I have cash of my own. I earned it by myself," Mari said proudly.

"That will be just fine. I can have it all wrapped up, and you can pick it up later when you are ready to go back to the ranch," he said as he took her money and rang it up on the cash register. "Here is your change and receipt. See you this afternoon."

"Thanks a lot, Mr. Blanchard. Nice seeing you."

Mari walked over to the other side of the store where the house-wares and gifts were on display. She moseyed around looking at all the beautiful dishes and kitchen gadgets, wondering what she could find next.

She spied a beautiful vase of blue glass. She picked it up and looked at the price. Three dollars. That would fit in her budget. Sarah would like a vase for the cabin. Well, maybe not. She wasn't even there but to sleep at night. Mari wandered around a bit and decided to pursue the idea of making aprons for her mother and Sarah.

She walked down the street looking in the windows as she passed the stores. All of a sudden, she saw the reflection of Beth across the street going into a bookstore. Mari quickly jaywalked across the street and darted into Shaw's Mercantile. She went to the back of the store to look at the fabric.

"May I help you today, young lady?" came a soft voice from behind her. "Well, hello, Mari. Nice to see you. Shopping to make something new?"

"Yes, I want to make a couple of aprons. I have this idea they should be made of all sorts of different pieces of material. The skirt of it should be one piece, the top another, the straps another, the pockets something else. It should be bright and durable," she explained.

"Well, this will take some time and be a fun challenge," the lady said.

Mari pulled several bolts of material off the shelf and laid them on the cutting table. She talked it all out with the lady and planned each color and pattern carefully.

"I think we have it! Now let's figure how much fabric of each you will actually need in order to cut all the pieces out," the lady said as she took out a large piece of paper. She sketched out a picture of an apron: the bib, shirt, straps, ties, and pockets. "This piece will go here, so we will only need a half a yard for it. This one will go here, so we will need a yard for that."

On and on she went with Mari figuring out the design and how much she needed, cutting each piece from the bolts she had chosen. Mari went over to the counter where the thread was and plucked out four different colors of thread she would need.

"I think we did it. This will be a great work of art, Mari. Who are the lucky ladies getting these lovely aprons?" The lady folded each piece up as she talked.

Mari watched carefully and replied, "My mom and Sarah."

"Who is Sarah? A special aunt?" she asked.

"Oh, she is our cook and housekeeper up at the ranch. She and her husband, Fred Bender, have been with us now since this fall," Mari explained. "I don't know what my mom would do without her now. My mom has more time for 4-H and helping my dad with business things," Mari said proudly.

"I think your mother and Sarah were in here earlier shopping for Christmas too. Everyone in town today shopping?" she said as she rang up the bill. "That will be ten dollars please."

Mari handed her a ten-dollar bill. "Egg money from my 4-H project. Earned it myself!" she said with pride. "Thanks for all your help. I couldn't have done it without you. Thanks awfully!" She picked up her package and walked around the store.

She wandered around the shop for a bit. Then it occurred to her: Sarah needed a new cardigan sweater. There were some really nice ones folded up on a table.

"May I help you, Mari?" a voice came from behind her. "I saw your mother a little while ago. What are you looking for today?"

"Did you see the lady she was with? I want to buy a cardigan sweater for her for Christmas. It will be a surprise," Mari said as she laid her package down on top of the sweaters. She picked up a pretty beige one with all sorts of flowers embroidered in bright colors on the front and back. It had green edges all around the sleeves and down the front by the buttons and buttonholes. "I like this one. Do you have one that would fit her?" Mari asked as she held it up to herself. "She would need a larger size than I am," she mused out loud. "She isn't fat or anything. Well, you saw her. What do you think?" Mari smiled.

"This one will be the right size, I am sure. Would you like it?" the lady said, accommodating her.

"How much is it? I have a budget today. I have to stay in my budget," Mari said with assurance.

The lady replied, "These sweaters are on sale today for fifteen dollars. Would that be in your budget?"

Mari thoughtfully added up what she had already spent in her mind: eight, ten, and fifteen. That would really stretch her. "May I put this on R. G. Rogers's account please?" she said with confidence.

"Of course, I have been instructed by your mother if you or Beth came in, you would be allowed to use the account. Would you like me to wrap this up for you as a gift?" The lady picked up a sweater that would be the right size and showed it to Mari. "This one will be perfect for your secret present." They walked to the counter where the lady made out the bill and handed the receipt to Mari. "You can pick this up later after you have lunch. It will be waiting here with the rest of your mother's packages."

Mari peered over the counter and saw several wrapped packages. "Those all for my mother?" she said in surprise.

"Why, yes. She and your cook were having a wonderful time shopping. We haven't seen your mother in several months. It was really nice to see her. She looked wonderful," the lady said cheerfully.

"Thanks a lot. See you later." Mari picked up her little package of fabric, put it under her arm, and walked around the store. She looked out the window to see if anyone was around. "No one in sight!" she whispered to herself. Out the door she ducked and down the street to Weston's Men's Store.

She darted in and quickly looked around to see if anyone was there.

"Hello, Mari!" came a voice from the back of the store. "See you and the family are shopping today. What can we do for you?"

"I need to get something special for my dad," she said quietly. You know my dad and what size he wears. I think he needs a nice plaid shirt. Maybe a Pendleton. What do you have?"

"They are over here, dear. This is his size. What you see in this area are all in his size. What color would you like for him?" Mr. Weston pulled two different shirts down and laid them on the table.

"You will have to put this on my dad's account for me today. But I want you to label it 'Mari's account' under my dad's name because I will be paying for this myself. I have egg money in the bank, and I just have to get it out to pay you later. Will that be all right with you, Mr. Weston?" Mari asked as she held up a green shirt.

"I can certainly arrange that for you, young lady. Your word is good enough for me. I will make your own personal account and not put it under R. G. Rogers's name at all." Mr. Weston took the shirt from Mari. "I can gift wrap this for you, if you like. You may pick it up after lunch. I understand you are all meeting at the Sweet Shop for lunch," he said wisely. "Nadene is meeting Daniel there too. I gather there will be a gang of you, from what I heard when Daniel and your dad were here earlier."

"That is true. I guess that's not a secret. My brother has a big mouth. He and Nadene will sure look cute at the Christmas ball. Those little kids will have a good time that night." Mari smiled shyly. "We all will. Thanks a bunch for wrapping the shirt. It will look really beautiful under the tree. Not like the white tissue paper and curly ribbon we usually have." She waved goodbye as she stuffed her package of fabric under her arm.

"I think you better get over to the Sweet Shop pretty soon, dear. It's about time you met your dad and the gang there," Mr. Weston shouted as she opened the door to leave. He hoped she had heard him as she moved quickly out the door.

Mari counted the money up in her head, muttering to herself, "I overspent my wad for sure. I know I have to get Fred something and Mark. Beth too." She got to the Sweet Shop and opened the door. What a great smell. The shop was warm and comfortable. Right away she saw her dad, Fred, mama, and Sarah at the big round table in the back. Daniel and Nadene were at a table by themselves. She walked back, package under her arm. "Have you seen Beth? I saw her earlier and lost track of her," Mari said in excitement. Just then, Beth and Mark walked in the door.

Mari scooted in the booth behind Daniel, saving a seat for Steven. Beth and Mark slid in across the table. Not a package in sight! Mari strained to look around to see if Daniel had anything with him. Nothing!

Steven suddenly slipped in next to her and gave her a kiss on the cheek. "Hello. Happy Thanksgiving, merry Christmas, happy birthday!" he whispered in her ear.

She kissed him back on the cheek. "Hello. Glad you could come. Shopping is really hard work. Have you done any Christmas shopping?" she inquired.

"Matter of fact, I already have all my shopping done weeks ago," he bragged. "I had more time than you since I live here in town. I could take my time and think about it after school and weekends. Hi, Mark. Hey, Beth. How are you guys doing today?" Steven said politely.

Beth had her menu up, looking to see what she wanted to order. "We're all hard at work shopping for surprises for everyone up at the ranch. Like Mari said, it's hard work shopping." She laid her menu down and looked at Mark. "How are you doing? Got everything you wanted?"

Mark looked at Steven. "Want to go look at a car with me after lunch? They have a really great convertible down at the Ford dealer. She's a beauty!"

"Sure. We should all go. That would be a blast!" Steven nudged Mari. "Want to?"

"Actually, I really don't have the time. I have too much to do yet. As I said, shopping is hard work. I think I would rather feed the chickens and gather eggs." She giggled.

Beth agreed. "I still have lots to do too. You guys go on and have a look at the car. We'll look forward to having the first ride in it when you buy it." She snickered.

"May I take your orders today, guys? Oh, hi, Mark. Not with Robin today?" the waitress said smartly.

"Just take our order, Diane. It's a family day today, not a date. These are my sisters Beth and Mari, who is here with Steven Haskell. My dad, RG, will be picking up the tab for our table and my brother behind us with Nadene Weston. I'll have the double hamburger with lettuce, tomato, pickles, no onion, with a side of french fries. May I have a Pepsi with no ice please?" Mark said confidently.

Steven said, "I'll have the same, thanks. But I would like a chocolate shake, please."

Mari said, "Same here. Only with a vanilla shake, please."

Beth hemmed and hawed. "Can't make up my mind. Oh, what do I want?"

Mark pushed her arm. "She'll have a pine float and a hamburger like ours with a strawberry milkshake. Please. Thank you, Diane."

"Cumin' right up with that pine float!" She smiled and winked at him.

Mari giggled. She pushed Steven under the table. "Pine float, what a special treat, Mark," Mari said sarcastically.

"Every girl deserves a pine float when they can't make up their mind what they want," Mark said, smiling.

"Good thing you know what you want, Mari. I like a girl who knows her own mind," Steven teased. They all laughed.

Mark started to push the buttons on the jukebox to pick out some music. They sat around and sang along with the music while they waited for their food.

Daniel and Nadene were having a great time being big kids all alone at their own table. Everyone chowed down their hamburgers and fries. The milkshakes were really thick and creamy. Beth laughed at her glass of water with a toothpick in it.

"Well, this has been really wonderful. I really have a lot to get done before we leave town. There isn't much time left. I don't want to be left behind like I almost was this morning." Mari pushed Steven to let her out of the booth. "You and Mark go and look at that car. Maybe you could come up to the ranch after Thanksgiving." She kissed him again on the cheek and put her package under her arm. Walking over to see her parents, she thanked them and explained she still had a lot to accomplish. "What time will we meet, and where is the car parked?" she asked quickly.

They decided when and where they would meet at the end of the day. Off she hurried out the door, intent on finishing her difficult job of shopping.

"I'll never complain again about doing my chores at home," she spoke out loud as she walked down the street,

"Daniel, Mama, Sarah, and Dad—what for Mark and Beth?"

She walked by the sporting goods store. But changing her mind, she dodged in the door quickly, looking around, trying to get an idea. Walking to the back of the store, she saw a letter jacket hanging on a special rack. "How does a person get one of these jackets?" she asked the man behind the counter. "Do you know my brother Mark Rogers? He has never had one of these jackets. He has all sorts of stuff he could put on a jacket like this. This is really beautiful! I have seen the other fellas at school wearing these and never knew where they got them." She felt the sleeve as she talked. It had leather and fabric with the school colors of red and white.

The man behind the counter came around. "I do know your brother. I often wondered why he never got his jacket yet," he said inquisitively.

"My parents don't get into town much because they really work hard and are always busy. I don't think they even thought about this at all. My brother would never think to ask for such a thing either. Is this a lot of money?" Mari asked shyly.

"Yes, I would say so. We would have to sew all his awards on it and pin his medals in all the right places for you. That would take a day or so," the man explained it all to her.

"I'll be right back, mister. I have to go and find my dad and mother real fast." Mari turned and ran up the street to the Sweet Shop. She dashed in the door, looking to see if they were still there. "Dad, Dad, you have to come with me right now. I have something to show you. It's really important!" Mari said with great excitement. "Here, Mama, hold my package. Don't squeeze it, you might break it. Come on, Dad, hurry up."

"What on earth can be this important and be in such a hurry, Brat?" he said as he got up from the table, kissing mama on the cheek. "Guess I have to go. See you later."

Mari tugged his arm and pulled him along. "Come with me, Daddy, to the sports store. I have to have something really important," she said anxiously.

She opened the door and pulled him to the back of the store. "See this! Mark has to have one. We have to go home and get all his patches and medals and bring them back into town, and they'll put them on a jacket like this one just for him with his name on it. Look, Daddy! We have to get one for Mark for Christmas. All the other guys at school have them but Mark. He never ever has asked for one," she pleaded.

"Take it easy, Brat. What the hell is this thing anyway?" he held the sleeve and felt the leather.

The man behind the counter came around and explained, "This is a letter jacket for the athletes at the high school. I wondered why Mark hadn't had one yet since he is such a star player," the man said with pride.

"Well, I am sorry, I didn't have a clue. I missed the boat on this one." RG took his handkerchief out of his pocket and wiped his face and nose. "If we came in tomorrow, would you have this thing ready for Christmas for us?" RG was humbled.

"No, sir, Mr. Rogers, we're closed for Thanksgiving. I'd be proud to have it ready for the boy next week. A great surprise for him, sir. Thanks to the little one here." He patted her on the arm. "I know just what size your boy takes, sir. I know the right size."

RG was actually overcome with emotion and turned away for a moment. "Better get out of here, Brat, before the boys see us in here. Guess I better hightail it home right now and get those medals and bring them back to town today."

Mari replied quickly, "Oh, they went down to the Ford dealer to see the car Mark likes."

"Oh, that's not a good thing!" RG said as they walked out of the store and looked down the street.

"Why is that, Daddy?" Mari asked as she took his hand.

"I bought the damn thing, and they put a Sold sign on it. I was going to pick it up later in a few weeks with Fred. He'll be really upset to see someone already bought it." RG walked at a brisk pace. Mari was holding on to keep up.

"That's okay, Daddy. Think about it. He'll really have the best surprise ever! More than anybody. How neat is that?" She was getting out of breath keeping up with him. They got to the Sweet Shop just as mama and the others were coming out.

"What the hell time is it, Helen? Pick up all your packages and gather up all the kids. We have to get home. You can come back after Thanksgiving and finish up. Mari and I have something important to get done right away."

They all ran around town and picked up their packages, met Fred at the car, and piled in. RG hightailed it down to the Ford dealer in the truck. He got there seeing Mark and Steven looking at the yellow convertible, his heart in his chest. "Don't you say a word, Daniel. Keep your mouth shut and behave yourself for once in your life!" RG said sternly.

They got out of the truck and walked over to the car. Steven and Mark were standing in front of the car looking at it. "Look, Dad.

Someone already bought the car. I guess I missed out again." Mark was devastated.

"We'll find another one, son. One that will be just as great. You wait and see. The right one will come along." RG patted him on the back.

Steven patted him on the back. "He's right, Mark. The right one will come along, and you'll love it more than this."

They all piled in the truck and took Steven home. The trip home was quiet. Daniel kept the secret, for once in his life doing the right thing, keeping his mouth shut.

"Where does Mark keep all this stuff you are talking about, Mari?" RG asked her when he got in the house.

"I can sneak in his room now while he is feeding the calves," Mari answered quietly.

Mari snuck into Mark's room and found all the patches and medals in a drawer. She got down to the kitchen where her dad was. He had explained to mama, he and Mari had to run back into town before the store closed to take care of something important.

They raced into town and got in just in time before closing. "When will it be ready for us, sir?" RG asked in an urgent manner.

"Oh, I'll have it ready by Tuesday, RG," the man said proudly. "An honor to have this ready for your son. We're all very proud of him."

RG wiped his face with his handkerchief and smiled. "I'll be in town on Tuesday. I'll make a special trip from Napa just for this. Thank you very much."

Mari and her dad walked out together. Her dad held her hand as they walked to the truck. The ride was not long this time. They had a nice time talking about all sorts of things that had been going on.

"I like your friend Steven, Brat. Nice kid! Behave yourself, and things will be all right," he said caringly.

CHAPTER 18

Daniel

THEY ALL CAME RUSHING IN the dining room one at a time. "Must have been really busy at something important," mama said as Daniel was the last to sit down.

"I just got some more new bunnies. I'm gunna be rich. Wait and see?"

"Did you see the ducks sitting on their eggs, and now one has started to hatch some babies? I bet I can sell more and get some money to put in the bank!" Beth joined in, just as excited.

Fred and Sarah came in with the serving dishes and set them on the table. "Beth gave us one of her ducks for Thanksgiving, and Daniel gave a rabbit. We have a great feast for us all."

The table was loaded with wonderful dishes, cranberries Mari had prepared, carrots with sweet brown-sugar sauce, green beans with little onions and bacon, mashed potatoes, and gravy. Everything was beautiful.

"Oh, give thanks to you, O Lord, for this bounty. You are great and good, amen!" RG prayed. He stood and cut the meat up on the platter.

"I think everyone is planning a great day tomorrow. We will be ready at eight o'clock in the morning. You will be proud, RG," Fred said proudly as he helped serve and then sat down at the end of the table with Sarah.

"Proud? Well, well! Wonder what has been going on all week?" RG prodded everyone. "Heard there has been some conspiring to go into town again and do some more Christmas shopping. Anyone need to make any phone calls to special people and make arrangements about anything?" He laughed out loud as he passed the potatoes to Mark.

"I don't need to call anyone, but I think Mari might need to call someone, Dad," Mark said as he served himself up a huge portion of potatoes.

"Yes, Daddy. May I call Steven and see if he could have lunch with us at the Sweet Shop again?" Mari asked, passing the green beans to Daniel. "We have business to take care of first, and then we're all going to go shopping. I think Fred alerted you ahead of time, so don't kid us. We know you know." She smiled as she looked over at him.

"Yes, your mother and Sarah said they have some things to do in town also. So we'll all make it another big day. Daniel, you stick with me."

Friday morning, Fred took the ladies in the big car, and the boys rode in the truck with RG. He inquired about what the boys had planned. "What didn't you get done, Daniel? I thought you sold a lot of rabbits. Why are there more rabbits in the box in the back today? I see we have to stop in Oakville at the market with Beth's ducks too. I assume Mari took her eggs in again also. You are all becoming big business here in the valley. Hope you do well," he said in a jovial manner.

"We're making a killing, Dad. Everyone really likes the rabbit for the holidays, and the duck meat is really going over big too. We didn't know it would be such a great hit," Daniel expounded with enthusiasm.

"We need to plan a nice deal for Mari's birthday, Dad. I know Mama already gave her that nice outfit, but everything has been all about the Christmas ball. Mari's birthday is in the middle of the week, and we want to make it special just that day. We seem to pass it by every year because it's your wedding anniversary," Mark explained.

"Your mother and I are not going to do anything special yet. This is our seventeenth, in case you didn't figure it out. I think we will make a trip into the city, just your mother and me, after Christmas. You kids can stay home alone with Fred and Sarah," explained RG.

"We can do her chores that day, Dad," Daniel said brightly. "She would really like that. And we could ask some friends to come up on Saturday after her birthday. Maybe we could let her buy some lunch at the student store and not have to take a bag lunch," Daniel offered thoughtfully.

"Yeah, I know she really hates a sandwich. She really never eats it anyway," Mark added. "She always gives it away to Robb. She's done that for years."

"Really? Don't tell your mother. That would hurt her feelings." RG laughed out loud.

They pulled in to the butcher in Oakville and took Beth's ducks in. Adalfo was waiting. "Wonderful, wonderful! I have many orders for these ducks. We're the only one in the valley who has them, and they are top prime. Wonderful! Wonderful! Where is my little partner today?"

"She and the woman are in St. Helena Christmas shopping sir," Daniel spoke up proudly. "We helped her this week. We were a team!" Daniel was holding the box on the counter. "How much you giving her this week since they are top prime ducks and the only ones in the valley?" he said bravely.

"You sure do have your partner's interest at heart, young man. She should know you are going to make a bargain with me today," Adalfo said as he took his pencil out from behind his ear. "Now let me see, how many did she make ready for me? I have many orders, you know." He counted the ducks. "I can sell every one of these today. Since she has gone into partnership, I must pay more today?" he said wisely.

"Yes, sir. She requires one dollar more for each duck," Daniel insisted.

"You drive a hard bargain, son. I pay you one dollar more for the pretty little girl since she work so hard for me. Just for holidays! Make this very special, no? Yes!" He laughed as he reached in the drawer and got out a handful of cash. "Now, you be sure you give her all her money. A good partner does that." He counted out the money and put it in Daniels hand.

"Thank you very much, sir. It has been a pleasure doing business with you. We're here to serve you and provide only the best poultry in the Napa Valley." He reached out to shake Adalfo's hand.

Mark, RG, and Daniel left the store and piled into the truck. "I am proud of you, son. You did a really great job for Beth back there." RG patted him on the knee.

"You sure drive home a hard bargain, Daniel, that's for sure. Beth will really be surprised," Mark remarked.

They found their way to Charlie King where they dropped off the rabbits. "Think you will get any extra for them this week, Daniel?" Mark teased. "You don't have a pretty little partner to make it sweeter this time." He poked him on the shoulder.

"Doesn't matter anyway. She needs the money more than I do. I'm the richest one around here anyway," Daniel boasted again.

"I wonder about that, kid. You have never known what I sell my calves for," Mark touted.

"Now, that is quite enough, boys. No one needs to know your financial business. That is good business!" RG instructed firmly. "You never know what your sister has. She is really quite the businesswoman and going to go places. You just watch out for her," he almost boasted.

They drove around and parked the truck in town, looking for the girls.

Mari had business at the bank to finish. She was still hopping mad about the incident concerning her account. She walked in resolutely and insisted on closing her account. It took a while, but she did it. She quickly went down to the other bank and went right to the same person she had seen before. "I was too busy to get back to you the other day as there were several things that came up unexpectedly that kept me from finishing up my business with you. I know my father gave you a call and assured you that he supported whatever I needed to do with my money. I have fifteen thousand dollars here. It's a huge amount of money. I need to put most of this in an interest-bearing account. That's what my dad said to do. Then I need to open a checking account so I can have access to a smaller portion to run my business for this next year. He said you would show me what you have to offer," Mari said in a very businesslike manner.

"Yes, we're prepared for you today, Mari. We welcome your business. And yes, this is a huge amount of money for a girl your age," the lady remarked.

"Well, you see, I have never spent any of the gift money I have received all my life. But now I am going to be fifteen, and I have my chicken business. I need to run it by myself and not depend on my father to buy the feed and anything else it takes for the chickens," Mari explained. "I started the chickens when I was ten years old. Now it's really big, and I have to work hard every day to keep them up," she said proudly.

The lady gave her the paperwork and explained all about a special interest-bearing account her father had instructed her to open. She gave Mari her own checkbook and showed her how to keep records in the little register.

"I would like to keep one thousand dollars in the checking account for the year, only allowing that much this year and see if that will take care of everything I'll need for gifts and the chickens," Mari explained. "Thank you very much for all your help." She reached out her hand in appreciation.

Mari left the bank filled with high expectations and confidence. She now had to take care of her bills at the Mercantile and Weston's Men's Store. She walked in the Mercantile first, looking for the lady who had assisted her. "I would like to pay my account today, please," she said with confidence.

The lady behind the counter said, "You are Mari Rogers, correct?"

"Yes, there should be an account for the sweater I purchased the other day." Mari had her new checkbook in hand.

"Yes, that will be fifteen dollars please," the lady said as she laid the bill out on the counter.

Mari wrote out her first check carefully and signed it, *Mareen Jean Rogers*. She entered it in the register, then handed the check out to the lady proudly.

She quickly went on to Weston's, paid her bill, and proceeded to the Sweet Shop. Entering, she looked to see if Steven had arrived yet.

Beth was standing at the soda fountain counter about to take a seat. Mari came up next to her. There was a tall man with dark-black hair standing next to her. "Hello, girls," the man spoke softly. They both giggled.

Beth looked at Mari. "That's Clark Gable!" she whispered. Neither one could say a word.

"Having a soda?" he said, winking at them.

Mari giggled. "We're meeting our boyfriends and Christmas shopping."

He took his ice-cream soda and sat down on a stool. Just then, Steven came in the door. Mari quickly went over to him. "That's Clark Gable! He just spoke to us," she whispered. They all went over to a booth and sat down.

After they had their lunch, Mari asked Steven if he would like to go shopping with her. She still had lots to get.

"Sure. I think we will make a great team. I might even give you some good ideas." Steven nudged her warmly.

Beth went off on her own, needing to finish up. Helen had given her some money of her own to add to her duck money. The girls had arranged to meet up with Sarah and Helen by four-thirty so they could get home in time for dinner and chores.

Once they were home, Mark and the girls rushed up to see the new bunnies and check on the ducks. When they reached the ducks, they all stood quietly and watched. Mark leaned down and moved the big duck aside to see the eggs. There were a bunch of them cracked, and little yellow ducks were climbing out of them. "Whoa! Look at that! There must be a dozen of 'um!" he said, almost shouting. "Did you see, Beth? Did you look and see how many you got?"

By now Daniel was there too. "We're going to be rich, Beth! Rich! We hit the motherload!" He patted her on the shoulder. "Yahoo!"

Mari said in disgust, "Is that all you can think of is money?"

"Shut up, witch! You are just jealous because your stupid chickens don't do anything but lay stupid eggs." He danced around joyfully.

213

"Don't act like that, Daniel," Beth said. "You are all so lucky. Be nice to each other. You can be such a turd head. Don't spoil this for me. This is such a precious moment to see these duckies. I can build a pen and play with them."

"No, you're not!" Daniel shouted. "You will kill them just like the last ones!"

Beth started to cry. "You are so rotten! I hate you!" She turned and ran down to the house.

RG had seen it all. "Daniel! Get over here!"

Daniel walked over to the barn where his dad was standing in the door where the tractors were parked. He got there, and RG took him inside and rolled the big door shut. Mari and Mark stood in amazement. They stood quietly and listened. Nothing. Quiet. Then—yowling, hollering, crying! Daniel ran out holding his pants and ran down to the house to his room.

Mark said with a smile, "Guess he got what's comin'!" They snickered as they went down to the house and washed up on the veranda.

By then, everyone had rallied in the dining room for dinner and were seated. RG thanked God and slapped his napkin onto his lap. "What have we today, Sarah?" he blustered. "Where's Daniel? Helen, get that boy down here now!"

Helen rose and left the room. Soon Daniel and Helen returned.

"What do you have to say for yourself, boy?" RG said sternly.

"Sorry!" Daniel sat down and was silent the rest of the meal.

When everyone was excused, he left and went back to his room.

The girls went out to the veranda and sat in the big chairs under the bedroom windows facing the barn and the big oak tree. All they could talk about was the ball: who was going with whom, what they would be wearing, where everyone would go to eat, and who was bringing food to the ball. They knew about the stars and the blue theme, but didn't know what the theme song would be. Mark and his pals were in charge of preparing the gym and the decorations, but they had been left out of the details of how they would get it all done. As nosy girls, they just felt they needed to know.

Saturday everyone was secretly taking care of the gifts they had bought, lots of giggling and sneaking around.

Sunday morning, Mari and Beth were up early. "Think we could talk Mark into driving us to church today?" Beth whispered to Mari as they were dressing.

"If we could even just get a ride down the hill to catch the bus, that would be something," Mari replied quietly.

"I'm going to ask!" Beth insisted. She quickly went and knocked on Mark's door. "Mark! Mark! Please would you take us down the hill to the bus so we can go to church today?" Beth pleaded quietly.

"Sure, just a minute." Mark was up and ready in a flash.

"Well, aren't you the persuasive one? I could never get that to happen in a million years," Mari said, smiling. "What's happening to this family anyway?" she mused.

That afternoon, they walked up the hill together, quietly enjoying the green grass the rains had brought.

"It's not so bad walking up the hill when I have you, Beth," Mari said softly.

CHAPTER 19

The Christmas Ball

BACK IN SCHOOL THE WEEK after Thanksgiving, Friday couldn't come soon enough. Concentrating on classes was difficult. Everyone on the committee was on time Friday at six-thirty as planned to get started decorating the gym.

By ten o'clock, they got as much done as possible. "See everyone tomorrow at nine o'clock," Bill said with confidence as he stood in the middle of the gym floor, looking at an incomplete mess.

Bill's dad walked over and patted him on the back. "It will come together tomorrow. Don't worry, son. Maybe we should all be here at eight," he said with encouragement.

"Ya. Better be here by eight," Bill shouted with confidence. "See ya eight!" Everyone left feeling exhilarated and satisfied with all they had done.

Saturday, everyone arrived at eight, excited to get things finished. There were ten kids and five dads all set with their jobs to do. Bill stood at the top of the stairs to the gym. "I think we need to set out a plan on what still needs to be done," he said with confidence. "Mark has the stars in a big box, and that will take a lot of time to hang them all. The parachutes need to be hung first so no one will get in the way while the stars are being hung."

Harper stood next to him. "Us girls will make sure all the tables are set up with the flowers. We have to go into town and get them from the flower shop. Come on, girls, let's take my dad's truck."

Harper, Babs, and Robin all piled into the truck and took off into town for the flowers. The dads unloaded some ladders and took them into the gym.

By three o'clock, they had it all put together. The lighting was set up; the parachutes were draped all around the edge of the gym and up on the stage. The disk-jockey station was also set up on the stage. The stars were hung all over the rafters. Tables were set for the food and drinks just below the stage area. They had set up white picket fences with small white tables and chairs behind, surrounding an area to make the dance floor. Each table had a blue tablecloth. The girls had taken soup cans and covered them with blue paper and silver glitter to make vases for the white daisies and carnations tipped with blue. At the entrance, they made an arch with a picket fence on each side where everyone had to pass through to enter the ball.

Bill's dad stood in the middle of the dance floor. "I still have to get the sound system equipment set up properly. That will take me a little more time."

"I can help with that." George rushed over. "I know some about that sort of equipment." The two went up to the stage together.

"Who knew George knew anything about sound equipment?" Mark said in surprise.

"Who knew any of us knew how to do any of this stuff?" Harper replied with a smile. "I think we're just terrific! Don't you, Robin?" They stood and admired their handiwork.

"I think we forgot to put up the words of our theme. They'll be hanging in the stage over the disk-jockey station," Harper said in surprise. "Where are the letters? Who has them?"

Babs pulled out a rolled-up banner. "I have it! I thought I would save it till last. No one will know the theme and give it away before the ball. When everyone is done and only Bill and George's dad are here, we will hang it up on the stage." She waved the roll in the air high above her head.

"You are so clever. Has anyone opened their invitations yet? Has anyone seen their dance cards yet?" Robin asked.

"I don't think so," Harper spoke up. "I thought the guys weren't to give them out to us until we got to dinner or when we got to the ball."

"That's sure clever! Who would think any of them could keep that much of a secret?" Robin chirped.

"Maybe they're just too dumb to open the tickets and don't know any better," Babs replied. They all laughed.

Bill and the committee walked around inspecting everything to see that all was done and in order.

"I don't think we have forgotten anything. When will the rest of you girls be bringing in the food?" Mark asked Harper.

"Everyone's bringing their stuff to the home economics room at six o'clock. Then they'll bring it over once the ball is opened and people are arriving. That way, no one will see the theme before it starts," Harper explained.

"Great plan!" Bill's dad said, surprised.

"Who did we get to be the disk jockey?" Babs asked.

"Carl from the KVON radio station," Mark announced. "My dad knows him, and Carl said he would do it for nothing if he could broadcast the music on the radio. He would tell about the ball while we were dancing."

"What a crazy idea!" Robin squealed.

"Let's get out of here. We have to get home and relax before we go out tonight," Bill said cheerfully. "I have a lot to do. I have to pick up the prettiest girl in school in a few hours."

They all piled out of the gym, waving goodbye to one another as they got in their trucks and took off in a hurry.

Mari rushed around once she got home. She got her dress and shoes and laid them out on her bed. Beth was doing the same as they chatted cheerfully.

"Come into my room, girls," Mrs. Rogers spoke softly as she entered the room. "I have something for each of you."

Beth and Mari turned in surprise to see her. "What?" Mari said in surprise.

"I have something for each of you. I think you are both ready for this." Mrs. Rogers led them to her room across the hall. There were two flat boxes the size of a page of paper lying on her bed.

"I bought this for you when we were in the City. I think you are ready to wear nylons to this party." She was opening the boxes and held a pair of silk nylons up delicately.

"Oh my!" Mari put her hands to her face. "How do you put them on?" she asked timidly.

"Here, I'll show you." Mrs. Rogers sat on the chair next to her bed and pulled out a pair, taking both her hands and sticking her thumbs into the top of one of the nylons, gently gathering the fabric all the way down to the toe. She placed her foot in and gently pulled the nylon up her leg quickly. "That does it! Attach it to your garter like this." She pulled her skirt up a bit so the girls could see the garter.

Mari snickered a little. "Mama, I never saw you do that before."

"I'm sure. Since you aren't in my room when I get dressed, dear," she said with amusement.

Beth laughed quietly. "I've seen women do that. When I...well, you know...before."

Mari turned and looked at her. "Really?" She started to laugh. "Oh, you woman of the world. I am so stupid. I know nothing. I'm this stupid little country bumpkin!"

They all started to laugh. Mrs. Rogers handed them their little boxes with the nylons. "Try not to snag them when you put them on. I only bought two pairs each. Just in case."

Mari and Beth grabbed their boxes and quickly went out of the room to their bedroom.

"I'm in the bath first, Beth," Mari announced.

"Okay, I'll wait." Beth sat on the bed and looked at her box of nylons. She stood up and picked up her dress, held it up against herself, and twirled around, dancing.

Daniel peeked into the room. "Stupid girls." He ran down the hall laughing.

"You get out of here, you fart-face jerk!" Beth shouted. "I can't believe I said that!" She looked in the mirror. Beth left the room and went down the veranda to the path next to the clothesline and over the bridge to the cabin.

"Sarah? Sarah? Are you home? Can you help me?" Beth knocked on the door loudly.

"Yes, dear? What do you need?" Sarah said kindly.

"I need someone to help us—that is, help Mari and me fix our hair. Mama doesn't know how to as much as you do," Beth pleaded.

"Why, sure, dear. I will be right there. Get your bath, and I will fix you right up." Sarah gave her a pat on the shoulder.

Beth turned and ran quickly back to the house. By then, Mari was out of the bathroom and in their bedroom. Beth hurried as she explained that Sarah would do their hair.

Everyone was rushing to get cleaned up and dressed. Mark and Daniel were rushing to have their turn in the bath and getting ready. They had gone down to the living room to wait for the girls.

Mari and Beth were ready and came down together. Mari stepped into the middle of the room in front of her father.

"Oh dear! Who do we have here, Mama?" RG said in amazement. The look on his face was astonishment. He took his handkerchief and wiped his nose and eyes.

Mari stood with tears in her eyes. "It's me, Daddy! The Brat!"

Her hair was so blonde, flowing in soft waves down and off to the side of her face in a page boy, her blue silk dress flowing gently to the floor. With both her hands to her side, she stood very still. Her dad rose and took both her hands.

"You look great, Brat! Have a good time." He turned and saw Beth. "Now who is this?" he said in amazement.

Beth stood next to Mari in her green dress. Her strawberry-blonde hair was pulled back on both sides to the back of her head with a green ribbon tying it as it flowed down her back. She stood in great expectation.

"You girls have done it up big. Be sure of it. You have a good time and behave yourselves now, you hear?" RG said, holding back emotion.

Just then, two cars came up the drive and pulled up under the big oak tree by the barn.

"That's them!" Daniel jumped up and ran out to the veranda up the path to the barn. "They're down at the house waiting for you. Come on down. My dad is waiting to kill you."

The two guys piled out of their cars and walked down with Daniel. "Why would he want to kill us?" Dante said to Steven as they walked down the path.

"Don't worry. Daniel is just a jerk. RG is a really nice guy," Steven assured Dante. They entered the living room where everyone was gathered. Steven followed Daniel with Dante timidly behind.

"Whoa! Mari! I have something for you." Steven had a box behind his back. He brought it out and handed it to her.

"Open it for her, jerk!" Daniel said.

"Don't be rude, Daniel," Beth said quietly.

Dante stood back looking around at the great room, holding his box, waiting for his opportunity to meet RG.

"Well, come on in, son!" RG said sternly to Dante.

The room was buzzing with all the interaction—Dante meeting RG, Steven, and Mari fumbling with the box and the flowers he brought.

Dante stepped up and held his hand out. "Pleased to meet you, sir. I'm taking Beth to the ball. I'll have her home when you say," he said politely.

"Don't worry, son. I will be at the ball watching with all the rest of the parents. We always chaperone all the big dances in town," RG said as he shook Dante's hand.

Dante turned and stood in front of Beth. "Wow! You look like an angel. Are you my date?" Dante opened the box and handed her a corsage she could put on her wrist. "I heard you liked green, so I got you this orchid." He helped her slip it on her wrist.

"I love it. Thank you. Thank you. I never...I never...it is so beautiful." Beth was blushing.

Mari and Steven were on the other side of the room. Steven had figured out how to get the box open. Getting the wrist corsage out, he put it on Mari's wrist. "A little bird told me you didn't want an orchid, so I got you these little roses with a blue ribbon to go with your dress." Steven looked over at Mark and winked.

Mark anxiously said, "I think I better head on down the hill to get Robin, Dad. See you in town." He patted Steven on the back as he walked out.

"Get going, Daniel. Your mother and I are ready. Get our boxes out of the kitchen, and we'll meet you in front of the veranda by the kitchen."

"Okay. See you, Dad. See ya, Mama!" Daniel hurried out.

"We should be going too, sir," Steven said respectfully as he took Mari's hand to leave the room.

"Thank you, sir. See you in town then." Dante grabbed Beth's hand and pulled her to go. "I have reservations in Yountville. Alanso and Margot are with us."

"Bye, Daddy. Bye, Mama," the girls said together.

Steven and Mari sat in the car a moment before Steven started the engine. "I have something else for you tonight, Mari." Steven pulled out a long slender box with a blue ribbon on it.

"What on earth? What is it?" she said, surprised, opening the box gently. "Oh my! You shouldn't have." She lifted a strand of pearls out of the box.

Steven took them from her. "Let me put them on for you." He gently put them on her neck and attached the clasp. "You like 'um? Happy birthday," he whispered.

"Oh yes! That's the nicest thing ever. I love you, Steven. Thank you, thank you." She turned and kissed him.

"We better be off, hang on. We better fly off this mountain, or we'll be the last ones to meet up with Bill and Harper. I said we would meet them in Napa at six-thirty."

"Why are we going all the way to Napa?" Mari said as they went on down the road.

"We're going to Rufino's Italian restaurant!" Steven said as he navigated the curves and culverts in the dirt road.

They met in Napa in plenty of time and went into the restaurant together. They had a great meal, laughing and enjoying the new experience of being out on the town at a fancy place on their own. They drove up the valley admiring the cool evening air. The weather was perfect. Once in the parking lot at the school, Steven and Bill met at the door with the girls. They weren't the first to arrive but not late. Some of the other committee members were already there.

Mr. Brown was standing at the archway wearing a black suit and a top hat. "Will this do, sir?" he said with jest when Steven and Bill walked in.

"You pulled this off perfectly! Thanks for doing this for us." Bill shook his hand.

"Let's practice it once, okay?" Mr. Brown stood on the inside of the arch and shouted. "Presenting Bill Lambert and Harper Collins."

Bill and Harper entered the gym.

"Presenting Steven Haskell and Mari Rogers," Mr. Brown shouted again loudly as the couple entered through the arch. "Is that what you wanted?" Mr. Brown said in a jovial way.

"That was great! Everyone will hand you their tickets. They should have put their names on them. If not, they will have to tell you who they are before they may come in." Bill was excited now.

Bill and Harper walked around with Steven and Mari. George and Babs came in. Mr. Brown announced them. Everyone laughed.

They all walked around inspecting everything. Bill's dad had already been there with RG, Mr. Hanson, and Reverend Haskell getting the lights on and opening all the doors. Their wives were over at the home economics building arranging all the food.

Carl was already at the controls playing music. "We're live in St. Helena at the Christmas ball playing all your favorite music. This is Carl on KVON radio 1400 on your radio dial." He spun around in his chair and waved at the committee. "We're on the air! We're rolling!" he shouted with excitement.

Mr. Brown was announcing people at the door.

"Presenting George Hansen and Babs Collins!" he shouted out loudly. "Presenting Zack Chambers and Joan Barnes." Joan was wearing a purple dress. "Presenting Daniel Rogers and Nadene Weston." Nadene had on a blue-and-white print dress. "Presenting Mark Rogers and Robin Moore." Robin was sweet in her pink dress.

"Presenting Dante Martin and Beth Andrews." Beth twirled around in her green dress to draw more attention to herself. "Presenting Parker Morrison and Pauline Banks." Pauline had a shimmering yellow gown to go with her dark-brown hair. "Presenting Charlie Ash and—well on your own, Charlie?"

Charlie strutted in with wearing a dark-blue suit with a shiny blue tie. "Yeah, I'll find me a single after a while. You wait and see."

The room was filling up, and everyone was amazed at the beautiful decorations. The lights were dim with a hue of blue.

"Presenting Charles Chambers and Blayne Alexander."

Everyone stopped and took a moment to pay attention to Mr. Brown announcing the couples as they came in the door.

Blayne had on a stunning gold sheath dress. It complemented her tall, slender mature body, her dark-brown skin, and her black hair. Charles was a very tall handsome athletic black boy. Their popularity stood out especially this night.

The girls opened their dance cards and were getting them filled. The room was buzzing with excitement. The secret theme was out: "Star Dust"

Once the room was filled, Carl announced the theme and played the music. "Everyone, take your partners and hold them tight. You will have Start Dust in your eyes tonight."

Steven took Mari in his arms and held her tight. "You look great, Mari. Merry Christmas. *And* I didn't forget your birthday either," he whispered in her ear.

"Who told you that anyway?" She pulled back and looked him in the face.

"Oh, that little birdy who told me about the flowers." He swung her out and back in and held her as they danced around the floor.

"See you made it, Robb. Got a pretty gal there." George smiled as he and Babs danced by.

Robb pulled Jenny in close. "You're the prettiest girl here. I can't tell you enough. You and me Jen. *You* and me!"

She put her head close on his shoulder. "You and me, Robb. We will make a great team," she whispered.

Song after song, Carl bantered on and called out the names and artists. Chuck Berry and "Rock and Roll," Elvis and "That's Alright," Gene Vincent and "Be-Bop-A-Lula," Pat Boone with "April Love," The Everly Brothers with "Walk Right Back," and the Clovers with "Devil or Angel."

Carl spotlighted special couples as they danced on the floor.

"We have Dante and Beth kicking it up down there. Look at them go!"

The spotlight swirled around and picked up Charlie Ash. "There goes my baby!" Carl sung out. Charlie was dancing with Rue Alberts. Everyone applauded. He swung her around and showed off their stuff.

"I'm havin' some of that pie I was plannin' on. Come on, I need somethin' to drink," Zack said enthusiastically. "Come on, Joan. Help me out here." Zack tugged her to come along.

"Better go with him. He'll need someone to carry one of his plates. He only has two hands," George jested.

"Havin' fun, Robin?" Mark swung her around briskly. "The place really turned out great, didn't it!" Robin smiled as they danced.

Carl shouted out, "Parents, grab your partners and show us your stuff. *You* kids watch out! Give 'em a lot of room!"

A bunch of the parents who were chaperoning the dance hauled out and showed off their stuff. RG and Helen led the crowd.

"Go, Daddy! Go!" shouted Mark.

Mr. Lambert and his wife were out there with Reverend Haskell and his wife. Some of the teachers joined in. Mr. Brown took Mrs. LaBelle out for a spin, and everyone applauded.

"All right, you fathers, grab your daughters and give them a twirl!" Carl shouted. He played a slow dance this time. "Okay, now switch off and give your gals up to their partners." Carl changed the music: "Only You" by the Platters.

Carl then switched it up with "Rock Around the Clock." The place went wild. Then on to Elvis and "Jailhouse Rock."

"I think you all better take a break and have some of those pies and cakes the ladies made for us," Carl shouted. "After that, we'll come back swinging." He lowered the sound and put some nice background music on and stepped down from the stage to get some refreshments.

"Love the job you're doin', Carl." Bill came up and patted him on the shoulder.

Matthew Young and Gail Hanford, Clark Blanchard and Jane Barkley, John Bates and Marcela Banks all gathered around the table.

"Love your dress, Blayne!" Jenny walked close to her. "You look stunning! You and Charles make a perfect couple."

"You and Robb now?" Blayne replied.

"Yeah, me and Robb. We got it together after all," Jenny said a little shyly. "I made some cookies. Did you bring anything?"

Blayne moved quickly down the table. "Here, I made this cake. It has pineapple in the frosting. I made it from my grandmother's recipe." Blayne cut several pieces and put them on some plates. "Would you like one?" She handed it to Jenny.

"Oh, thanks. I'll share it with Robb." She took the plate and went back with Robb. "Look what Blayne made. It really looks good."

Robb guided her to a table close to the lunch gang.

"Can't wait to get out on the dance floor again," Charlie announced. "Me and Rue!" Everyone laughed.

"Better be careful, Rue. That Charlie plays a mean air band," Bill shouted over the tables.

Carl started up the music again, and some of the couples started out on the floor once more. By now, parents, teachers, and everyone were out on the floor dancing. They danced a slow dance and enjoyed the Star Dust decorations.

"Okay, change partners. Guys cut in and take another round the floor," Carl announced.

Confusion all over the room, some fumbling to switch.

"I'll take this one, Steven." Robb tapped him on the shoulder.

"I don't think so, bud. Find another." Steven danced away.

"That wasn't very nice, Steven. He didn't mean any harm," Mari said impatiently.

"I just don't want to give him any room. Sorry!" Steven insisted.

Bill danced up. "Switch with us, Steven, make it easy."

They swung their girls around and switched.

"Mari! You are really easy to dance with. Harper and I are always tangling with our feet." Bill smiled.

"Steven and I spent some time practicing at the dances after the ball games. We were pretty clumsy at first. I always want to lead." She laughed.

"Okay, give 'um back. Kick it up now with Little Richard and 'Tutti Fruitti'!" Carl shouted out. The music blared. Everyone swung into a jitterbug. They cleared the floor for Charlie Ash and Rue, Blayne and Charlie. Everyone applauded.

Everyone danced and danced. Carl apologized and announced, "Last dance, everyone. Be sure you have your best girl in hand." He played "Star Dust" while everyone held each other close.

"Hate to end. How about you, Mari?" Steven whispered.

"You'll come up to the ranch, won't you?" she replied softly.

"Be all right with your dad?" he asked.

"I'm sure. He'll put you to work." Mari laughed.

"Let's get out of here. Now!" Steven pulled her off the floor.

They drove slowly down the Silverado Trail. Mari sat close to Steven. They pulled in to find the big white gate already open. On up the dirt road. Steven stopped the car at the top of the hill at the flat part in the road overlooking the valley.

"Just look at that, Mari. What a sight!" Steven put his arm around her.

"We're not going to stop here long, are we?" Mari said strongly.

"I just wanted a few minutes more with you before I take you home," Steven pulled back. He reached in and kissed her on the cheek. Mari snuggled in and kissed him back on the lips.

"That's all. Now take me home!" Mari said with a giggle.

"Okay! You are really something!" Steven said as he started the car and laughed.

He walked her up to the veranda and held her hand. "I'll come up this week for Christmas and your birthday, okay?" Steven leaned in and kissed her. He turned quickly and got in the car. He honked the horn and drove down the road. Mari stood and watched the car as it got to the fork in the road and disappeared.

"Good night, Mari," a voice came from the far end of the veranda. It was Sarah.

"Good night. It was super!" Mari went upstairs to her room and plopped on her bed and looked at the ceiling.

A little later, she heard the others driving up returning from the ball. Everyone was whispering. She knew it was really a special night for everyone.

CHAPTER 20

Family Feud

ON SUNDAY, THE MUCH-NEEDED RAIN had finally come to the valley. Fred helped everyone with the animals early the next morning so no one would be late for the school bus. The thrill of the ball was still lingering in everyone's heart. Mari planned to wear the new outfit her mother had given her, but she had forgotten to buy herself the blue socks to go with the sweater. She would get them this weekend when she went in to sell her eggs.

Fred took everyone down the hill to catch the school bus. They sat in the town car to keep warm. "What a deal, never got to do this," Daniel touted, pushing against Mark in the front seat next to Fred.

"Well, just wait. Next year sometime, I'll have my own car, and we won't have to sit around waiting for the old bus anymore," Mark pushed back.

"I heard Steven say the yellow car was sold already. What kind of car do you want anyway?" Beth spoke up quickly.

"Maybe I'll get a Thunderbird! They are really hot. Then I wouldn't have to take all you kids with me 'cause there wouldn't be enough room for you all." He laughed. "Ha-ha!"

Just then, Robin and Anne walked up in the rain. "Jump in out of the rain, you guys," Mari said, opening the door. They squeezed in and giggled.

"Nice and warm in here!" Annie said, excited to see the inside of the town car.

"Better than an old truck, I would say," Robin said with a smile.

"I hear the bus!" Daniel climbed out of the car quickly and placed himself out on the edge of the drive near the road to be first on the bus.

"He never gets enough of being first, does he?" Beth shouted after him. They all ran through the rain and hopped on the bus.

Everyone was excited to great each other. "Hi, Jen. Hi, you guys," Mari greeted all the kids on the bus, adding, "I think we all ran between the drops and didn't melt."

Daniel snidely spoke up, "You're not sweet enough to melt anyways! Ha-ha-ha!"

Mari and Beth sat close to Jenny. "What time did you get in? Was Robb a gentleman? Did your folks have a good time?" Beth chattered on and on.

The bus pulled up to the Martins' place, and Dante rushed to get out of the rain. "There is my angel!" He scooted in next to Beth.

She spoke softly, "Where's your brother today?"

"Oh, he drove the truck into school. He and Margot, you see." Dante put his books to his side and leaned in closer to whisper to Beth, "They are in love. Big trouble at home."

"Really? Why is their trouble at home over that?" Beth whispered.

"Oh, my father. Well, he has plans, and Alanso he has plans. They had a big fight about it Saturday after the ball. I think he and Margot have plans."

Jenny was straining to try and hear what they were talking about. "Get your sticky beak back here, Jen!" Mari poked her on the back. "None of your bee's wax!"

Jenny straightened up and sat back. "Can't wait to see what that is all about," Jen whispered.

Mari whispered back. "For someone who doesn't want anyone to know about your life, it seems strange to me you need to know so much about other people's lives." They both sat quietly as the bus passed Margot's place without stopping.

The bus rolled up to the gray stone building, and everyone piled out, rushing to get out of the rain. Steven was under the porch by the door of the gray stone building, waiting out of the rain. Mari rushed up quickly. "Got something for you," she said as she pulled out a paper bag and handed it to him. "Thought you might like a duck sandwich I made. Not the usual thick bread my mother cuts. Made it thin cut, with homemade mayonnaise, lettuce, tomato, and some pickles left over from dinner."

"Oh, swell. I might eat it before lunch." Steven took it out of the bag, unwrapped the wax paper, and took a big bite. They walked over to their lockers. With his mouth full, he said, "Not going to run over to the gym with you in the rain, Mar. See you later."

She laughed and went with the other girls, who were running through the rain to the gym. Margot was running ahead of them. "Margot, wait up!" Mari shouted. She caught up with her as they ran up the steps and in the door.

"You and Alanso have a good time Friday night?" Mari said, out of breath.

Margot pulled her hand out. "See, I had the best time ever!" She wiggled her left hand. They both continued walking down to the lockers to change into their gym clothes.

"What have you gone and done?" exclaimed Mari.

"Nothing, nothing! We're making plans, that's all." Margot was all excited to show off her ring. "We sat in the orchard after the ball, and he asked me to marry him. I said yes. We'll get married this summer, then go to college together. He'll take the ranch on the Oakville Road and live there. He asked my father on Sunday."

At that point, all the girls were gathered around looking at her ring and listening to her. Mrs. LaBelle came and blew the whistle to get everyone up for roll call: all the seniors in their section, juniors in theirs, and the sophomores in theirs.

Mari stood next to Hydie Teasdale.

"Did you see her ring? What a huge stone!" Hydie whispered.

Mari whispered back, "They have a lot of money, I guess. He must love her a lot. I bet they have a big wedding this summer after graduation."

They all divided up in several teams to play volleyball. Mari and her soccer teammates ganged up on the seniors and whipped them good. The bell rang, and everyone ran down to take their showers and get dressed for class again. Mari made sure she got around to see Margot once she was ready. "What do your parents think about your plans? Are they happy for you?" Mari asked Margot as they walked across the gym floor, leaving.

"I have to say, my dad is really upset. He has other plans for me. My mom is very happy. I think Dad's going to go over to the Martin ranch today and talk to Alonso's father. I'm not Catholic, and they don't like me."

Mari and Margot ran across campus to their classes in the new building. "See you later, Mari. Talk about it later, okay?"

Mari was glad to see Steven at lunch. "I don't have anything else to feed you. You are on your own, bud," she teased him.

"That's all right. The student store is selling hot soup now. Wait here while I get some. Want a bowl?" he asked as he started to get in line.

"Sure, vegetable," Mari replied.

She sat down at a table toward the end of the room. The gang all piled in at the table around her. Joan, Hydie, Babs, and Pauline were all chatting about Margot and her huge ring. "What a ring!" Hydie declared.

"He must love her a lot!" Pauline commented. "Can't imagine what their parents must think, he being Catholic and all. What will happen when they have kids? What will they be? How will they go to college if they're married? I sure wouldn't want to worry about that."

Steven came with the soup and handed Mari her vegetable soup. "Got some crackers to go with it too."

Andrew spoke up and asked if he had seen Margot's engagement ring. "What? Engagement ring? No way!" Steven exclaimed. "There will be trouble now!"

Everyone had an opinion about it and expressed concern over the consequences of being young and the differences in their families.

Parker was quick to add, "I have to get my degree and have my career in order before I get that serious about anybody. I love Pauline, but we aren't going to get married now. Maybe never, maybe after college. Who knows?"

Pauline poked him. "Who said I would marry you anyway?" They all laughed. The bell rang, and they all parted, going off to their classes.

Steven and Mari walked together. "I would marry you, Mari. That's how I feel right now. But like it was said, I want to get my degree and have a career set before that."

She laughed. "Like Pauline said, who said I would marry you anyway?" She poked him. "I do love you, Steven. I think I could love you forever." They went into class and sat down.

When Mari got home, she met up with her dad in the barn after she finished checking on the chickens, helped with the rabbits, and fed the dogs. "Margot and Alanso are getting married, Dad," she announced as her dad was stacking some sacks of walnuts.

"What? You don't say! That will sure stir things up at the Martin Ranch. Can't think old man Martin will stand for that. I think I will have to have a talk with him before he and Schmidt get into a fight. They both have a pretty good temper and see things their own way." RG was perplexed.

"You really think they would get into a fight, Daddy?" Mari asked in surprise.

Meanwhile, Margot, Alanso, and their parents were meeting at the Schmidts' ranch. Alanso and Margot were sitting on the davenport sofa quietly listening to their fathers argue.

"You Methodists!" Mr. Martin's shouted in his heavy Italian accent.

"You Catholics!" Mr. Schmidt shouted in his heavy German accent.

They went back and forth. "My grandchildren aren't going to be no Catholics. We come from old country, and we're Protestants. We fought for that! We die for that!" Schmidt hollered.

Mrs. Martin stood up. "Now, Papa…now, Papa, you don't mean to be mad. Alanso and Margot get married and go to school. They will work it all out. Give him ranch on Oakville Road and be happy. He make wine like you. Maybe better. He will have many boys with Martin name. Margot is a good woman. She will go to college too.

She is really smart. She cook and sew. She will make good mama," she implored him as she took his arm.

Mrs. Schmidt took her husband's arm. "She is right. They will work it out. We came to this country to make a new life, and we have it here. They will make their own life. If that is what they want, I will stand by my Margot. I would not like my grandchildren to be Catholic, but if Margot want to, then she will do it." Mrs. Schmidt tugged at her husband.

"Sir?" Alanso spoke up. "I'll be sure Margot finishes school in June and graduates with me, then we will get married this summer here in your orchard. I plan to go to UC Davis and get my degree. Margot and I will both get our degree as you wish. Then we will make our home here in the valley. We have plans. That is what we plan."

Margot stood by his side, strongly holding his arm. "Yes, Daddy and Mummy. We have plans, and we're going to make a new life like you are doing." She was in tears now.

Her mother went over and touched her on the shoulder. It was not in their nature to be very emotional. "You are good girl. Don't spoil anything before you get married," her mother pleaded.

"Oh, I am a good girl, Mummy. We behave ourselves until we get married. Be sure of that," Margot reassured her mother and father.

"You treat her right, you hear! You treat her right, or else," Mr. Schmidt said strongly, not yelling anymore. He held out his hand to Alanso. He turned to Mr. Martin and shook his hand and held his arm with his other. "We be a family!" The men took out their handkerchiefs and wiped their faces.

"You go home now, Alanso, and get to work! You waste my time today," Mr. Martin ordered. He took his wife by the hand. "Come on, Mama. We go home and have some pasta."

They all walked out together. "Thank you, Mr. Schmidt. I will be good to Margot, I promise." Alanso kissed Margot in front of his parents and jumped in his truck and drove off quickly down the road. He waved his hand out the window in the rain.

He and Margot drove to school in his truck every day now. They studied together at the Schmidt Ranch. Alonso wanted to get acquainted with her mother and dad. Once in a while, Margot would go up to the Martin Ranch and study so she could get acquainted with Alonso's parents. She learned a lot about the wine industry. Her father's ranch had prune and walnut orchards and only table grapes.

One day that week, RG went down and visited with Mr. Martin. "Thought I would check in with you, Agusto. Heard your son is planning to be married. Congratulations. Things all right with you?"

"We shook hands. We don't like it much. We be happy anyway. Schmidt and me, we work it out. Them two young people have plans. We made plans in our day. They make plans now in their day. I got my way when I left the old country to come here. Now he have his way. But I still get my way later. He and me, we make wine together anyway," Mr. Martin said as he wiped his face with the palm of his hands.

"Glad to hear it. Glad to hear it. How is the place on the Oakville Road coming along? I bet you have your work cut out for you," RG said with great interest.

"We tear out a lot in old house and fix her up so Alonso and Margot can have it when they not in college. I will have lots of boy children from them, ha-ha-ha." He and RG laughed long and strong.

"How's the missus? You and she are welcome to come up to the ranch on Sunday afternoons. We always have a bunch of folks up for food and talk," RG said, encouraging him. "Your boy Dante is seeing our girl child Beth, you know. He is a real gentleman. Better keep it that way. I'm keeping an eye on him. You come up with him when he comes to see her. Do that now, okay?" RG spoke sternly.

"Good to know. We come up soon. They just kids. They play good together. That is good thing for now," Mr. Martin joked.

"Well, I'll be running along, Agusto. Take care. Good talk." RG jumped in the truck and drove carefully out the driveway and up the Trail.

He stopped in the kitchen and spoke to Helen. "Saw Agusto Martin. Things have simmered down with the Schmidts. They'll be coming up on some Sunday afternoon when Dante comes up to see

Beth. He says they play good together." He chuckled. He and Helen talked a lot about the young couple getting married and how they ran off and got married without permission. They hoped their kids would do it differently and have all the traditional wedding plans they had missed out on.

CHAPTER 21

Mari's Birthday

HELEN, SARAH, MARI, AND BETH still had some shopping to finish before Mari's birthday. They took the opportunity to take a few hours the two Saturdays they had before Christmas to make quick trips into town when Mari, Daniel, and Beth went in to sell their eggs, rabbits, and ducks.

Mari still had some gifts to buy. It was really difficult for her. She had to have time to sew the aprons and still get her homework done, along with all the rest of the chores. She kept forgetting to buy the blue socks she wanted.

"Come on, Beth. I have to go to The Elegant Closet and get those socks I want to match my new sweater Mama gave me for my birthday," Mari urged as she pushed to get on down the street.

They got in the shop quickly. "I need some of those blue angora socks to go with the new sweater my mom bought for me, Mrs. Alexander," Mari said, walking over to the rack where the socks were. "Oh, I don't see any here. Are you out? I was too busy and didn't get down here soon enough, I guess. Oh well, missed out," Mari said, disappointed.

"I'll have some in after Christmas, if you can wait," Mrs. Alexander said kindly.

"Oh well, that's okay. I really don't need them. I just wanted them to go with my new outfit. I do have other socks to wear." She laughed.

She and Beth looked around the shop. Everything was beautiful and expensive, far more than they had in their purses.

"We'll catch you later, thanks. Merry Christmas. Say hi to Blayne."

Off they went up the street. Mari had everything she needed. "I am done. How about you, Beth? I think we better find Mama and Sarah and get back to the ranch. I have to get some things done for Christmas that will take me some extra effort and time," Mari explained to Beth. "You need anything else?"

"No, I was just hanging around with you and enjoying looking at all the stores. I saw the movie *Giant* was playing at the theater and wondered what it would be like to go to the movies. Rock Hudson, Elizabeth Taylor, and James Dean are in it. James Dean! Rock Hudson! Dreamy! Maybe someday we can go. What do you think? Maybe Dante and Steven would go with us," she said hopefully.

"If we asked Mark, he would take us. Dad would let us go if Mark went with us, I bet," Mari said as they rushed up the street looking for mama and Sarah.

"I see them. They just came out of Shaw's Hardware Store. Let's run." Beth grabbed Mari by the hand. They ran up and insisted they go home since they had so much to do. "Well, look who are the busy ones now?' Sarah said. "Fred is waiting around the corner as we speak. We were just wondering about you two girls," Sarah said cheerfully.

"I couldn't get any blue socks at The Elegant Closet. They were all out." Mari pouted a bit. No one said a word.

"We finished up all we had to do. I think we're through with this job, shopping," Mama said as she settled back in the town car.

Mari closed her eyes and took a nap on the way home. Beth rested her head on Helen's shoulder. Fred turned the radio on to KVON. Carl was on. Fred laughed. "What a kid. He sure put on a great program for the Christmas ball."

Sarah leaned over. "Hush, they're all asleep."

Mari had to find Mark. She needed a place to secretly set up her sewing machine to make the aprons. She quietly went up to the library to see if he was up there. "Mark? Mark? Oh, there you are, I need a secret place to set up my sewing machine and make something for Christmas. Let me use your room. No one would think to find me in there," she pleaded.

"Well, what's in it for me? Gunna make something for me?" he joked.

"If you need an apron, sure." She laughed. "So okay with you?"

"Sure, just don't leave any pins on my bed or on the floor," Mark remarked.

She ran quickly to set up her sewing machine, shutting the door quietly. No one missed her the rest of the afternoon.

Tap, tap, tap—came a soft rap on the door. "Have to quit, Mari. Dinner will be on soon and chores. Get a move on!" Mark said softly.

She quickly put everything away in the corner of Mark's room where it wouldn't be conspicuous. She ran up to the barn and quickly tended to the dogs and her chickens. The rain had subsided a bit, but everything was dripping wet. "Oh, wet! What a mess!" she wailed out loud.

Daniel and Beth had already taken care of their animals, and RG was just coming down from milking Baby. "Thought you could help me separate the milk out in the milk house, Brat. We need some cream in the house. The butter churns are empty again. Mama and Sarah have been baking up a storm, using at least eight pounds of butter a week," her dad said as they walked down to the milk house together.

They entered the kitchen to find Sarah, Mama, Daniel, Beth, and Mark talking. They all stopped talking when they entered the room. Mari stopped short with the bucket of milk for the churns looking at everyone. "What's going on? What have I done now? What did I forget to do now?" she said defensively.

"Not to worry," Sarah said quickly. "Everyone was just telling me what they wanted for Christmas dinner, that's all." The kids all scooted out of the kitchen to the living room. They had been conspiring plans for Mari's birthday.

Mari went on and filled the two churns with milk and cleaned up the spills. She put the churns on the table, looking around.

There were signs of all sorts of cookies and things going on in the kitchen she had not had to be a part of since Sarah was there to assist her mother. She stuck her finger in some frosting sitting on the table.

Out in the living room, while Mari was busy, Daniel reminded Mark and Beth about his plan to let Mari off the hook and not have to do her chores. Mark agreed. They would all do them for her the rest of the week.

"When will we tell her?" Beth said quietly.

"We can leave her a note on her bedroom door Monday morning," Mark suggested.

"I'll feed her chickens and pick up her eggs. That's easy for me. I know how to do that," Beth offered.

Daniel said he would feed the dogs and tell her she didn't have to help with the rabbits.

"I'll drive everyone down the hill in the old truck that is just sitting out in the barn and leave it by the horse barn at Robin's place so she doesn't have to walk in the rain," Mark said.

"That's good for us all, stupid," Daniel snidely stated.

"Well then, I will pay for her to have lunch in the student store all week. I can afford that," Mark boasted.

"Well, that's settled. I'll make a fancy note to put on her door," Beth said, all excited. "Since when is it that there's an old truck in the barn that's just sitting there and we haven't been using it? We've been walking in the cold and rain all this time getting drenched, packing all the stuff up the hill like packhorses, and that has been sitting there all this time?" Beth spoke up loudly, disgusted. "I never!" she huffed.

"Never gave it a thought 'til now, kid," Mark replied thoughtfully. "Now that I drive, I just thought about it. Since I'm not going to get the yellow car anyway, we could just clean it up and use it. I'll talk to Dad about it today."

Beth went to her room later and secretly made a very pretty sign to put on the bedroom door. She got some glitter blue paper left over from the Christmas ball.

Happy birthday, Mari!

This certificate gives you a week of no chores:

1. Daniel will feed the dogs for you every day this week. You will not have to help him with the rabbits.
2. Beth will feed your chickens and collect your eggs.
3. Mark will pay for your lunch all week at the student store.
4. We will all have a ride up and down the hill in the old pickup truck out in the barn.

Signed,
Mark, Daniel, and Beth

Mari's birthday was on Wednesday, but they wanted her to have the whole week of fun. She was one of the youngest in her class. Most of the kids had already been fifteen and turned sixteen in the fall. She was smart for her age but had to work harder for her grades since she had so much work to do up at the ranch.

Monday morning, Mark, Daniel, and Beth were up and out doing all the chores before Mari even got up. Fred was out helping along too. "Beth? Oh, gone already? I must be late," she spoke out loud to herself. She quickly ran across the hall to the bathroom. Returning, she then noticed the note on the door. She peeled it off the door, reading it out loud. "Well, I never! This is all Beth's doing, I know. She is so sweet." She went into her room and searched around for a special outfit for school.

When she reached the kitchen, Sarah and mama were mixing up french toast and stuff. Mari stood next to the kitchen table and asked, "What can I do to help? I have been relieved of all my chores and have nothing to do."

Her mother replied, "Just sit there and watch. You are free to have a happy birthday all week, according to the kids."

Sarah added, "Queen for the week, my dear. Enjoy it while you can."

Mari really didn't know what to do with herself. She ran up to Mark's room and got her sewing out. She had all this time to work on her aprons. They would be all finished in time now. She was excited and worked swiftly. She hummed along, being very pleased with herself and the design she had created. She looked out the window and saw the kids all coming down the path from the barn. She quickly put everything away and went and sat at the piano as if she had been there ideally enjoying herself.

Daniel came up and into the library. "Stupid songs, you and your Jesus songs." He went out and down the hall to his room to change his clothes. Mari could hear him howling, making fun of her.

"Figured he couldn't be nice very long," she said out loud as Beth entered the library.

"I'm going to clean up and meet you down for breakfast. Hurry up now, queenie," Beth teased Mari.

Mark peeked in the library. "See you got some more done in my room. I really like what you have done," he said with a smile.

Steven was waiting by the big redwood tree when she got off the bus. "You wouldn't believe what my brothers and sister did for me for my birthday this week," she said enthusiastically. "For one thing, I get to buy lunch at the student store all week, compliments of Mark. Daniel and Beth are doing all my chores morning and night. I'm sewing some presents for Sarah and my mother. They don't even know how much this gives me time to get it all done. They think I'm just sitting around up in the library playing the piano." She giggled.

Steven grabbed her books and walked her out to the gym. "See you at lunch. You can buy me soup today, on Mark." He turned and laughed as he ran back to his class.

The day went well for her, no drama from Jenny. Nothing was hard for her for a change.

She met Margot at the gym. "Things going well now at home? I am really excited for you. I can't imagine all you have on your mind. Graduation in June, a wedding, planning college. You and Alonso both going to UC Davis?" Mari said quietly.

"I'm planning to be a high school home economics teacher. That way, I will have time in the summer to do all the things I will have to do at home for a family," she spoke in such a grown-up manner.

Mari really admired her and looked up to her. She and Margot had been friends in 4-H for a long time. They had gone to church together all this time. "I think I would like to go to college somewhere else. There are other schools to consider. I would really like to go wherever Steven goes. He and I are really close. I think I understand how you and Alonso feel about each other," Mari said as they walked across the campus.

"I fell for him right away when he asked me to the ball. He was so cute about it. Then we just hit it off, and everything we talk about just clicks as if we have known each other all our lives," Margot said frankly.

The girls parted and went on their separate ways. "See you later, sweetheart." Margot raised her arm and waved as she was walking away. Mari paused, looking at her in admiration.

She and the gang all had lunch as usual. Steven got the soup and put it on Mark's bill. Everyone was amused at Mari getting off from doing her chores.

"No one going to do your homework, madam?" Zack teased her.

"Still have that to do! Wouldn't have it any other way. Get my own bad grades. Don't need anybody doing it for me," Mari joked as they all laughed.

Joan poked her. "You make out like you're so dumb, and yet you are so smart, clever, artistic, musical, and the most thoughtful person in our group. I think you should play the piano for us and have a concert of your own at one of our assemblies."

Pauline and Joan agreed. Joan chimed in, "After Christmas, we'll make arrangements for Mari to have a fancy recital and play some of her best works."

Pauline added, "I think Mari plays better than anyone else in our school, and no one seems to know about it. Why is that?"

Steven jumped in with a mouthful of crackers. "'Cause she's so shy and kind to everyone else all the time. That's my girl."

Mari got up and put her empty bowl away. "I don't know, you guys. I just tinker around on the piano in my spare time." She walked away, filled with emotion.

Robb spoke up, "I've heard her play, and she is a concert pianist, in my opinion. Better than any old air band I've heard." Everyone laughed and got up and went off to class.

Mari went up to her room quickly when she got home. She had nothing to do but finish the aprons and play the piano. "Well, look at that. Pajamas!" New pajamas were neatly folded on her bed with a note from her mother: "Happy birthday. Wouldn't want to leave you without this. Love, Mother." Mari sat and cried as she held them up to her face.

Dinner was special that night. She told everyone how the gang had wanted her to do a concert for them. "Just think, I could wear my blue dress again if I performed for them."

Daniel made scathing remarks, "They don't get to hear you howling like I do."

"What a nice thing, Mari. Your gang found out about your secret. I bet Robb told on you," Beth interjected.

"Maybe that kid isn't so bad after all," Mark said quietly.

Just then, Sarah and Fred jumped up from the table and went into the kitchen. Out they came with a cake blazing with fifteen candles. Everyone sang "Happy Birthday."

Mari teared up and sat back in her chair. "This is all because of you, Beth. Thank you. This is really special." She looked at the candles. She made a wish and blew hard. They all went out in one breath. "I'll get my wish. Thank you!" She cut the cake, and Sarah served everyone ice cream as she passed the dishes around. Mari was pleased.

"We have a couple of gifts for you, Brat!" RG said with gusto. He reached in his pocket and pulled out a little box. "This is from my mother's collection, and you are old enough to have it now."

Mari took the little box and opened it. It was a ring with a turquoise stone set in sterling silver. "Oh my. This is my birthstone."

"Yes, your grandmother Rogers's birthday was December 21. My father always gave her fancy jewelry every year that I can remember." RG wiped his face with his hand.

Daniel got up out of his chair to come and look at it. "Can't feed the chickens wearing that!" He patted her on the shoulder and sat down.

Mark sat back in his chair and smiled. "I knew you were going to get it, Mari. Dad showed it to me last week. Here, I have something for you." He pulled out a package wrapped with fancy paper, obviously done up by a store. He passed it down to her.

She opened it carefully, saving the paper so she could use it again. "Oh, look! A pretty box." She opened it, and music began to play. "A jewelry box! Well, I never! Perfect, just perfect!"

"Here, Mari, something from me." Beth reached out with a little package in white tissue paper with curly ribbon.

"Whoa! More?" she squealed. She whipped the paper off quickly. She started to cry. "I was such a pout puss, and look, you had them all the time." Mari held up the pair of blue angora socks she wanted. "Thank you, thank you. This is the best birthday ever! I will never forget it." She put the ring on her right hand and held it out, admiring it. "Can't do dishes with this either."

They all laughed.

"Christmas can't get any better than this," Fred said as he whipped his face with his handkerchief and went out to the kitchen to start cleaning up. "Never had a family like this, Sarah. Never in my life."

He held her in his arms close for a moment.

Everyone was ready for the Christmas break. Friday at lunch, the gang all gathered around. "Last lunch on Mark, everyone. Go and have a small treat for Mari's birthday," Steven announced, standing at the end of the table. Everyone applauded and laughed.

"What's this I hear?" Mark walked up and put his hand on Steven's shoulder.

"Yes, sir, we all thank you for Mari's lunch treat. Have a seat, and we will serve you up a milkshake—on your account," Steven said smartly.

"Don't mind if I do." Mark sat down.

Robin walked up and sat down next to him. "I hear ya all are celebrating a fifteenth birthday all week. A history-making event at the Rogers Ranch, I hear."

He kissed her on the cheek. "I don't think we celebrate her enough sometimes," Mark said quietly.

CHAPTER 22

Christmas

MARI WAS OUT IN THE middle of the barn sweeping up the glitter from the stars they had made for the ball. She stopped and listened for a moment. A beautiful melody. It was RG.

> *Ihr Kinderlein, kommet,* (Ye children come)
> *O kommet doch all!* (O come ye all!)
> *Zur Krippe her kommet* (Come to the cradle)
> *In Bethlehems Stall.* (in Bethlehem's stall.)

She had never heard her father sing like this before. Her heart in her throat, she ducked around to the other section of the barn where he was cracking some walnuts. He was sitting on a large log he had stood on end with another in front of him. Carefully holding each nut and hitting it just right, he split it and tossed the meat into a large bowl.

"Hello? What is that you are singing, Daddy?" Mari asked quietly.

He stopped suddenly and looked up. "Oh, just times of my youth. Days long gone, I'm afraid." He had tears in his eyes.

"'Ihr Kinderlein kommet' boasts a beautiful melody that brings the family together, that's all. We don't keep the German anymore since the war. You are too young to know it." He cracked some more walnuts.

"Why don't you teach that to us kids, Daddy? It's so beautiful. I could play it on the piano, and we could all sing some of your old songs together," Mari said quietly.

"I think listening to old man Schmidt has brought me back to my youth. His family and ours fought for the church against the Catholics. I can see his passion even now that he is here in this country." He stopped and looked up at her. "You sneak off on Sundays and think I don't know it. That is your right, your freedom to choose for yourself, your own religion. I will not keep you from it. Schmidt and Martin want their children to follow them in their religion. I won't do that to you and the boys. You learn and choose for yourself, like you are doing. But there will be no German spoken in the house! Not now, not ever!" he said strongly.

"Yes, Daddy, all right. I love to hear you sing it though," Mari said softly.

She left the barn, quite stunned at her father's words. She went up to the library and sat and played the piano for a while. Beth came in and sat in the big green chair, taking up a book as if to be reading it. She listened for a long while.

Mark had been in his room resting on his bed. He lay there listening too. He got up and came in the library and sat down in the other big wing chair and picked up a magazine, which he pretended to read.

Fred came in with some firewood, stoked the fire, and sat on a stool for a bit and just listened as Mari played. Sarah walked up the hall, heard her, and snuck in, sitting down with the rest.

Soon Helen came in and sat on the chair next to the fireplace. They all sat spellbound while Mari played.

"Did anyone see my logbook for my rabbits?" Daniel burst into the room suddenly. "What is all this racket?" he spoke loudly.

"I think you are being very rude, young man!" Fred stood up quickly, walking over to Daniel. He grabbed him by the shoulder and marched him out of the room into the hallway. Everyone could hear him speaking strongly to Daniel. He came back into the library. "I'm sorry. I just couldn't help myself, Helen. I know he's your kid and all," Fred apologized.

"Someone has to straighten him out. I sure haven't had any luck with him," Helen said softly.

The door shut down the hall. "Where is everyone? I have about ten pounds of walnuts ready for you," RG blustered as he walked down the hall to the library.

"We're all in here listening to Mari play the piano, dear. You missed out," Helen said as she rose from her chair. "I guess we all should get back to the kitchen and make some candy. Come on, Sarah. You too, Beth. I want to make some divinity today."

"Actually, divinity is my specialty, Mama," Mari said as she scooted off the piano bench. "I'll be showing everyone how it's done. No one has ever made it better than I do." Mari showed more pride than usual. "My fudge is the best also. Dad and I just separated the milk this morning, and we have lots of cream today."

Off they all went to the kitchen. Beth shouted out, "Daniel, get out here and help in the kitchen!" He took this opportunity to make up for his rudeness and try to be nice. Besides, he just wanted to have the chance to lick the bowls.

Everyone spent the rest of the day in a huge production of making cookies, candy, and little packages Helen always put out for all the people RG did business with. She had saved up the flat lids from shoeboxes, greeting cards, her nylons, and other things they had purchased during the year. Then she had the kids line them with white paper doilies.

She and Sarah had already started baking all sorts of fruit cake and all the family cookie recipes in November. Most of the old-time German recipes called for butter, walnuts, pecans, raisins, currants, and candied fruit. There were Russian stripes, cinnamon stars, apricot hearts, Mexican wedding cakes, plain old chocolate chip cookies, lemon bars, bourbon balls, candy, and fruit cake. Everyone pitched in setting up an assembly line: first, lining the box lids with the doilies. Then everyone had their cookie, candy or fruit cake to put in a box. All were laid out in a decorated pattern. Then one person wrapped red or green cellophane around and taped it down. One person at the end put curly ribbon on each package. Helen and RG always addressed each one personally on a little card.

By the end of the day, they had thirty packages all ready to deliver that next week. Helen and RG always drove around personally to present the thank-you gifts to all their friends and clients.

"This year, everyone has really made this easy for me," Helen said as she wiped the table clean. I really had much more fun this year. Thank you. Thank you, everyone. Now wasn't that more fun than being ornery, Daniel?"

"Sure!" he took a cookie and stuffed it in his mouth and ran out the door.

Christmas was on Tuesday that week, which gave them Sunday afternoon and Monday to get them all delivered. Sunday morning, RG rapped on Mari's bedroom door. "Rise and shine, Brat! I'm taking you down the hill this morning. You don't have to ride the bus today."

Mari rolled over, stretched, looked at Beth. "What? Can't believe it. You going to church with me?" she replied.

"No! Mother and I have to deliver packages and have a job to do," he replied through the door.

Everyone scurried around quickly in order to get a ride with RG. They went into St. Helena and dropped the girls off at the little white Baptist church. "You catch a ride with Pastor Bob, Brat. See you tonight." RG and Helen drove off quickly.

They had made an appointment with the Ford dealer for that morning. "I thought I would trade the old truck in and get this one, Helen. This one has a heater and a radio in it. It's bigger and will hold more grapes. They walked around a big green truck. It already had a sign on each door that said "The Rogers Ranch, R. G. Rogers, contractor and architect. Phone: 6333-R."

Helen stood in amazement. "Oh, Robert, she's a beauty. She came around to the tailgate. It had big letters: HERCULES. She burst out laughing. "Can't ever give up that name for your trucks, can you?"

He wiped his face with his hand. Had old Herk here for too many years. Hard to let him go."

The man from the Ford dealer handed him the keys to the truck. "Have to clean out your old one now and load him up, RG."

They both set out and transferred all the boxes of packages, the toolboxes, and the bench from the back of the truck. They shook hands and climbed into the new truck.

"This really rides so smooth, dear. How do we turn on the heater?" Helen started to fiddle around with the dials on the dashboard.

They drove around town and delivered all the packages to the folks in town, then drove on down to Oakville and Napa. By three o'clock, they had delivered most of the packages with only a few left for the next day.

"Better get home to milk Baby, Helen. Your packages are always a hit. Everyone always seems to be surprised when we show up with them." He reached over and gave her a kiss.

"Fred? Fred?" RG called out as he walked across the bridge to the little house. Fred came to the door. "Hey, what's up?"

RG raised his voice. "We need to get into town tomorrow for that last job that needs doing." The men stood out on the porch of the little house. "Helen and I only have a few packages to deliver in Napa. We can get that done in the morning, and you and I can sneak into town when we return. That good for you?" RG spoke quietly.

"Sure, I'll be ready when I see you," Fred replied.

"Have to come up to the barn and see something. Come on. You'll like it." RG stepped off the porch. Fred followed. They went over the bridge past the clothesline, past the milk house, past the woodpile, and in through the back of the barn. RG slid the huge door to the back of the barn. "What do ya think?" he said proudly. The men walked around new Hercules.

"He's a beaut, have to hand it to you! Still have the old rusty one here. Saw the kids driving it last week. Guess we're keeping it?" Fred ran his hand along the top of the back of the truck. "Green again, I see. Got your name on this one!"

RG replied, "Green, only color I ever have." All his tool handles were green, and the toolboxes were painted green with his name of them.

The men examined the truck from top to bottom, pushing buttons and checking the lights. Mark and Daniel walked in the barn to see what was going on.

"Wow! Can I drive him?" Mark shouted out in amazement. "This one will hold a lot more grapes. Won't have to make as many trips to the winery now."

"I'll be drivin' this one when I get my license! Look at that name on the door! He's a beaut, Dad!" Daniel said in excitement.

Pretty soon everyone was out in the barn admiring the new truck—walking around, climbing all over it, getting in the cab.

"Look at this. I bet four people can sit across this seat," Mari shouted. "A heater, a heater! Jeepers, Dad. You really did it. A heater!"

Beth and Daniel piled in to see if they all fit in the big cab. Daniel scooted behind the steering wheel as if to be the driver. Beth started to laugh. "You can hardly see over the wheel, Daniel. We'll have to prop you up with a pillow."

Daniel snarled back, "I'll be as big as my dad before you know it. Just you wait and see!"

Everyone got down to the house where Sarah had prepared a light supper. "How much excitement can we all take?" she said in a lighthearted manner.

That night, everyone said they were going to bed early. Each one had plans. Fred and Sarah had already snuck some gifts under the tree. Helen had put some under already too. She was in her room still wrapping some little packages with white tissue paper and curly ribbon.

RG came in and kissed her and patted her on the butt. "Still sneaking around this late? Santa still has to come yet." They took the packages down together. "This year is really special, dear. You have had a huge year with business. The ranch is well taken care of with Fred and Sarah. Mark is managing the vineyard beyond my expectation. Mari and Beth are so sweet together. Daniel...well, Daniel, his business is growing, but we still have to get him under control," Helen remarked as they looked at the tree together.

They left the room and went into the kitchen. They could hear the door to the living room creak. Someone was sneaking in and putting gifts under the tree. The door shut. Soon they heard another— *giggle, giggle, giggle, shh, shh. Whispers.* The door shut again. They listened quietly. Not a sound. "I think we're safe." They snuck out the door to the veranda and up to their room.

Early Monday, Christmas Eve day, Helen and RG went off in the big town car and down to Napa with their packages.

Fred, being left with the kids, instructed firmly, "I want you and the kids to drive up the hill to the Hanford place with their Christmas packages later today, Mark. They will be there after four this afternoon. See to it you get there about that time. See to it, all right? You take all the kids with you in the old truck and say Merry Christmas to them. They will be up for the holidays this week."

"Sure, we haven't been up there in quite a while. Mari and Beth will love to see their horses," Mark replied respectfully.

RG and Helen arrived home about one-thirty that afternoon; Fred was waiting. He and RG quickly drove off in the new truck, hoping they wouldn't be noticed. Helen kept the kids all in the kitchen, making some pies. Mari and Daniel sat grinding away on the churns, making more butter. Beth was learning how to make flakey pie crust. Mark sat on the windowsill eating some fruit cake with some frosting he found left over from the cinnamon stars.

With his mouth full, Mark said, "Fred said we had to get up to the Hanford place this afternoon. You kids have to come with me. Beth, you'll love seeing all their horses. They have Arabians. We all learned to ride their old horse Chummy. Have to be back here in time for dinner."

"No rush, Mark. Sarah and I plan a late supper. Nothing big. Just be back by six," mama said quietly.

Daniel spoke up with authority, "They have two older girls and one boy a bit younger than I am. We got into a lot of trouble last summer with Mrs. Hanford. They have a gillion feral cats up in their barn. Wouldn't want all that here, that's for sure." He cranked along in rhythm with Mari, churning away.

"You stay out of trouble today! Hear?" Mark ordered. "Don't need any of your guff on Christmas Eve. Santa will put coal in your stocking!"

"Huh! Ain't no Santa!" Daniel sneered.

252

Beth chimed in, "It still is fun to pretend. I have never had such a great Christmas like we're having. You shut up, Daniel!"

"Now, everyone, don't spoil the day," admonished mama.

The kids piled in the old truck with the packages for the Hanfords a little after four that afternoon. Helen and Sarah watched from the veranda as they rounded the dam. "Got them out of the way safely," Sarah said with a smile. "I think we can put Beth's special ornament on the tree without being seen."

They returned to the kitchen making some cold cuts and treats for the light supper. They both went into the living room, put the special ornaments they had, turned on the radio, sat down, and admired the tree as the fire burned brightly.

"Thank you, Sarah, for the wonderful time you have been here. I can't believe I have done everything without you all these years. You make it so much easier to manage things around here. Will you and Fred want to go someplace and see any family of your own for Christmas? You most certainly deserve the time off," Helen asked quietly.

"Actually, Helen, we have no family left. Our son, Randy, died a few years ago in an automobile accident and our son, Frank, is in Europe in the air force. Our parents are both gone now for several years. You are our family now, if you'll have us?" Sarah said with emotion.

"I feel you are my family, Sarah. Sisters, like Mari and Beth." Helen held out her hand, reaching over to Sarah. They sat enjoying the peace and quiet, listening to the music on the radio.

Soon they heard the truck rumbling up out under the big oak tree in front of the barn. The dogs were barking all over the place at the new truck. Sarah and Helen quickly went up and stood waiting as a yellow convertible smoothly rolled up in front of the big barn door. Fred got out of the truck and rolled open the big barn door. RG pulled the car clear to the back. Fred, Helen, and Sarah rushed in quickly.

"Look at that! Yet another new vehicle!" Sarah exclaimed.

"What a Christmas this is!" Fred exclaimed.

"We have never had one this big. This has been a great year for us. I sold fifty houses in the subdivision in Napa, and Mark did well with the price of Zinfandel grapes this year at Charles Krug. We're greatly blessed and grateful," RG said as he and Fred covered the car with a tarp. They all walked out, and RG pulled the huge door shut. They strolled down the path, Dagwood in tow.

Sitting in the living room now as if they had nothing to do, RG opened a bottle of sherry and poured a glass for everyone. They sat and talked for a little while when they heard the old truck drive up.

Fred jumped up running to the barn to meet Mark before he shut the engine off. "Just park it out here by the watering trough. We need to clean it up this week" He waved his arm to direct him.

The kids all piled out, excited, talking all at once, telling everything about their visit with the Hanfords.

"Better get to your chores now, you kids. I'm not helping you today. Clean yourselves up and put some clean clothes on before you come in for supper," Fred ordered and then walked slowly down the path to the house, smiling to himself.

The kids all worked quickly and got down to the house, cleaned up and dressed in a hurry. Everyone met in the living room and sat down. The fire was blazing, the radio played music softly. Helen and Sarah were sipping their sherry. Fred and R.G. had settled in with a glass of Jack Daniels. Mark, Daniel, Mari and Beth came in and sat around with a bottle of root beer, admiring the tree and all the gifts. More than they had ever had in any year.

"Do we have to wait for Santa?" Beth piped up. "I think it's almost too much to spoil everything the way it looks. We should keep it like this. Just look at it," she said wistfully. Suddenly she stood up near the tree. "Look at this! Look at these ornaments. This one has my name on it. Here, *Daniel.* Oh, look, *Mari* and *Mark* too."

"Well, I think we could allow you to open just one present tonight," mama said as she put her glass down on the end table.

She rose and went over to the tree near Beth, reached down, and picked up a very small package with white tissue paper and curly ribbon on it.

"This says, "To Beth from RG." Mama handed it to RG.

"Here, kid, just a little something." RG stretched out his arm with the package.

Beth sat on the floor at his feet now. Tears in her eyes, she took the little package and held it on her lap for a moment. Everyone in the room was still, waiting quietly. She slowly pulled the curly ribbon off the white tissue paper, setting it aside. Carefully, as if she didn't want something in it to break, she pulled the tissue off. "Oh my. Oh, look!" She opened a long flat box with a label on it from the jewelry store in St. Helena. "I never had such a beautiful necklace ever in my life." She leaped forward and hugged RG around the neck.

"Put it on! Put it on!" Mari said, all excited. "Let's see it. What does it look like?" The other kids crowded around her to see it.

RG carefully took the gold chain with a gold cross that had a pearl in the middle of it out, putting it around her neck. She held her chin up so everyone could see it.

"*Wow!*" Daniel exclaimed.

"That is really special, Beth. It really is perfect for you," Mark said quietly.

Mari hugged her. "I bet you'll wear it every day," she said, smiling.

"I believe that's your birthstone. We found papers from school that had your birthday on them. June 20. Mari, you wanted to know," mama spoke up softly. "You'll be fourteen then."

Beth had tears running down her cheeks. "I really didn't remember when my birthday was. No one ever talked about it."

Everyone in the room was stunned at such a thought. Daniel jumped in kindly, "I bet we can have a big party next summer. We'll fill the watering trough under the oak tree in front of the barn with water and swim in it."

Everyone laughed.

Mark suggested, "We would do better down at the dam in June."

"Not with fish and frogs all over the place," Mari said excitedly.

Beth thanked RG again and went back to her chair and took a big gulp of her root beer.

"I don't want to open anything, Mama," Mari said, getting up to take her bottle to the kitchen. "I want to wait and see what Santa will bring me in the morning."

Mark agreed, got up, and followed with his bottle.

"Aw! Stupid Santa!" Daniel huffed into the kitchen and plunked his bottle on the counter, shouting as he went out the door to the veranda. "Stupid Santa!"

Mark gave him a punch as they walked up to the bedroom wing of the house.

Mari was in her room getting her new pajamas on when Beth came in the room. "I think I will wear this for the rest of my life." She plopped on her bed, lying back looking at the ceiling. They crawled into bed that night very tired, filled with great peace and joy.

Very early Christmas morning, Daniel pushed open their door, yelling, "Santa was here! Santa was here! Come and see what I saw!"

The girls rolled over and looked at him. "What time is it anyway?" Beth demanded.

"Why are you hollering at us at this time of the morning?" Mari said, grabbing her bathrobe from the end of her bed, trying to get her foot into a slipper.

Mark was up now and at her door. "Better come and see this. You won't believe your eyes! Santa had to have come for sure," he said, encouraging Beth.

"Oh, silly, I know Santa didn't come." Beth was pulling her robe on and getting her feet into her slippers.

They all hopped down the stairs where they all stood in the middle of the room. There were even more presents under the tree than last night. Fred and Sarah came in with a cup of coffee in their hands. "Keep it down, you kids. You will wake up the dogs," Fred joked.

At that point, mama and RG came in the door. "What's all the commotion about? Can't anyone get some sleep around here?" RG blustered with a big grin.

Sarah went out and got them each a cup of coffee. Everyone sat around while Fred added some kindling to what remained of last night's fire, getting it started again.

"I think Santa was here," Mark insisted. "Look at that big box. It wasn't here last night! See, Beth? Santa had to have done it."

"Oh, cut it out. I know it wasn't Santa. But look and see who did put it under the tree. It has a card on it."

Mark and Beth went over leaning down to look at the card. It read, "To Mark, from Mari and Dad."

"Well, look at that. What could you be up to, Mari?" Mark said, joking around. "That is a pretty big box for something you may have made all on your own."

"Sit down, everyone," mama insisted. "Your dad will hand out the gifts the way we always do it."

Daniel would gather all the wrapping, fold it up, and save the ribbon. She turned the radio on to some Christmas music to play softly while they opened their gifts.

One by one, RG passed out the gifts, announcing whom they were for and whom it was from. Everyone watched with curiosity as each opened their gift. The whole family had done a great job of keeping secrets so no one would know what was in each package.

"This one is for Sarah from Mari," RG announced.

Sarah got up, surprised. "Really? For me?" she said, very surprised. She squeezed the package and held it up. "I don't think it will break." Carefully saving the paper and ribbon, she pulled the apron Mari had made out and held it up.

"Wow!" Daniel said loudly. "That's a work of art!"

"Shut up. This is her moment." Beth pushed him.

"It truly is a work of art. I don't think I could get it dirty in the kitchen. I will save it just to look pretty in," Sarah said in all her excitement.

"Oh no, it's made of very durable fabric and meant to be used every day," Mari said, all excited.

"Well then, I will use it every day. Thank you, this is really wonderful. You did all this by yourself without anyone knowing about it? How clever," Sarah said as she held it up to herself.

"Well, since I had my birthday week, I had lots of time to work on it," Mari confessed. "I hid out in Mark's room while everyone was doing the chores for me." They all laughed.

RG continued handing out the gifts one at a time. Daniel was pleased with the tackle box from Mari. He was grateful for all the new clothes from his parents. Beth gave him *Frog Went A-Courtin'*, the Caldecott Medal Winner for 1956, by John Langstaff and illustrated by Feodor Rojankovsky. Mark gave him the 1955 award winner, *The Thanksgiving Story* by Alice Dalgliesh and illustrated by Helen Sewell. Mark thought Daniel would like it because it was a story about country people who were farmers, weavers, and hardworking people like those in the Napa Valley. They wore simple clothes with bright colors and made their own knitted hats or plain cloth caps. RG gave him a beautiful world globe for the library.

All the kids got clothes from RG and mama: jeans, shirts, socks, underwear, and of course, pajamas. Everyone laughed when Fred gave Mari an umbrella. Sarah gave Mari and Beth a cookbook with her favorite recipes. Fred and Sarah got good stuff too: a vase from Beth, a picture for the cottage from Helen, and a fishing pole from RG.

Beth had a pile just for her. Mama and RG gave her some extra clothes from The Elegant Closet since she needed so much. Mark gave her a jewelry box; Daniel gave her a big box with six pairs of socks in it. Mari gave her a little bracelet with a half a heart engraved: "Sisters Forever. Love, Mari." And another one with Mari's name engraved with the same thing, but "Sisters Forever. Love, Beth."

RG gave her a little white Bible with a little piece of paper taped on the front. "We found your name in the records, *Irene Elizabeth Andrews*. If you would like us to have it engraved, it can be done next week."

She wept, "I never knew that. I always hated Elzbeth. I prefer Beth. That is so much prettier. Just *Beth Andrews* would be fine. I think I remember all that now. Thank you, thank you so much." Everyone was excited for her.

Mark was always pleased each Christmas, with all the clothes he got. The work gloves from Daniel were much appreciated. Beth surprised him with a picture frame sporting a photo someone had taken at the Christmas ball of all of them dressed up with their dates.

"Daddy?" Beth begged. "Who is that big box for? And what is that big thing there?"

Mari lunged forward. "Oh, this one is from me to you!" She grabbed it up and tossed it to her. Beth fell over as she was sitting on the floor, laughing as she caught it.

"This is not heavy! It's really soft. What is it?" Beth tore in to the paper quickly, giggling. "What? How wonderful!" She held a big pillow up to her face and squeezed it.

"It's goose down, not from your ducks but really good ones from the store," Mari said in excitement. "Thought you might enjoy it." Everyone laughed.

The kids gave RG and mama all their gifts. Mari gave mama her apron. Everyone loved it. The Pendleton shirt was a real hit. Work clothes and warm socks all round and jewelry for mama.

"I think we have to see what's in this big box. Don't you think, Daddy?" Mari said as she scooped it up and shoved it over to Mark. Everyone sat at attention, curious with anticipation. No one knew what the big secret was.

Mark was stunned to think there could possibly be much more under the tree for him. He paused and looked at it. It was a pretty big box. He lifted it, slightly heavy, and shook it. Didn't rattle.

"Well! Open it!" Daniel shouted impatiently.

"Yes, open it!" Beth pushed his back.

Mari was sitting on the floor at her father's feet, watching quietly, holding her excitement. RG pushed to the edge of his seat and put his hand on Mari's shoulder.

"Mari is the one responsible for this one, son. Give her all the credit."

Mark knew it had to be really special since it didn't have the ordinary white tissue paper and curly ribbon on it. He carefully took the paper and ribbon off to save it. Observing the plain brown box, he lifted the cover. His face turned red; tears swelled in his eyes. Lifting the letter jacket up high to show everyone, he jumped up and quickly put it on. He was speechless. Everyone clapped their hands.

"What a jock!" Daniel said proudly. "That's my brother!"

Mark looked down at the jacket with all the patches and medals. "I guess I didn't realize I had all this stuff. How did you get it?"

"Mari snuck into your room and took it out of your drawer," RG said with a laugh.

"Well, I think you all need to get out to the barn now and get your chores done. I bet the animals are wishing for their Christmas too," RG said abruptly.

"Yes, I will help you kids today," Fred added.

"I think I would like to see all the little bunnies and baby ducks," mama joined in.

"I'll go with you, Helen," Sarah added.

"Come on, everyone, get going!" Fred ordered.

"Aww, always have to work!" Daniel moaned.

"We can come back and look at all our stuff in a while when we get done," Beth said, encouraging him.

They all got up and casually walked out the door into the veranda, Daniel in the lead with RG right behind him.

"Keep your mouth shut. Don't say a word!" His dad put his hand on his shoulder.

"Oh, oh," Daniel whispered.

Mark was following behind everyone. Suddenly he pushed past, yelling, "The yellow convertible! You did it! You're the one! Gee, Dad! She's a beauty! A 1953 Chevrolet Bel Air convertible! She's the one, Dad! She's the one! You are the greatest dad in the whole world."

"You earned it. Every bit of it, son. The vineyard is your money now. You run it like you did this year, and you will do just fine. License, insurance, and gas all taken care of. Just don't get into any trouble racing it around showing off, you hear!" RG said strongly.

Everyone walked around the car. All the dogs were there smelling it, wagging their tails.

Daniel jumped in the back seat. "We don't have to ride the bus anymore."

"We'll see about that, kid! I might not take it to school just yet. Maybe just for special occasions. Maybe just on Friday nights!" Mark sat behind the wheel with his letterman's jacket on.

Mari had her camera and quickly snapped a photo of him with everyone standing around admiring it.

"What a Christmas for a hardworking family, Fred. Think it can go on like this forever?" Sarah said as they walked down the path to the house arm in arm.

About the Author

Photo by Glynis Buschmann

Mary Carol came from the rich culture of Northern California, born in Fort Bragg and raised in the Napa Valley. Her two genius parents read books to her by great authors like Mark Twain, Lewis Carroll, Rudyard Kipling, Robert Louis Stevenson, Edgar Allan Poe, and so many more, who gave her a great imagination. She would entertain her classmates with tall tales and make them laugh with her ability to imitate the different accents of the characters she told about.

When she married a man in the Lutheran ministry, it took her out of her sheltered country life in the Napa Valley to almost every part of the United States and Australia. This gave her an even broader view of the different cultures of the world, only to find that each community and its characters would give her more stories to create. Her love of vocabulary and words allowed her to recreate her imaginations, expressing her characters' emotions, which she found always exciting.

The hardships of country life in all the rural communities of America and Australia have given her a bounty of experiences to spin more and more stories. She found that each community has the same secrets, which people hide from each other.

The formal education she was given has only enhanced her desire to finally do as so many have asked of her, and that is to write. Teaching, drawing, designing her clothes and sewing, gardening, raising her own children and foster kids, being the wife of a Lutheran pastor, being his personal administrative assistant, and becoming the business owner of a flower shop and now a tutoring center have only added to her rich life experiences.